MR NICE

JOHN NICHOLL

B

Boldwood

First published in 2020. This edition first published in Great Britain in 2022 by Boldwood Books Ltd.

Copyright © John Nicholl, 2020

Cover Design by Head Design

Cover Photography: Shutterstock

The moral right of John Nicholl to be identified as the author of this work has been asserted in accordance with the Copyright, Designs and Patents Act 1988.

A CIP catalogue record for this book is available from the British Library.

Paperback ISBN 978-1-80426-634-2

Large Print ISBN 978-1-80426-630-4

Hardback ISBN 978-1-80426-629-8

Ebook ISBN 978-1-80426-627-4

Kindle ISBN 978-1-80426-628-1

Audio CD ISBN 978-1-80426-635-9

MP3 CD ISBN 978-1-80426-632-8

Digital audio download ISBN 978-1-80426-626-7

Boldwood Books Ltd
23 Bowerdean Street
London SW6 3TN
www.boldwoodbooks.com

1

Megan woke with a start, opening one bleary eye and then the other, as the banging got louder, reverberating throughout the entire house, the front door shaking in its frame. She turned her head on the pillow, tired eyes narrowed to slits, glancing at the illuminated numbers on the digital clock to her left. Megan screwed up her face, swearing crudely under her breath as the clock's face came into gradual focus. 2.03 a.m., and here he was again, pissed out of his tiny mind no doubt, hammering on the door like the place was on fire. Would he ever see sense? Would he ever grow up? It seemed that even the threat of imprisonment couldn't control the fool's drunken excesses.

Come on, girl, up you get. Just get rid of him. Send him on his way. He won't sod off otherwise. The idiot never did.

Megan threw back her summer-weight quilt. She rose wearily from the bed, pulling on a cotton T-shirt and a pair of loose, knee-length, linen shorts, before approaching her young daughter's bedroom, across the small landing at the front of the Victorian house, with a view of the little garden and street below. As the banging became even more insistent Megan entered the room, to find her daughter perched on her single bed with the curtains only slightly ajar, peering down, half-hidden, at her drunken father below. A single tear ran down the young child's freckled cheek as she turned to Megan, her face perfectly framed by her pale-yellow hair.

Lottie smiled thinly as she met her mother's tired eyes, but there was an unmistakable air of sadness about her that made Megan's heart sink. It seemed the breakup and everything that went with it was taking its inevitable toll.

'Is Daddy cross again? Have I been naughty?'

Megan reached out, pulling Lottie towards her and hugging her tight as she carried her towards the larger bedroom at the back of the house, away from the street.

'No, sweetie, it's not your fault. It's never your fault. Daddy is being silly again, that's all. I'm going to tell him to go away, and then we can get back to sleep. Try not to worry. Everything is going to be just fine. I'll look after you. I love you very much.'

Lottie climbed into her mother's double bed, pulling the quilt high, hiding from the world, not wanting to see Megan leave the room. 'Can I sleep in your bed all night, Mummy?'

Megan forced an unlikely smile, nodding twice, her blue eyes flickering like a faulty bulb, tears flowing despite a determined desire to remain stoic in times of adversity. 'Of course you can. I'll tell Daddy to go back to his flat and then we can cuddle up together. Now, close your eyes, ignore the silly noise and think nice thoughts. We can go swimming together tomorrow, at the pool, just you and me. You'd like that, wouldn't you? And maybe we'll call to see Granny on our way home. You can feed the fish in the pond.'

'And the frogs?'

Megan relaxed slightly, full of hope as the banging stopped. She stood and listened, clutching her stomach, rocking in one place. Had the fool finally given up on the hope of a response?

Megan placed the palms of her hands together in front of her at shoulder level, fingers pointed upwards. *Please, God, let it be so.*

But, no. Bang! There it was again. Bang! Megan swallowed hard, a twitchy feeling in her extremities. 'Yes, Lottie, we mustn't forget the frogs. We like the frogs. Now, close your eyes and put your hands over your ears. I'm going to send Daddy on his way. That's it, hold them tight, as I showed you, like the last time. I'll be back as quickly as I can.'

The little girl opened her eyes wide. 'Where's Teddy?'

Megan crossed the room, looking back, speaking as calmly as possible, desperately attempting to introduce a semblance of normality to a situation that had become all too familiar in recent weeks. 'I left him in your room. That was silly of me. I'll bring him with me when I come back, promise. Now, hold your hands over your ears like I told you and close your eyes tight shut. That's it, perfect, what a good girl you are. I'll be back before you know it.'

'Will you leave the light on?'

'Yes, I'll leave the light on.'

Lottie was entirely hidden under the quilt when Megan left the room a few seconds later, closing the door behind her. Megan wanted to stay to comfort her daughter. She so wanted to hold Lottie close and whisper sweet words of reassurance into her ear, but what would that achieve? Her idiot ex-husband was still out there, banging, banging, banging, and no doubt getting angrier and more frustrated. It was always the same. His misplaced sense of entitlement, the indignant rage that seemed to define him. Just like the last time. Just like every time. For the briefest of seconds, Megan considered running down the stairs, opening the front door and telling Dale exactly what she thought of him in unambiguous language even he couldn't fail to understand. But she changed her mind at the very last second. What would be the point? The man was drunk and very likely beyond rational thought. Her words would be wasted.

And worse than that, he might well push her

aside. Force his way in. Rush upstairs and disturb Lottie. He'd done it before. The potential pay-off just didn't justify the risks. Keep him out. That was best. Encourage him to go.

Megan noticed that her hands were trembling as she re-entered her daughter's bedroom seconds later, her gut twisting and her heart thumping in her throat. She clenched her jaw as she knelt on the bed, urging herself on, rather than giving in to the temptation to curl up in a ball and cry.

She threw back the curtains, opened the window wide and glared down at her ex-husband, as he turned away from the door and began kicking it mule style. Megan watched, feeling a mix of anger and grief as her ex stumbled forwards, almost falling before regaining his footing, a look of triumph on his unshaven face. She shook her head slowly to the right and left, shouting just about loud enough to ensure he heard her in the street below. 'What the hell do you think you're doing?'

He peered up at her, hands held wide, palms forward. 'So you've finally heard me, have you, you stuck-up bitch?' He burped at full volume. 'It's about fucking time.'

Megan's reply was immediate. 'Oh, the entire street has heard you, Dale. It's past two in the morning, in case you hadn't realised. And you've woken Lottie. She's five years old, for goodness' sake. What were you thinking?'

'What's the problem? She wants her daddy, that's all.'

'Are you completely deranged? You've scared her! She's lying in bed, crying her eyes out because of you. And she doesn't want to hear her mother called a bitch. It upsets her like it upsets me. What part of that don't you understand?'

He peered up with a drunken, supercilious smirk that Megan found infuriating. She knew exactly what was coming next. It was a tactic he used often, good guy and bad guy all rolled into one, anger followed by pleading, as predictable as night and day. 'Just open the fucking door, there's a good girl. Please, I've only had a couple of pints. I'll soon cheer Lottie up.' He took a bag of sweets from a jacket pocket, holding them up in clear view, shaking the packet above his head as if they were the most fabulous prize in the world. 'I've bought her some sweets, jelly babies, her favourites. Come on, open up. She wants to see her daddy.'

Megan closed her tired eyes for a beat before speaking again, holding the window frame with a white-knuckle grip, digging in her nails, taking out her frustrations on the plastic. 'You can't be here, Dale. Have you forgotten the injunction? Do you remember what the judge said? Look around you. People are putting their lights on. Curtains are opening. I suggest you sod off home before someone calls the police. Because someone will, they definitely will. It's just a matter of time.'

'Interfering bastards!'

'What else do you expect when you behave like a total prat?'

'They can all go fuck themselves.'

'You won't be saying that when you're dragged off in handcuffs.'

Dale returned the sweets to his pocket, succeeding on the second attempt. 'Oh, come on, open the door. This was my home too, not so very long ago. I paid for half of it. Open the door. It's not too much to ask, is it?'

'Go away. Go while you've still got the chance. Do you want to be locked up? God knows you deserve it.'

He gagged once, then again, spitting vomit before looking up and smiling, a thin line of drool running down his chin. 'Oh, come on, Meg. I want to see my girl, that's all. She's my daughter as well as yours. We made her together.' He began thrusting his hips back and forth in slow rhythmic motion, his open hands positioned as if holding a lover's hips, penetrating her from behind. 'Surely, you must remember?' He started moaning loudly, as if in the realms of sexual ecstasy. 'I'm coming. I'm coming. I can't recall you complaining at the time.'

Megan sucked the still-warm summer air deep into her lungs, swallowing her fury, forcing it back down her throat. She steadied herself, telling herself insistently that a more conciliatory tone may help calm him down if she chose her words with care. 'Oh, come on now, Dale, it's the middle of the night. You know the score. You can see Lottie once a week by prior arrangement, and that's if, and only if, you're sober. You can't be here now. And especially not in that state. Sort yourself out. You're breaking the conditions of the injunction.'

'Fuck the injunction! I can't understand why you took me to court in the first place.'

'Come on now. Someone will have dialled 999 by now. Go before the police arrive. Turning up here in that state in the middle of the night doesn't achieve anything at all.'

He threw his arms out. 'I just want to see my girl.'

This time Megan's words spewed from her mouth in a torrent, rising in pitch and volume as she glared down at him, eyes popping. 'No, no, no! It's two in the damned morning. Lottie needs her sleep. How many times do I have to say it? It's time to grow up. I've had enough. Just shut your stupid mouth and go away.'

'I'm not going anywhere until I've seen Lottie.'

Megan shook her head. 'Do you want to upset her? Do you want to break her heart? Because that's what you're doing.'

'You're full of shit, woman.'

'Lottie needs a daddy she can rely on. A daddy to be proud of. Just give up the booze, and you can be that person again.'

'What harm do a few bevvies do?'

'If you're trying to ruin your daughter's life, you're succeeding. Is alcohol really more important than her happiness? That's what you need to ask yourself. Because it seems that way to me.'

He looked up and yelled. 'You're talking crap, total fucking crap. Lottie is missing me, that's all! Open the fucking door. I'll give her a hug and a kiss and then I'll be on my way.'

Megan gritted her teeth, hissing her words. 'We can arrange something in a few days, if, and only if, you leave now.'

Dale picked up a sizeable stone from the well-tended flower bed bordering the small rectangular lawn, intending to smash the glass panel in the door, to force entry. But he dropped it almost immediately on hearing a siren wail in the distance, getting gradually louder. He peered up at Megan as angry as she'd ever seen him, tense muscles changing the contours of his face. 'You phoned the pigs. You have got to be kidding me. Why would you do that? You bitch, you total fucking bitch!'

Megan shook her head once more, feeling somewhat conflicted. A part of her was grateful to whoever had called the emergency services; a part of her bemoaned her ex's continued decline into alcoholism. 'No, I didn't ring the police, not this time. But don't think I won't in future if you turn up here in that state again. Now go before the police get here. Sleep it off. We can talk when you're sober. If you don't go now, you're going to be locked up. None of us wants that.'

Dale bowed in mock obedience. 'Yeah, yeah, I hear you. Anything you say, your majesty.'

Megan went to close the window but pushed it wide again as he staggered towards his vehicle, keys in hand. 'Walk, for goodness' sake! You're way over the limit. Do not get in that car. Now go before it's too late.'

2

Megan crept into her spacious bedroom a short time later, both surprised and gratified to see that Lottie was asleep and lost to her dreams. Megan yawned, bent stiffly at the waist and gently kissed her daughter's forehead before tucking her favourite chocolate-brown teddy bear next to her under the quilt. Megan looked down at her young child for a few seconds more, studying her features, her impish face, her light-blonde hair, recalling happier times in the not so distant past, before Dale's gradual decline into alcohol addiction ravaged their previously ordinary lives. Before his selfish nature tore their relationship to pieces.

Megan brought her rumination to a sudden end, considering her thought process pointless at best. Going over it all yet again didn't change anything, not a damned thing. She had to look forward. Megan tiptoed from the room ever so slowly, ever so quietly, a look of resigned acceptance on her face. *Please don't wake up, Lottie. Please don't wake up.*

Megan shuffled into the family kitchen on tired legs, in search of aspirin to alleviate her nagging headache. She popped a soluble tablet into her open mouth, switching on the kettle on autopilot, before picking up her mobile, seriously considering contacting her mother despite the early hour. It would be so good to talk to someone who actually cared. But in the early hours of the morning, really, was that even remotely reasonable? Most likely not; why not have a quick cuppa and give it some further thought.

She dropped a teabag into a favourite pottery mug, poured in the water, added a splash of unsweetened soya milk from the fridge, and slumped back down into the nearest chair, still weighing up the pros and cons of making the call. *Oh, what the hell, Mum won't mind. She never does.*

Megan nearly ended the call before her mother answered, guilt almost getting the better of her, but she suddenly heard her mother's familiar voice at the other end of the line. 'Hello, Megan, what is it, love?'

Megan took a deep breath, filling her lungs, exhaling slowly before speaking. 'I need to talk.'

'What, now? It's the middle of the night. Can't it wait until morning?'

There was a moment's silence as Megan began weeping without words.

'What is it, love, what's happened? I know there's something.'

Megan sipped her tea, wetting her mouth, wondering why her throat felt so very parched. 'He's been here again.'

'Dale?'

'Well, yes, who else?'

'Oh, for God's sake, not again! What's he done this time?'

'He turned up here pissed out of his tiny mind, as usual, hammering on the door and demanding to see Lottie at the top of his voice. What sort of father does that? In the middle of the night!'

'I'm so sorry. It's hard to believe he's the same

man you married. Dale's changed so very much in such a short time. I know he lost his father, followed by his job. It was hard on him. But we all have to deal with life's problems. No-one is immune, not you, not me and not Dale.'

Megan cradled her mug, taking comfort in the residual heat. 'It's less than two weeks since the court proceedings. I thought the injunction would make a difference. But it seems not. It's Lottie I feel most sorry for. It's knocking her confidence, confusing her, setting her back. She's even started wetting the bed again. Dale knows all this. How is a five-year-old little girl supposed to understand what's going on? I want to explain. But what do I say? It's tearing me apart, Mum. I don't know what to do for the best.'

Megan heard a deep sigh at the other end of the line before her mother spoke again. 'You two used to be so very close. Dale's such a nice boy when he's sober.'

Megan stiffened. 'Yes, but not so much when he's drunk. Why doesn't he stop pouring poison down his stupid throat? If he doesn't want to stop drinking for himself, why not do it for us? Aren't we enough? It's like the real Dale walked away from us and never came back.'

'It's an illness. Your father was much the same. This is like travelling back in time.'

'Dale promised me he'd stop drinking. He said it to my face as we left the courtroom. For my sake and Lottie's too, that's what he said. Do you know, I actually believed him this time. But it didn't even last a fortnight. Maybe one day he'll live up to his empty promises.' Megan paused. 'I'd still like to think he will.'

'All the good intentions in the world are meaningless unless Dale acts on them. Your father made his share of promises over the years, most of them worthless.'

Megan wiped away her tears with the back of one hand. 'I know, honestly, I know. Dale's a liar; I can't believe a single word that comes out of his stupid mouth. I'm beginning to think that moving away's the only real option left open to me. I could ask work for a transfer. Somewhere far away at the other end of the country, Plymouth maybe, or Truro. I've always liked the West Country. If it weren't for you, I'd do it, I really would.'

'I'd miss you and Lottie terribly.'

There were a few seconds of silence before Megan spoke again, her voice resonating with raw emotion. 'The police came.'

'What?'

'The police, they came here tonight, two uniformed constables, a man and a woman, siren blaring, blue lights flashing. They left a few minutes ago. I'm a solicitor, Mum. I knew one of them by name. I'd seen her in the magistrates' court. I've never felt more embarrassed in my life. When's it all going to end?'

'Did you call them, the police? Did you call them?'

Megan shook her head in reflexive response. 'No, it must have been one of the neighbours. I was annoyed at first. But I can't blame them. Dale was making one hell of a racket, yelling, banging the door. People aren't used to that sort of thing. I can't believe it's me in the spotlight. It's the sort of thing I deal with professionally. You know, the sort of thing that happens to other people. Everyone's going to be talking about me, and not in a good way.'

'What does it matter what people think? That's the least of your worries.'

'It's a work thing, Caerystwyth's a small town, my reputation's important to me. My clients need to know they can trust me.'

'Is Lottie asleep?'

Megan massaged the back of her neck, her hand moving in jerks. 'Yes, I don't know how, but she managed to get off somehow. The poor thing must be totally exhausted.'

'At least there's no school. She can have a lie-in. That's one positive... are you going to report him?'

'What, Dale?'

'You've got to put a stop to all this sometime. Maybe now's the time, this could be the opportunity.'

Megan exhaled slowly through pursed lips, shifting on her chair, crossing and uncrossing her legs, unable to get comfortable. 'He's broken the conditions of the injunction. He's in trouble enough as it is. A part of me still loves him; God help me. I don't want to make things even worse than they already are.'

'Not even after everything he's done?'

'No, I don't think so.' Megan laughed despite herself, but her tone betrayed her true feelings. 'I thought me and Dale were in it for the long haul. I thought we'd grow old together. How wrong can one be? I don't trust my judgement any more, that's the truth of it.'

'Everyone feels a bit like that when life takes a difficult turn. I know I did when, well, you know, when your father went off the rails. The girl was twenty-one years old, for goodness' sake. Maybe they're all as unreliable as each other. Or perhaps we've both been unlucky. There must be some good men out there somewhere.'

Megan stretched and yawned, pushing her mug aside, still three-quarters full. She closed her eyes for a second or two before opening them again, glancing at the clock.

'Are you still there, Meg?'

'Yes, I'm still here. I nearly drifted off. I've taken a sleeping tablet.'

'Give me a ring after breakfast. We can talk again then. Why don't you come and visit? I've bought Lottie a new colouring book. You know, one of the ones she likes with the shiny stickers. I'd love to see you both.'

'I did say I'd take her swimming and then call with you on the way home. She wants to feed the fish.'

'I'm in all day, call any time, you're always welcome.'

'Thanks, Mum, I love you. I don't know what I'd do without you.'

'I love you too. I'll see you in a few hours' time. Now, it's late, off you go to bed. Things will get better, promise. Nothing lasts forever, not even this.'

3

Megan woke at just after seven that morning, as a shard of bright sunshine broke through the marble clouds, bathing the house in light. The events of the night came into sharp focus, playing behind her eyes as if in real-time, as she went to hug her daughter. Megan turned first one way and then the other, reaching out to pull Lottie close. But all she found was the soft toy, lying next to her under the quilt. Megan was on full alert in that instant, her protective mothering instincts sending adrenaline surging through her system, energy and blood redirected to her muscles as she sat up.

Megan's eyes darted from one corner of the room

to the next, to right, to left and back again, every instinct telling her that something was amiss. Where was Lottie? Where on earth was she? She usually slept until woken. And on those rare occasions when she'd been the first to wake, she'd called out 'Mum!', sought her out and shaken her.

Megan jumped from the bed, checking the bathroom first without success, and then Lottie's room, hoping she may be playing with her dolls, but no, she wasn't there either. Megan called out Lottie's name, once, then again, louder this time, with concern in her tone. But Lottie didn't reply.

Where is she? Where on earth is she? Megan hurried downstairs two steps at a time, her blood pressure soaring to a savage high as her anxiety continued to escalate. Megan called out her daughter's name time and again as she rushed from one room to the next, but all was silence. A strange pervasive silence that seemed to mock her, sending imaginary icy fingers running up and down her spine as she continued her search.

In the kitchen, she stopped and stared, slack-jawed, mouth hanging open, her eyes fixed on the large, open window as if a spotlight were shining upon it. Someone had opened it wide. They'd climbed through the gap. It was the only thing that made any sense, the only logical explanation.

How hadn't she heard? Was she that tired? She'd only taken the one sleeping tablet. Oh no, what was she thinking? She shouldn't have taken anything at all.

Megan stood, statue-like, her mind still racing as she searched for an explanation that made any sense at all. Oh, shit, it was Dale. It had to be Dale. He must have returned after the police left. Or he could have hidden. Maybe he'd hidden. Perhaps he'd waited, bided his time. The bastard, the absolute bastard! He'd broken in. He'd actually broken in.

Megan pictured her drunken ex scrambling through the open window in the semi-darkness of the night. She pictured him ascending the stairs, one cautious step at a time, and then lifting Lottie from the bed while she slept sedated next to her.

How dare he? He'd gone too far this time. What the hell was the idiot thinking? Was he really that irresponsible?

Megan reached out, picking up her smartphone from where it was charging. She rung Dale's number, cursing loudly and crudely when she didn't receive a reply. She rang twice more but with the same negative results. Megan briefly considered leaving a message, something that left her ex in no doubt as to her extreme displeasure.

But no, it made more sense to drive straight to his recently rented home. To bang on the door and keep banging until he answered. See how he liked that, some of his own medicine when nursing a hangover. It was time to pull on some clothes and get out of there just as quickly as she possibly could. Should she ring her mum? No, no, that could wait. Mum wasn't getting any younger. She needed her sleep. There was little point in worrying her even more than she already had. Now, where were those car keys?

Megan rushed from the kitchen and towards the stairs, spotting the bunch of keys on the dark, wooden hallstand next to the front door. Her mind was still racing as she climbed each step. The behavioural effects of the alcohol would have worn off by now. Lottie should be okay. She was safe.

Yes, Lottie was with her dad. The sober dad, the sensible dad, the dad she'd known before the strong drink gradually sunk in its claws, taking hold and ruining everything they had one painful day at a time.

As Megan picked up a pair of faded blue jeans, her mind leapt, one thought after another tumbling in her head, in search of reassurance, cathartic, a self-therapy of sorts.

Dale was immature and reckless, but he wasn't a bad person, not deep down where it really mattered. He wasn't one of the truly evil bastards she sometimes encountered in her legal role: the haters, the destructive, self-obsessed men who felt no concern for anyone but themselves. Dale had a conscience. He wasn't entirely devoid of goodness. He'd never hurt Lottie, not intentionally and certainly not physically. No, no, of course he wouldn't. He'd always loved their daughter in his way. And he'd be wide awake by now – suffering, wracked with guilt, full of heartfelt regrets.

Lottie was safe. She'd be sitting on the sofa watching one cartoon or another, eating a favourite sugary cereal without a care in the world. Lottie was safe and sound. Megan told herself she'd soon have her back. They'd be off to the pool together, making the most of the day ahead.

4

Megan started her small but sporty Arctic-white Italian hatchback on the second turn of the key. She headed towards Dale's rented flat on the outskirts of the pleasant west Wales market town, driving a lot faster than was sensible as the rain began to fall.

Within ten minutes Megan was turning into Dale's modest terraced street, searching for a suitable parking space to the right and left as she slowed, the windscreen wipers battling valiantly with the increasing volume of water, seemingly coming from every direction at once. Megan parked half on and half off a low kerb about one hundred yards from her ex-husband's first-floor, two-bedroom abode.

When she reached Dale's shared front door
Megan was panting hard, her chest rising and falling
with a steady pulse as she pressed the top bell of two,
holding down the white button, hearing the shrill
tone ring out. She allowed the bell to ring for a full
thirty seconds before banging on the door with the
side of a clenched fist, increasing the force and regu-
larity of the blows with every few seconds that
passed. The last thing she wanted to do was to upset
Lottie. The events of the early hours had done more
than enough of that already. But she had to get an
answer. Why no reply?

Why on earth wasn't Dale answering the
damned door? They'd both be awake by now. No-
one could sleep through that noise. Was Dale hiding? Was he choosing to ignore her, embarrassed by
his drunken behaviour, and keen to avoid con-
frontation, an argument he couldn't win? And what
about Lottie? Surely, she'd open the curtains. She'd
peer out. Guess it was her mum. Why were the curtains still closed after all this time? Megan shuddered, her entire body trembling from growing
apprehension as opposed to cold. She looked up at
each first-floor window in turn. Oh, God, what on

earth was going on? Maybe they weren't in there at all.

Megan looked up and down the street, suddenly acutely aware that she hadn't seen Dale's aged, rust rotted estate car at any point since her arrival. She looked again, hoping she'd missed it, eyes darting from one vehicle to the next, but it was nowhere to be found. Megan wanted to scream, she wanted to stomp and shout, but instead, she reached into her bag, searching for her mobile with frantic fingers, as large raindrops continued to fall, water running down her face and soaking into her clothes.

She bounced a foot on the pavement as she dialled and began striding back to her car as the rain eased slightly. She picked up her pace, avoiding the many puddles with quick dancing feet, speaking as she walked, phone in one hand and car keys in the other as the sky darkened. 'Mum, Dale took Lottie last night after I rang you.'

Her mother's tone was urgent. 'Took her? What do you mean he took her?'

'The bastard broke into the house and took Lottie from the bed while I slept right there next to her in my bedroom at the back of the house. I left the kitchen window open, just slightly, on the latch. I forgot to close the damned thing after boiling some soup. It was a warm night. Why wouldn't I leave it open? We live in a low crime area. And he took full advantage. He broke in and took her away!'

There was a second's silence. 'Are you sure?'

Megan's voice betrayed her frustration. 'Yes, of course I'm sure. I couldn't be surer.'

The response was immediate this time. 'Have you rung him?'

Megan unlocked the car, jumping into the driver's seat to escape the rain, which had started falling more heavily again. 'Yes, I've rung him. And I'm at the flat now. But there's no reply, and his car's not here. I've searched the entire street. I don't know what the hell to do next. I'm starting to panic, Mum. This isn't like anything he's done before. If he's capable of breaking into the house, what else is he capable of? He must be having some sort of breakdown.'

Megan detected a hard edge to her mother's voice when she spoke again. A hard edge she hadn't heard for quite some time. 'Right, now you listen to me. I want you to go straight to the police station, and I want you to tell them exactly what's happened, word for word, as you've told me. Make it official. If Dale gets into serious trouble, he's brought it on himself. If he's locked up, that's down to him too. It's no more than he deserves.'

Megan paused. When she spoke her tone was reticent, 'Do you really think that's necessary?'

'Dale's broken into your house. Think about what you've told me. He took that little girl in the car and drove when he was drunk. He put her life at risk. And you don't even know where she is. It's time to put her first. She's the only thing that matters now. What's Dale capable of? You asked the same question yourself not a minute ago. You need to get Lottie back before she comes to any harm, deliberate or otherwise. Go to the police station and tell them everything. I can't say it any clearer than that.'

Megan dropped her chin to her chest, exhaling slowly as she started the engine and turned on the wipers. 'Yes, okay, I know you're right. I'll go straight to the police station right now. If someone had told me the idiot was going to do something as stupid as this, I wouldn't have believed them. It's got to be down to the drink. It's twisted his mind – addled his brain. The man needs professional help. I could slap him sometimes and slap him hard. He's breaking our hearts.'

'You're doing the right thing. Talk to the police. Dale's forced your hand. No-one can blame you.'

Megan talked as she drove, holding the phone to her face with one hand while steering with the other. 'Right, I'm on my way.'

'Okay, we can speak again later. If there's anything you need, I'm here for you.'

5

Megan visited West Wales Police Headquarters on a regular basis in her role as lawyer, to represent one client or another, offering legal advice, sitting in on interviews.

But this time was different, very different, and as she stood in reception, curling her toes, fidgeting with her cuff, Megan felt like a fish out of water. Her usual professional assurance had been stripped away by the personal nature of her purpose. She was about to shine a light on her private life, something she'd had to do all too often in the recent past, and the prospect filled her with morale-sapping doubts and apprehensions.

But she repeatedly reminded herself that her mother was correct. Lottie had to come first. Dale had crossed a line. Perhaps some time in a cell was precisely what he needed, shock therapy. Maybe then he'd get off the booze once and for all. Perhaps he'd become the man he'd once been – the man she loved.

Megan rocked back and forth where she stood, shivering slightly in her soaked clothes, unable to settle in the one place as she anticipated what was to come. When the receptionist finally appeared behind the grey glass security screen, her friendly face was familiar, but even that didn't help Megan relax even slightly. As Megan chose her words with care, she feared they might stick in her throat. She'd never felt more out of her comfort zone, never more ill at ease. 'I... um... I... err... I need to speak to a police officer.'

The receptionist smiled with what looked like genuine affection. 'It's still raining then?'

Megan pushed her wet fringe away from her eyes and nodded. 'Yes, I think it's getting worse as the morning goes on.'

The receptionist pointed to her left. 'There's some paper towels in the ladies' toilet if that helps.'

Megan shook her head. 'No, I'm... I'm all right, thanks. I've got some tissues in my bag.'

The receptionist smiled again, this time without parting her lips. 'I haven't seen you here for a while. How are things? Are you keeping busy?'

Megan searched her busy mind. What was the woman's name? Susan, Sandy, Sandra, yes, Sandra, that was it. 'Can I just speak to an officer please, Sandra? I haven't got time to chat.'

Sandra stiffened, her smile disappearing as quickly as it appeared. 'Do you want to speak to anyone in particular?'

Megan dabbed at her face with a paper hanky before dropping it back into her bag. 'No, I'm happy to speak to whoever's available. But if I can see somebody quickly, that will be appreciated.'

Sandra rolled her eyes. 'If you could give me an idea of what it relates to, I'd have a better idea who's best.'

Megan's brow furrowed. 'It's a domestic issue.'

'I need a little more than that.'

Megan responded in a whisper, her nose almost touching the glass. 'My ex-husband, he's... he's abducted our daughter. I've got legal custody. He doesn't have the right to take her. I don't think he'd hurt her, not deliberately, not physically, but I can't be entirely sure. He was drunk when he took her. I need her found, and quickly. I feel sure you understand.'

Sandra nodded. 'You're in luck. I saw DI Kesey a little earlier. She's not usually in on a Saturday.' Sandra picked up the phone. 'Give me a second. I'll try her office number.'

Megan forced a brittle smile. 'That's appreciated, thank you.'

Sandra dialled and waited.

'Hello, ma'am, it's Sandra on the front desk. I've got Megan Weller here with me, the solicitor, she says her ex has abducted their daughter. She's got custody; the father was drunk. She's concerned as to the girl's safety.'

Kesey's tone was urgent. 'When exactly did he take her?'

'Give me a second, ma'am.'

Sandra lowered the phone, turning her attention to Megan, who was blowing out a series of short breaths as she stood gripping the counter's edge. 'When did the alleged abduction take place?'

Megan tensed at the use of the word 'alleged', but she decided to let it go. Maybe she was being over-sensitive. There was little point in delaying matters for the sake of argument. 'He broke into my house sometime in the early hours of this morning and took Lottie from my bed when I was sleeping right there next to her. She's only five years old. The man's gone far too far this time. I don't know what the hell he was thinking. I can only put it down to the drink.'

Sandra provided the detective with the required information, adding the child's age, rushing her words, keen to convey efficiency.

'Okay, thank you, Sandra, that's helpful. Are any of the interview rooms free?'

'Rooms one and three.'

'Okay, put Ms Weller in room three, offer her a hot drink, and tell her I'll be with her in two minutes. If she thinks she's having a bad day, it's about to get worse.'

6

Detective Inspector Laura Kesey sat opposite Megan, separated only by a small rectangular table, looking across at her with obvious concern. When Kesey spoke, it was in nasal Brummie tones that some Welsh locals found challenging to decipher. 'So, let me see if I've got this right? You got into bed with your daughter Lottie in a bedroom at the back of your house in Picton Street shortly after the officers left your address, yeah?'

Megan was quick to respond. 'Yes, as I said. That's exactly what happened. I had a quick cup of tea, rang my mother, and then went back to bed. Lottie was already fast asleep when I climbed in next to her.' Megan dropped her head, looking away. 'I hate to admit this, but I'd taken a sleeping tablet. If I hadn't, well, you know what I'm about to say, I'd have woken. I'd have heard him; I'd have stopped him, simple as. We wouldn't be here talking now.'

'Don't beat yourself up. My old DI often used to say hindsight's an exact science. You couldn't possibly have known what was going to happen when you took that tablet. Not unless you can see into the future.'

'No, I know. I've told clients much the same thing myself. But it doesn't make me feel any better. Maybe I'll remember that next time I'm tempted to say it. I feel as if I've let my daughter down.'

'About how long do you think it took you to get off to sleep?'

Megan crossed and uncrossed her legs, gripping one hand with the other. 'Oh, I'd say a couple of minutes, maybe a little longer, no more than five minutes at most.'

Kesey made a scribbled note on a sheet of A4. 'And then you woke at just after seven this morning, yeah?'

'Yes, that's right; it was ten past to be precise. I

can say that with certainty. I glanced at the clock on my bedside cabinet before, well, you know, before searching for Lottie, heading downstairs and discovering the wide open window in the kitchen. I knew then that she was missing. My heart sank. It hit me in the gut like a physical blow. Dale had taken her. It has to be Dale. Nothing else makes any sense. I can't believe he went that far. He's never done anything this stupid before.'

Kesey paused for a second or two, considering events in her analytical mind. 'So, if someone broke in and took Lottie from your home, they must have done it sometime between 2.30 a.m., and 7.10 a.m., correct?'

Megan jerked her head back, her voice raising an octave. 'Someone? You said, someone! Aren't you listening to what I'm telling you? It was Dale, my ex; I thought I'd made that crystal clear. He must have come back after your officers drove off. He came through the side gate and into the back garden. I'm guessing he tried the back door, found it was locked, and then spotted the partially open window. I bet he couldn't believe his luck. He was desperate to get into the house. He'd made that perfectly obvious with his drunken ranting. He opened the window wide and climbed in. It's the only thing that makes any sense at all.'

Kesey rose to her feet. 'Finish your tea. And stay exactly where you are. I need to check my facts before we continue the interview. I'll be back with you as quickly as I can, ten minutes, maybe fifteen at most.'

Megan felt her heart pounding in her chest as a cold sweat formed on her brow. 'Is there something you're not telling me? Has something happened? Has there been some kind of accident? Oh, God, is Lottie okay?'

'Try to relax, Megan. I'm not aware of any accident, but there is something I need to discuss with you. Have you got a photograph of Lottie? Something that clearly shows her face?'

Megan's entire body stiffened, each muscle tensing. 'What? Why would you need a photograph? Just find Dale. Get Lottie back. That's all you've got to do. What the hell's going on? You're starting to worry me.'

Kesey raised an eyebrow. 'Look, I appreciate that none of this is easy. I have a young child myself and can only imagine how I'd feel in your place. But please try to be patient. I'm following a well-established protocol because it works. Now, the photo, please, it really would help. The quicker we progress matters, the better the chance of finding your daughter.'

Megan reached into her bag with a trembling hand. She took out her phone and began quickly scrolling through the many photos until she found one she thought suitable. She handed Kesey the mobile, Lottie's pretty face almost filling the screen: her shoulder-length blonde hair, her bright blue eyes, smiling, in happier times before the recent separation. 'How about this one?'

Kesey glanced at the screen as she approached the door. She looked back as she turned the handle. 'Yeah, thanks, that's perfect. I need to ask you what Lottie was wearing at the time of her disappearance?'

'She was wearing green pyjamas, a top and trousers.'

'Green?'

'Yes, I know they're a bit unusual. My mum's got a garden pond. It was full of frog spawn, then tadpoles and finally, tiny frogs that were hopping all over the lawn. Lottie loved them.' Megan stalled, choking back her tears before speaking again. 'Her pyjamas are covered in cartoon images of smiling frogs sitting on lily pads. I'm sorry, I haven't got a photograph of her wearing them. Is that going to be a problem?'

Kesey shook her head, picturing the missing child in her mind's eye, feeling the mother's angst. 'Just tell me where they were bought. I can always obtain a pair. It may be useful if we decide to appeal to the public for information.'

Megan looked increasingly puzzled. 'I bought them in the new children's clothes shop in King Street, the small independent place close to the library on the opposite side of the street, but why would you—?'

Kesey spoke without allowing Megan to complete her sentence. 'I'll be back with you as quickly as I can. I need to be certain of my facts. As I said, there are things we need to discuss.'

Megan paced the room, first one way and then another, her mind leaping from one unwelcome hypothesis to the next, searching for answers she couldn't find until Kesey reappeared about twenty minutes later. The look on the officer's face only served to send Megan's pounding heart soaring to a new and savage high.

'Take a seat, please. There are things we need to talk about.'

Megan appeared frozen, rigid, unable to move as if welded to the spot. She opened her mouth to speak, but no words came.

Kesey reached out, taking her witness's arm, guiding her to her chair. 'Sit yourself down, Megan. I'm keen to continue as quickly as we can.'

Megan slumped into her seat, forcing the words from her mouth as her gut churned and twisted. 'What is it?' She swallowed hard. 'What's happening here? Has something happened to... has something... has...?'

Kesey met Megan's eyes, holding her gaze, resisting the desire to look away. 'I need to inform you that Dale was arrested within approximately twenty-five minutes of leaving your home address in the early hours of this morning. He was driving erratically. He mounted the pavement and was seen by an officer. His vehicle was stopped, he was breathalysed, arrested and brought directly to the police station. He provided a second positive sample and was then placed in a cell after throwing a punch at the custody sergeant. I have confirmed that Dale is still in the cells. He'll be interviewed very shortly. Hopefully, he can clarify matters.'

Megan's voice raised in pitch as she looked back with an incredulous stare. 'So... so if Dale's here, if he's locked up, you must have found Lottie. Just tell me where she is. What are you waiting for? For God's sake, put me out of my misery.'

Kesey leaned forward in her seat. 'Please listen to what I'm telling you very carefully. I've just spoken to the officer who made the arrest. He's adamant that your ex was alone in the car when his vehicle was stopped. Wherever Lottie was, she wasn't in the car.'

Megan dry gagged, swallowed, and gagged again. 'What?'

'I'm sorry, I can only repeat myself. Lottie wasn't in Dale's car when it was stopped in the early hours of this morning. If she had been, the officer would have seen her. Your ex was alone.'

Megan reached out, grabbing Kesey's wrist, holding it tight. 'Did the officer look? Did he search? It's an estate car. An old wreck of a thing always full of rubbish. Lottie could have been asleep in the back.

Under a blanket, maybe, or a coat, something like that. He can't have looked closely enough. You need to look again.'

Kesey made no effort to pull away. 'I'm sorry, I know this isn't what you want to hear. But I don't believe that's the case. Lottie was not in that car.'

The tendons stood out on Megan's neck, a pulse visible as she struggled to compute the unfathomable. 'Where's the car now? She's on her own. The poor girl must be terrified. You need to look again, please, you need to look again!'

'The car's here in the police pound right now. I've had it checked. Your daughter is not in the car. I can say that with absolute certainty. I'm sorry, Megan, but the facts are the facts. I know it's not what you want to hear, but we have to deal with reality.'

The colour drained from Megan's cheeks, the skin bunching around her eyes as the tension changed the contours of her face. She looked suddenly smaller, older, as if her life-force were draining away. 'But that can't be. It's just not possible. There has to be some mistake. Dale took her. Talk to him, for goodness' sake, talk to him! If Lottie wasn't in the car, where the hell is she? What on earth has he done with her? Talk to him now. What are you waiting for? You've got to make him tell you.'

Kesey's eyebrows gathered together in a pained expression she couldn't hope to hide. 'Dale will be questioned as soon as this interview is at an end. He may have taken Lottie. He could have left her somewhere between the time of leaving your home address and being stopped by the officer. It's not inconceivable. But it's not a good idea to make any assumptions or jump to any conclusions before we know the full facts. We have to consider every possibility as the investigation progresses. Failing to do so would be a failure on my part. I'd be letting Lottie down, and that's the last thing I'd want to do. Do you understand what I'm telling you?'

Megan clenched her hands into tight fists, digging the nails into her palms, oblivious to the pain as the full implications of Kesey's words slowly dawned. 'Oh, God, where is she? I can't bear it. Where's my little girl?'

Kesey wanted to comfort Megan. She wanted to say just about anything that relieved her inevitable feelings of dread, even slightly. But the detective knew from hard-won experience that brutal honesty was best. False hope was no hope. There was a window of opportunity where a missing child was concerned – the likelihood of finding them alive diminished with every hour that passed. There was no room for ambiguity, no room for sentimentality, however well-intentioned. It was time to get on. 'I'm going to do everything I can to find your daughter. That I can guarantee you. Let's get a statement down on paper as quickly as we can. I'll then interview your ex personally, and we can proceed matters from there. Are you ready to continue?'

Megan nodded frantically, her eyes staring but not seeing, shoulders tight. 'Yes, I understand.'

Kesey handed Megan back her phone. 'I've already asked my sergeant, DS Raymond Lewis, to issue a missing person notification to all officers within the force. It will be circulated on a nationwide basis later today if that proves necessary.'

Megan's shoulders curled over her chest as the stark reality fully sank in. She'd never felt lower, never more desperate. Her face was ashen as she spoke again. 'You... you... you don't think Dale took Lottie, that's what you're implying. You think... you think somebody else took her. Some stranger, some monster who broke into my house.'

Kesey looked back at Megan with a pained stare. 'Let's get the full facts down on paper.'

'Oh my God, I'm right, aren't I! You think Lottie's been abducted by someone else entirely. A stranger who invaded my home.'

Kesey took a thin sheaf of papers and a pen from the cluttered drawer below the tabletop. 'If Dale did take her, she was only in his car for a matter of minutes. That's a hypothesis we can't rule out entirely. But as I said, we need to consider all possibilities. Now, let's start with a written statement. You know how this works. You've been here often enough. We need to record everything that happened from the time Dale arrived outside your home address to the time you discovered that your daughter was missing this morning. Once that's done we can continue from there.'

Megan wiped away a tear with the same tissue with which she'd dried her face. 'You will find her, won't you? Lottie is going to be okay, isn't she? I couldn't bear to lose her. She's got her whole life ahead of her. She's only... she's only five years old.'

Kesey poised her pen above the statement form. 'Most missing children are found safe and sound.'

'Yes, but not all of them.'

Kesey shook her head slowly, first one way and then the other. 'No, not all of them, but I'm going to do all I can to ensure that your daughter isn't one of those unfortunate children.'

'You've got to find her, Inspector. I'm begging you. Please find my little girl.'

7

Kesey sat alongside DS Lewis, with Dale flopped in a chair on the opposite side of the interview room table.

Dale was nursing a hangover. He appeared distracted, focused on his physical suffering, only mildly concerned by the potential legal implications of his actions, as he raised a hand to his face, shielding veined and bloodshot eyes from the electric glare of the fluorescent light above his head.

Kesey glanced towards her older but less senior colleague, keen to expedite matters. A child was missing and very likely in peril. 'Switch the tape on,

Ray. The quicker we get this done, the happier I'll be.'

Kesey stated the time, date and location, rushing her words, and then continued, her tone conveying her concern. 'My name is Detective Inspector Laura Kesey. Also present is Detective Sergeant Raymond Lewis, and the suspect Mr Dale Weller. I need to remind you, Mr Weller, that you are still subject to caution. Anything you say could be used in evidence in any subsequent court proceedings. Do you understand what I'm telling you?'

Dale nodded once, looking away as if uninterested, his eyes narrowed to slits as he massaged his temples with the tips of his fingers.

'For the tape, please, Mr Weller, we need to hear you say it.'

Dale met her eyes before lowering his gaze. 'Yeah, I understand. Happy now? Can we get this shit over with? I need to get my head down.'

Kesey spoke again the moment he finished his sentence. 'And can you confirm that you have declined the offer of legal representation?'

Dale emitted a long, deep audible breath. 'I was

pissed; I acted like an idiot. You've got all the evidence you need. There's no point in my trying to deny any of it. There's fuck all a solicitor can do for me now. Stop pissing about. Interview me, charge me, and let me get out of here. I could do with a pint to take the edge off.'

'So, you don't want a lawyer?'

'No, I don't want a fucking lawyer. Is that clear enough for you?'

Kesey tilted her head at a slight angle, holding his gaze right up to the time it was no longer comfortable. 'As long as you're sure?'

'Yeah, yeah, I'm sure. Just get on with it.'

Kesey drummed two fingers of her left hand on the tabletop. 'Where's your daughter?'

He opened his eyes wide. 'What?'

'Just answer the question.'

Dale raised himself in his seat. He appeared more animated now, Adam's apple bobbing as he made a strange noise in his throat. 'Why the fuck would you ask me about Lottie?'

'Where is she? That's all I need to know.'

A look of genuine concern dominated Dale's features. 'I'm assuming she's with her mother, or maybe

her grandmother. Unless you're telling me something different.'

'You were outside your ex-wife's house in the
early hours of this morning.'

'What's your point? I haven't denied it.'

'You confirm you were there?'

'Yeah, I was there. I said so, didn't I? But what the
fuck's that got to do with Lottie?'

Kesey moved to the very edge of her seat. 'You
hammered on the front door; you repeatedly de-
manded to see your daughter. That's true, isn't it?
Isn't that what happened?'

'Yeah, but so fucking what? Megan refused to let
me in. She told me to sod off home. She's like that
sometimes, unreasonable.'

Kesey softened her tone. 'Ah, okay, now we're getting somewhere. Unreasonable how?'

'I'm a good father, a loving father, but it seems
the miserable cow can't see it. She thinks she's better
than me with her posh job and paper qualifications,
that's the problem.'

'How does that make you feel?'

Dale cleared his throat. 'We were close before she
got a degree, soulmates. It was all downhill from

there. A simple plumber isn't good enough for her any more. No doubt she wants some stuck-up tosser with a load of money in the bank. A walking fucking suit and briefcase.'

Kesey glared at her suspect, studying his body language, trying to read his thoughts. It was time to up the pressure. 'But Megan qualified years ago. Your separation was far more recent. You're making no sense at all.'

'It's my life. What the fuck do you know? The problems began when she left university. Nothing was the same after that.'

'Are you telling me she doesn't think you're good enough?'

'Of course I fucking well am.'

'Does that make you angry, Dale? Is that what happened? Did you hurt Lottie in an uncontrollable rage? Did you lose control?'

He shook his head frantically, wincing as a stab of pain fired behind his eyes. 'Don't be so fucking ridiculous. Why would you ask me that? I've never raised a hand to Lottie, never once in my life.'

Kesey rested her elbows on the table, leaning towards her suspect, focused on him and only him. 'I think that's exactly what you did. It may have been the first time, or maybe not. Only you know the answer to that one. But you've done something this time. I know that much. I just need you to tell me what.'

'No, no, no, for fuck's sake no! I saw Lottie looking down from her bedroom window at one point, and that was it. I drove off as soon as I heard the siren. And then one of your pig friends stopped me on my way home, a big bloke with a beard and glasses. But then you already know that. That's why I'm here. Why not just charge me with drink-driving and let me get out of here? If something's happened to Lottie, I need to see her. The girl means everything to me. Charge me and let me go.'

Kesey glared at him as he rocked in his seat, nostrils flared, chest thrust out, sweating. 'You've forced your way into your ex-wife's property before now. It's on record, in the files. Perhaps this time you did something you now regret. I've interviewed Megan. She described your behaviour in specific detail. You were way out of control. It seems as if you were angry enough to me.'

'I haven't got a fucking clue what you're talking about.'

'Lottie is missing, Dale. You need to take this seriously. I want you to tell me exactly what you've done with her. You need to do the right thing. It will go better for you in court if you do. It's the only card you've got left to play.'

Dale repeatedly clenched and unclenched his hands into tight fists below the table, as his bravado melted away. 'What the fuck are you saying? I've got no idea where she is. Get out there and find her. If she's missing, it's got fuck all to do with me.'

This time it was DS Lewis's turn to speak up. 'We have good reason to believe that you either hid in the vicinity and waited until the two officers left your ex-wife's home address, or you left the area and then returned very shortly after the officer's departure.'

'No fucking way, that didn't happen.'

'You broke in through the kitchen window, you climbed the stairs, and then you took Lottie from your ex-wife's bedroom at the back of the property. It's time for some honesty, time to come clean. Where is she, Dale? What have you done with your little girl?'

Dale jumped to his feet, knocking back his chair, his arms held wide. He was shouting now, his voice breaking as the tears began to flow. 'If some bastard has taken Lottie from the house, you need look for her.' He lurched forward, throwing himself over the table, grabbing the lapels of Kesey's navy jacket with both hands and pulling her towards him, foreheads touching, skin on skin. 'Did you hear what I said, you stupid bitch? I want out of here. I want to look for my daughter. If some fucker took Lottie, it wasn't me!'

Lewis moved with surprising speed and agility for a man of his age and fleshy build. He pulled Dale off Kesey, forced an arm up his back, and then used his superior strength and weight to push him to the floor, pinning him there with one arm while searching for his handcuffs with his free hand.

As Lewis dragged Dale upright, both wrists tightly secured, Dale was still yelling, a stream of tears running down his sullen and ill-tempered face. 'Find my daughter! That's all I'm asking you. If someone's got her, you've got to find her! I'm begging you. She's five, just fucking five! Do something useful for once in your fucking lives. Find my little girl.'

As Lewis shoved Dale back towards his cell,

Kesey sat back in her seat with her feet on the table, gathering her thoughts. She was only slightly shaken by the physical nature of Dale's protests. His overt aggression hadn't surprised her a great deal. She'd seen it all before and coped with worse.

No, it was the implication of Dale's emotional words and demeanour that bothered Kesey most. She'd always thought the chances of Dale being the perpetrator she was looking for were slender, and now she was sure of it. If Dale was lying, he was a world-class actor.

This wasn't a case of parental abduction following family breakdown. It was more than that, much more. If Lottie was still alive, she was in terrible danger.

They'd examine every inch of Dale's estate car for forensic evidence. And they'd look for his fingerprints on the window frame too. They'd follow procedure as all good detectives did. But they wouldn't find anything implicating Dale in the crime.

They were looking for someone else entirely, a hunter who preyed on the innocent.

8

Detective Chief Superintendent Nigel Halliday pushed up the sleeve of his bespoke, charcoal-grey pinstripe jacket, and looked at his high-end Swiss watch, making it obvious, before turning his attention to Kesey, as she sat and waited in his excessively large office. 'Right, what can I do for you, Laura? Please try to be as concise as possible. I'm rather pushed for time.'

Kesey silently acknowledged that almost everything about the man's outward behaviour and bearing annoyed her immensely. She'd disliked him since their first meeting. 'I'm sorry, sir, this is far too important to be rushed.'

Halliday studied his watch for a second time as if willing their meeting to end. He sighed before stifling a yawn. 'It might be an idea to let me be the judge of that. You do rather ramble on at times. Try to outline the key points as succinctly as you possibly can. Other matters are demanding my attention. We can always reschedule if necessary. I can't spend all my time talking to you.'

Kesey's tone hardened as she held his gaze. 'We've got a child abduction case. A five-year-old girl taken from her home in the early hours of this morning. She's the daughter of a local solicitor, Megan Weller. She's with Rundle and Evans in Curzon Street.'

All of a sudden Halliday appeared more interested, but only slightly. 'Are we talking about a family-perpetrated abduction? Most are in my experience. I dealt with several while with the Met.'

Kesey shook her head, asking herself why he always felt the need to mention his time in London. And all those academic certificates on his office wall. Small dick syndrome. 'I thought it was likely initially, but early enquiries suggest otherwise.'

He appeared far from persuaded. 'And you say that why exactly?'

'The girl lives with her mother. There have been recent custody issues involving the father; there's an injunction; and he seemed the obvious suspect, but he was in our custody for most of the night on a drink-drive charge. If he took his daughter, she was only in his car for a matter of minutes. I can't see that happening. The timeline doesn't fit. We're looking for somebody else.'

Halliday looked at Kesey as if she'd stunk out the room. 'Stranger abductions are extremely rare, particularly in this part of the world and from private property. Are you sure of your facts?'

Kesey imagined herself kneeing Halliday between his legs, hard, bang, right in the balls. 'Rare, yes, but they're not unknown. DI Gravel told me he'd investigated a very similar scenario a few years back – before my time – involving a psychiatrist, a Dr David Galbraith, one evil bastard if ever there was one. It shook Grav, even with all his experience. He said it was the worst case he's ever dealt with.'

'Are you suggesting that this Galbraith is a suspect in the girl's disappearance?'

Kesey shook her head. 'No, that's not what I'm saying.'

Halliday looked down his nose at her, shaking his head slowly. 'Oh, for goodness' sake, try to stick to the point, Laura. I've told you my time's valuable. Have you even interviewed the father?'

Kesey scratched an eyebrow. 'Yes, he's been interviewed, charged with drink-driving and assaulting a police officer. He was released on pre-charge bail pending further enquiries relating to the abduction about an hour ago.'

Halliday made a peculiar humming noise before speaking. 'Released? Do you think that was wise?'

'The man appeared genuinely shocked when told of his daughter's disappearance. We can't rule him out completely, not at this stage, not without further enquiries. But I think it's highly unlikely he had any involvement.'

'If you're certain?'

Kesey felt sure she'd detected a hint of sarcasm in Halliday's tone, which didn't surprise her in the slightest. 'All I can do is follow the evidence. I'm as sure as I can be that he's not our man. In my opinion, we're looking for somebody else. I can't make it any clearer than that.'

'Why assume it's a man? You could be looking for a female. Never make assumptions, Laura. It's unwise in our line of work.'

Kesey felt her entire body tense. 'It was a manner of speech, that's all, nothing more.'

'Words matter, please remember that. This isn't the first time we've had a conversation along these lines.'

She bit the inside of her lower lip hard, resisting the almost overwhelming desire to tell him exactly what she thought of him. 'Can we focus back on the case, sir? You've said your time is limited.'

Halliday raised a hand to his freshly shaved chin. His right eye was twitching slightly when he spoke again. 'Speedy and efficient action is crucial in this type of case, whatever the motive. I shouldn't need to tell you that. A child's life may hang in the balance. Screw this up, and it won't do your career any favours. I'm assuming you've made the relevant notifications.'

And just when she thought she couldn't like him any less. 'Yes, a full description and photograph have been circulated both within the force and on a countrywide basis.'

'An all-ports alert?'

'That's what I said.'

He made that same humming noise. 'Very well, Laura, that seems like a reasonable start in the circumstances. Where do you suggest we go from here?'

Kesey glanced up at the wall clock to her right. 'I've got a planning meeting arranged for just under an hour. I know exactly what we need to do, I'm fully familiar with standing orders pertaining to this type of investigation, but I'm going to need additional resources.'

'Budgets are tight. Finances have to be carefully managed. There's no money to waste.'

Kesey fingered the silver chain hanging around her neck, her eyes cold and flinty. 'What I suggest is that we set up a dedicated team of officers to focus on this case and nothing else until we find Lottie Weller alive or otherwise. I require at least another six officers under my command. I'll also need you to reassign my current cases for as long as necessary. I'm in court on Tuesday, there's no avoiding that, but that aside, I'd like to focus exclusively on heading up the task force with DS Lewis as my second-in-command. He's got both the experience and dedicated work ethic I need in the circumstances. I'm very much hoping you agree.'

Halliday screwed up his face. 'Don't you think this is all a bit over the top? We're not exactly awash with resources. There are other priorities I have to consider.'

Kesey couldn't quite believe what she was hearing. She asked herself if he was simply winding her up, taking pleasure in being obstructive, annoying her because he could. Or was he as useless as he sometimes seemed? 'Whatever the perpetrator's motive, money, sex, or even worse, the child is in danger. And that's if she's not already dead. You said it yourself. This type of case can destroy careers. I'm sure that applies to yours as well as mine.'

Halliday made an unnecessary adjustment to his silk tie. 'Very well, I'm happy to agree to your proposals in principle. But I want a full written report on my desk, with costings, by four o'clock this afternoon at the latest. I want to keep the chief constable fully apprised of the facts. Now, is there anything else before we bring this meeting to a close?'

'If we haven't found the girl within seventy-two hours, I'd like to hold a press conference. I'd want the parents there, and I'd want the media well represented. Are you in agreement?'

'Talk to the press officer. She should be able to help you with the arrangements.'

'Do you want to be involved?'

The shake of his head was barely perceptible. 'No, I don't think that's necessary, not at this stage, I'll leave it to you.'

Kesey stood, keen to get out of there. 'Thank you, sir.'

'Keep me fully informed, no surprises. Have I made myself clear?'

Kesey spoke as she walked to his office door. 'Yes, sir, loud and clear. When anything significant happens, you'll be the first to know.'

9

Kesey was attempting to exude an air of confidence she didn't feel when she entered the conference room later that day. She looked around the brightly lit space, pleased to see that all the required officers were seated and waiting, except for the six additional officers she had requested, but she wasn't expecting them to attend. Changes had to be made to shift patterns, leave cancelled. And, like it or not, that was going to take a bit of time.

The chatter stopped almost immediately when Kesey stood at the front of the room, raising an arm above her head, hand open, fingers spread, palm faced outwards. She looked from one officer to the next, silently mourning the limited resources at her command. The curse of small forces.

'Right, listen up, everyone. It's time we made a start. It's now almost six hours since Megan Weller discovered that her five-year-old daughter, Lottie, was missing from their family home in Picton Street here in town. An all-ports notification has been circulated as per procedure. Scenes of crime officers are at the house as we speak, and will report any significant findings. I will then share those findings with you. I've spoken to the lab, who will rush things through.

'Dale Weller, the father, has been interviewed and is an unlikely suspect. We may well be dealing with a stranger abduction. I'm sure I don't need to tell you that prompt and efficient action greatly increases the chance of a successful outcome. We all want Lottie Weller found safe and well. And we're going to assume she is alive unless proved otherwise. You've seen the photograph. You know who we're looking for. Lottie is young, and she's vulnerable. There's no room for cock-ups. I need you all to be crystal clear as to the nature of your duties.' Kesey paused for breath and then continued, 'As of now, this case is our number one priority.

Nothing is more important. Not until we find her. With that said, are there any questions before I continue?'

No-one said a word.

'Okay, let's get on. I'll quickly apprise you of developments so far and then allocate your duties. I will be the senior investigating officer for as long as the case continues, with DS Lewis as my second-in-command. If there are any significant developments, we need to know about them immediately. Don't even think about sitting on anything. Is that clear?'

Everyone indicated their understanding in one way or another, a nod of the head or a verbal response.

'SOCOs have examined Dale Weller's car, and, as I said earlier, are at the Picton Street address. DS Lewis has already contacted the hospitals but without success. We have nothing to indicate who took Lottie Weller or where she was taken.'

A long-serving career constable seated in the back row raised a hand.

'Yes, Mike?'

'What about CCTV?'

'There are no cameras in Picton Street or the immediate area, but it may well be worth checking the town centre cameras. If there were any known or suspected offenders about at the relevant time, anyone with a history of offences against children, we need to know about it.'

'That's something I'm happy to do if that helps.'

Kesey nodded. 'Thank you, Mike, make a start as soon as we're done here.'

'Will do, boss.'

'DC Thomas, I want you to go through the list of all known and suspected paedophiles in the force area. The abduction could have a sexual motive. Look at how each offender operates and put together a shortlist.'

Thomas nodded less than enthusiastically. 'Any idea of how many nonces are on the list?'

'We're talking close to four hundred. That's known and suspected abusers. If anyone can be ruled out for a good reason, do that, and then go through the rest of the list as quickly as you can. If any of them has any link to the Weller family, we need to look at them closely. The quicker we can check them out, the better.'

Thomas nodded for a second time. It was going to be a long day.

'PC Rees, PC Evans and PC Price, you'll be making house-to-house enquiries under the supervision of DS Lewis, starting in Picton Street and then moving on to the surrounding streets. Dale Weller made one hell of a racket in the time before the abduction, which was followed by the police siren. It's usually a quiet residential area. A lot of people will have been woken. Someone may have seen something significant. It's your job to find out if they did.'

Kesey turned and pointed to a map of the Picton Street area she'd prepared in advance of the meeting. It was a technique she'd learnt from her much-loved mentor, DI Gravel. She tapped a biro repeatedly on a large blue X marked close to the centre of the map. 'This X indicates the location of the Wellers' semi-detached Victorian home, the crime scene.' She tapped the map again. 'This first circle, the black one, indicates the area those of you not yet allocated a task will search first. I need you to search bins, out-buildings and the like, each and every location where a child could hide, or a body could be concealed. A dog handler will assist you. This work isn't glamorous, it isn't exciting, but it is crucial. Let's get it done as quickly and efficiently as possible.'

Kesey turned her attention back to the map and continued. 'This larger circle, the green one, marks the additional area that those of you allocated the task will search if nothing is found within the black area. So, to be clear, you'll examine the area within the black circle first and then move on to area two once that's completed to DS Lewis's satisfaction. Please thoroughly familiarise yourselves with the geography before you leave the room. If we don't find anything today, we will search again tomorrow and the day after that, and the day after that until we do. Lottie Weller has to be somewhere. Hopefully, she's still alive. It's our job to find her.'

10

Later that day, Dale was standing at the bar, sipping a glass of sparkling water less than enthusiastically, when Megan entered the quiet Caerystwyth Rugby Club. He turned as the busty bottle-blonde barmaid nodded at Megan, acknowledging his ex's arrival with a wave. 'All right, Meg, I'm glad you came. Thanks for agreeing to meet me, it's appreciated. It's fucking horrendous. We've got to stick together.'

Megan looked pale, tired, dejected. As if the stuffing had been knocked out of her. 'Why here? Why a bar of all places?'

'Oh, come on, give me a break. I played for the first team for years. And we used to come here when we were courting. It seemed the obvious place, neutral territory. What's it matter?'

Megan stared at the glass in his hand. 'What are you drinking?'

He placed his half-empty glass on the bar, throwing his hands up. 'It's water, just fucking water. Taste it if you want to. Do you really think I'd get pissed with Lottie missing fuck knows where?'

Megan frowned hard, and for a moment he thought she may start weeping. 'I don't know, Dale, you've changed so very much in recent months. I don't know what to think any more; life's been blown apart.'

'Do you want a drink or what?'

'I can't eat, I can't drink, I've thrown up more times than I care to count. My stomach's doing somersaults. I've been walking the streets for hours, just looking, just hoping I'd spot her. Why would I want a drink?'

'I'm talking about a soft drink. Don't read anything into it. We've got a difficult time ahead of us. You've got to keep your strength up.'

Megan sat at the nearest table, shoulders

bunched, arms folded across her chest. 'My mum said much the same thing when I rang her.'

'So, what are you going to have?'

'Get me a coffee. I'll try to force it down.'

'Good girl, that's the spirit. Milk and sugar?'

Megan nodded, dabbing at her tear-stained eyes with a paper hankie taken from her bag. There was audible stress in her voice when she spoke. 'I really couldn't give a toss. Anything will do. However it comes.'

Dale ordered, paid, and joined Megan at the table. 'There you go, love. Try your best to drink it before it goes cold. You look as if you could do with it.'

She chose to ignore his use of the endearment. There were bigger battles to fight. 'Why am I here, Dale? You said it was urgent. You'd better not be wasting my time, not now, not with all this going on. I'd never forgive you if you are.'

He lowered his eyes, fighting to control his emotions, focusing on the beer-stained carpet at his feet for a beat before speaking again. 'I've... err... I've made some posters on the computer. I printed them off. Twenty to start with. But I can make more if we need them. I'd just need to buy some more ink.'

'What are you talking about?'

'Isn't it obvious? Posters, posters of Lottie, you know, saying she's missing and telling anyone who knows anything to contact the police as a matter of urgency. I thought you might think it's a good idea.'

Megan gripped the table's edge with both hands, clinging on as if for life itself. 'Look me in the eye, Dale. I need you to tell me you didn't take Lottie. I need you to swear it on your mother's life. I need to hear you say it right here and now to my face. And I'll know if you're telling me the truth. You never were a very good liar.'

He tugged at his sleeve with restless fingers. 'I can't believe you're even asking me that question. Of course I didn't fucking well take her. I know I've been a prat since my dad died, but come on. What the hell do you take me for? I wouldn't harm a hair on the girl's head.'

'Do you swear it? Do you give me your word?'

His eyes filled with tears. 'For fuck's sake, woman, how long have you known me? Of course I swear it. I love Lottie to bits.'

'Did you take her, yes or no? It's a simple enough

question. And one that requires an answer in case you were wondering.'

'No, how many times do I have to say it? No! Of course I fucking well didn't take her. I'm tearing my hair out. Can't you see it? I'm crapping myself. I'm as worried as you are.'

Megan studied his face, that oh so familiar face, the face she'd once loved above all others. And the longer she looked at him, the more she believed she knew the truth. Dale was innocent. 'I've got to believe she's okay. What are we going to do? How can we find her?'

He slurped his water, draining the glass. 'So, now you believe me?'

Megan nodded her head. 'Yes, yes, I do. I know you're telling the truth. I think I knew it all along. I didn't want to think anybody else had her. Someone has taken Lottie. I couldn't deny that, however tempting. I wanted it to be you.'

Dale's relief was almost palpable, a degree of tension draining from his face. 'Well, thank fuck for that. Things are bad enough without you doubting my integrity.'

'What are we going to do?'

'Right, I thought you could drive us around town. You know, we could ask various shops to display posters in their windows, and the Post Office. A lot of people go there. There's always people waiting at the counters.' He pointed at the wall to the right of the bar. 'I've already put a poster on the notice board. See? The one above the team sheet.'

'It's a good idea, I'll give you that. But it's not enough.'

He dropped his chin to his chest. 'I know that. I know I've let you down. And I've let Lottie down too. If I hadn't fucked everything up, I'd still have been there to look after her. I know posters aren't enough. But I've got to do something. Just sitting and waiting is driving me round the fucking bend.'

For the first time, Megan felt some empathy for his shared loss. They were both suffering, him as much as her. She could see it in his eyes. 'Maybe the police will come up with something soon. They took fingerprints at the house. They could identify whoever broke in. Find him, and they'll find Lottie.'

'I'll beat the bastard to a fucking pulp if I get my hands on him.'

Megan picked up her cup but returned it to its saucer without drinking.

'What is it, Meg? Tell me what you're thinking. I can see there's something.'

'I don't know if it's of any relevance, but I guess it could be. I've been thinking about the various clients I've worked with over the years. There was one named Peter Davies, a sex offender accused of the indecent assault of a six-year-old boy in the Llanelli area. I can remember him looking at a framed photo of Lottie on my office desk. The man made my skin crawl. He was almost drooling. You know, like when a man looks at a good-looking woman in a bikini on the beach. It shook me up. I took the photo home after that. I can't believe I was ever that naive. Some truly evil offenders have come through my office over the years. Sharing anything about your personal life is never a good idea. What the hell was I thinking?'

Dale clenched his hands into tight fists. 'Do you think the bastard may have taken her?'

'I don't know. I'm thinking out loud. This is like a nightmare that's become a reality. I keep thinking I'll open my eyes and it will all have been a bad dream.'

'Did you mention this Davies bastard to the police?'

'Not during the interview, I only thought about him on my way home. But I spoke to DI Kesey by phone as soon as I could get hold of her. She said they'd just finished a planning briefing and were getting on with the investigation. Screw client confidentiality. If I lose my job, what does it matter? I told her everything I know.'

'What did she say?'

'Nothing specific, nothing significant, but I got the distinct impression that she knew exactly who I was talking about.'

'Where does the bastard live? If he's touched Lottie, I'll tear his fucking balls off.'

Megan's expression darkened. A part of her regretted saying anything at all, but only a part. 'It's just a thought, that's all, nothing more. We've got to leave it to the police. Davies may have nothing at all to do with Lottie's disappearance. I just figured if the police found his fingerprints, well, they'd have their answer, God forbid. I pray it doesn't come to that. He's not the sort of man you want anywhere near our daughter. Or any other child, for that matter. He's a predator who feeds on the innocent.'

Dale reached across the table and clutched her hand. 'Where does he live? You may as well tell me. I can find out easily enough. I know a lot of people in this town. I'd just have to ask around.'

She wanted to tell him. She so wanted to tell him. 'I'm sorry I said anything at all now. You're in enough trouble without making it even worse for yourself. I've told Kesey. She'll look into it. Why wouldn't she? Let's leave it at that.'

Dale increased his grip, oblivious to crushing her fingers. 'What if the bastard has got her? What if he's hurting Lottie right now?'

Megan felt her gut spasm. It was too much to bear, too terrible to contemplate. She blurted out her reply, almost without thinking. 'He lives on the council estate near to the park. You know, the one on the hill with a view of the river. It's number eighteen or nineteen. I can't remember which, but it's definitely one or the other.'

Dale released her hand, rising to his feet. 'I'll fetch the posters. I left them on the bar. You take care of them, and I'll do the rest. If the police ask, this conversation never happened. You never mentioned Davies, not to me.'

'Oh, God, does that mean what I think it does?'

'If Lottie's there, or if I find anything out, I'll let you know.'

She touched her bottom lip. 'Yes, okay, but don't use your mobile.'

'I'll get a cheap pay-as-you-go. I'll ring your land-line in a couple of hours.'

Megan stood and hugged him, pulling him close and holding him tight, finding comfort in their shared adversity. 'Thank you, Dale. If the police ever ask me, we were together all afternoon. You say the same if you ever have to, and let them prove other-wise – either that or stick to a no-comment interview. And avoid the main streets on your way to his house. You don't want to be caught on camera. You know the area as well as I do.'

'Okay, I hear you. That's not going to be an issue.'

'We've got to find her. We've got to find her alive. Do whatever you need to do, no holds barred. I'll un-derstand, and I'll do all I can to protect you. What would we do without our little girl?'

11

DS Lewis banged on Peter Davies' front door without reply for a full thirty seconds before resorting to yelling. He could clearly hear the sound of the radio coming from inside the semi-detached house, Radio One or maybe Two, music and chatter, so why no reply? Lewis called out one last time before peering through a ground floor window.

He saw a man meeting his suspect's description lying prone on the floor of a dated, sparsely furnished lounge. The man had dark blood seeping from his nose and mouth. He glanced up with swollen eyes when Lewis tapped the glass, and then quickly looked away. The detective grinned as the man attempted to crawl behind the sofa, but he didn't try to rise and run.

Lewis threw his not inconsiderable bulk against the front door, once, then again, cursing loudly and crudely as a jolt of pain fired down one arm. He took a backward step and then hurled himself forward again, this time with success as the metal lock fractured in the wooden frame. The DS stumbled into the hall, falling to his knees, and then raising himself upright with the aid of a wall decorated with peeling wood chip paper.

Just being in the house made Lewis feel dirty. He'd dealt with paedophiles before, more than he cared to count, and it was a part of the job he loathed. Lewis was glad he didn't understand them. He was happy he didn't share their deviant tastes. He silently observed that scum like Davies destroyed so many lives. They preyed on the innocent. As if children were worthless. As if they didn't matter at all.

'I'm coming in. It's the police.'

Davies spat a large globule of partially congealed blood from his mouth as Lewis entered the lounge, with its charity store furniture and frayed floral carpet. 'Thank fuck for that. I thought he might have come back.'

Lewis glared down at his suspect, feeling nothing but revulsion. Davies looked so ordinary, so un-threatening. *What a shame men like him don't come with PAEDO stamped on their foreheads in large letters people couldn't miss. Or maybe they should carry a bell. Unclean, yeah, maybe carry a bell. A warning to stay well clear.* 'You thought who might have come back?'

Davies raised a hand to his face, wincing on touching a torn lip, a part of which hung down onto to his bloody chin. 'The bastard who did this to me. Who do you fucking think?'

Lewis strolled around the room, peering from one place to another, spotting a laptop, asking him-self if it was worth looking at. Maybe the tech team could find something useful. Something to put the scrote back inside where he belonged. 'Mr Peter Davies, I presume?'

'What are you going to do about the fucking state I'm in?'

'Well, now, let me think. I'm assuming someone found out that you're a filthy little nonce. Am I right?'

Davies looked away. 'I want to press charges.'

Lewis smiled as he slowly approached him. 'I'm guessing you were beaten up by someone with kids of their own. Someone like me who can't stand the sight of you. Someone who doesn't want a nasty little pervert like you anywhere near.'

'What the fuck do you want?'

'I know what you're up to, you dirty little paedo. I saw the play area on the corner, the slide, the swings, the climbing frame, the mothers with kids in tow. That's why you moved here. That's why you chose this house. I'd be willing to bet your landlord doesn't know your history. Unless he's a nonce as well, of course. Shit sticks together. It's as predictable as night and day.'

'I said I want to press charges.'

'This is a nice neighbourhood, a family neighbourhood. I suggest you fuck off somewhere else. It's not a place for the likes of you.'

Davies visibly tensed as he lost control of his bladder. 'Look at the fucking state I'm in. I need help. My ribs are broken. I'm losing blood. I want to press charges.'

Lewis laughed. 'There's only one thing as low as a nonce in the eyes of the criminal classes, and that's a grass. I'd forget about making any allegations if I were you. I could put the word out, let people know. And as for helping you, I wouldn't gob on you if you were going up in flames.'

'I've served my time. I've got rights. I'm no different from anyone else. I want the bastard who did this prosecuted.'

The big detective stood on the fingers of his suspect's right hand, pressing down hard until he yelped. 'Oh, I don't think so, Peter. We wouldn't get anywhere with the investigation even if you did make a statement. I've got more important things to do with my time. A case that matters a lot more than you do. That's why I'm here. Your name's in the frame. I'm looking for a missing child. A child with links to you.'

Davies pulled his hand away as the detective took a backward step. 'If a kid's missing, it's got fuck all to do with me. Ask the probation people. I completed the sex offender course over a year back. I haven't offended since, not even once.'

The big man chuckled to himself. A cold laugh that had nothing to do with humour. 'Yeah, like that's going to make any difference. Give me a fucking break. You haven't been caught yet, that's all. People like you don't change. You can't make a straight man gay or a gay man straight. And you can't turn a nasty little nonce git like you into anything different. You're always going to be a risk to kids, all your miserable life. It's who you are. Those courses are as fucking useless as you are; if anything, they make things worse.'

Davies shifted his position as the urine pooled under him, soaking into his clothes, staining the frayed carpet. 'I haven't done anything, I swear it, what more can I say?'

'In that case, you won't object to me having a good look around this shithole, will you, you dirty little pervert?'

Davies grimaced on shaking his head. 'Look wherever the fuck you want. I've got nothing to hide. I just want you out of here.'

Lewis turned away. 'You stay right there where you are, there's a good nonce. Don't move an inch. Just lie there and stink of piss. I'll shout if I need you.'

Davies called out as Lewis approached the open door to the kitchen. 'When did the kid go missing?'

'Are you trying to be funny?'

'No, no, not at all, it's a serious question. If you tell me, I may be able to help you.'

The detective walked back towards his suspect, flexing his powerful biceps, cracking his knuckles. 'Waste my time, and I'll show you what a proper beating feels like. It's something I'm good at, something in which I excel... speak up, Peter. I'm not a patient man.'

Davies pressed himself against the base of the sofa, making himself smaller. 'I'm not that stupid. I want you gone. I'll do anything I can to help. Just say the word.'

Should he say something? Was it a good idea? Yeah, what the hell, it would be all over the papers soon enough anyway. 'The child disappeared some time in the early hours of this morning.'

The merest hint of a smile appeared on Davies' bruised and battered face. 'Did you say this morning?'

'What's so fucking funny?'

The thin smirk on Davies' face gradually became a broad, full-blown grin as he ignored his pain, endorphins providing a natural high. He wanted to laugh. He so wanted to laugh. But the big man was looming over him. 'I flew into Cardiff airport at twenty to nine this morning. My old mum paid for a holiday in the sun. You can check the flight schedule. It's over there on the sideboard with the boarding pass next to the clock. It's all there in black and white.' He raised a finger to his face. 'I told the nutter who did this to me the same fucking thing when he stopped beating the crap out of me so I could speak. You're pissing in the wind, Detective. I wasn't even in the country. If a child's missing, I couldn't give a shit. It's got fuck all to do with me.'

Lewis crossed the room, flinging Davies' computer forcibly to the floor and then stamping down on it with the heel of a black leather brogue. 'Oh dear, sorry about that, Peter, I've always been a bit on the clumsy side. Buy another one, and I'll be back. And start planning your move. To somewhere without a nearby school or playground. Somewhere you're less of a risk to the community. You've got four weeks from today. If you're still here after that, I'll be back. And the local hard cases are going to find out exactly what and where you are. You won't last very long after that. Not in one piece anyway. They'll tear your balls off and stuff them down your throat until you choke.'

'You can't do that. You're a copper; there're laws, rules you have to follow. I'll make a formal complaint. I'll report you. You'll be out of a fucking job.'

Lewis laughed again, this time with genuine amusement. 'I'm a decorated officer with over twenty years of service, and you're a nasty, dirty little nonce cunt who's served time on a sex offenders wing. I looked up your record, gross indecency, indecent assault, thousands of indecent images of children, many in the most extreme category, including torture. One of your victims was four and another six. Complain to whoever the fuck you want to. Who are they going to believe, you or me? If you're still here in four weeks, I'm coming for you. That's my rules, that's my law. Suck it up and accept it, nonce. It's the only choice you've got.'

12

'Bless me, Father, for I have sinned. It has been eighteen years, nine months and three days since my last confession.'

The pencil-thin, grey-haired priest peered through the screen in the semi-darkness of the confessional, his gold metal-rimmed glasses perched on the very tip of his nose. 'That seems very specific if you don't mind me saying so. Is there something in particular that brings you back here after all this time?'

The man moved a little closer, inching himself forward, sitting on the very edge of his chair and looking back with an intense, fevered stare. 'Don't you remember me, priest? You should do. I re-member you. You were a friend of my father. He was as depraved as you are.'

The priest raised a clammy hand to his chest, making the sign of the cross. 'Henry? Is that you?'

'Ah, so you do remember me. It's Martin these days, Martin Heath to be precise, but, yes, I was known as Henry in my youth.'

The priest looked up, asking God for strength as the hairs rose on his arms, pressing against his shirt-sleeves. 'You sat in that same seat all those years ago and told me that you'd killed your baby sister. You'd drowned her in the bath. Murder, you actually used the word. You held that poor child's head under the water until she breathed her last breath. Everyone believed it was an accident, but you told me different. You shared that awful burden with me at the age of only twelve years old and said you felt no remorse. You rocked me to my very core that terrible day. That's a hard thing for a man like me to forget.'

Heath giggled to himself, taking pleasure in the older man's obvious discomfort. 'Ah, yes, little baby Pamela, I still think of her sometimes when the mood takes me. I can picture the terror in her eyes as she looked up at me through the bathwater. There was the light of life in those eyes, and then it faded away to nothing as if she became a doll. She'd have been nineteen by now, had I allowed her to live. She'd be all grown up and doing who knows what. Oh, dear, how very sad! Do you think the wee small thing realised she was about to die as I pushed her under? I like to think she did.'

The priest retreated slightly in his seat as damp patches formed under both his arms. 'You committed a truly awful crime, an evil offence, an abomination in the sight of God. And at such a young age. Do you not realise that? Do you not appreciate the heinous nature of your wrongdoing?'

The giggling continued.

'What is there to laugh about? One day you'll face God's righteous judgement. Ask Him for mercy. You need to pray for your soul.'

Heath cocked his head at a slight angle. 'Do you really think so?'

'You took a life, an innocent life with all the promise that held. For God's sake, man, consider what you've done. Take responsibility for your actions before it's too late to save your soul.'

Heath broke into a smile that lit up his face. 'I can remember it all as if it were yesterday. My parents were utterly distraught, and particularly my mother, who couldn't stop weeping. And that was the point. Can you understand that in your very different world? Pamela was always the favourite, mummy's little angel, the centre of attention. And I hated her for that. I hated both of them. I wanted them to suffer, mother and baby daughter. And they did. I made it happen, me, all by myself. And after I killed my sister, I insisted on attending her funeral. My parents resisted the idea at first, but I prevailed, I was there. And it turned out to be one of the greatest days of my life. I could see the sorrow in my mother's eyes when they lowered the small white coffin into the ground forever. I tore that woman's heart to pieces. I ripped it to shreds. Mother was never the same person after that day. She was broken and beyond repair. She blamed herself for leaving the bathroom, leaving me, a mere child, to look after my sister. I planned, I waited for my opportunity, and I took it. Everything worked out exactly as I'd pictured it in my mind's eye.' He laughed again, louder this time, virtually manic. 'Pamela became an angel for real, up there somewhere in eternity, or simply rotting in the ground, and I was number one again. The boy who tried to save his little sister. The boy who did his best to resuscitate her, breaking her little ribs in the process. It was all in the papers, all over the news. I'd been through a horrible ordeal. That's what the fools said. It's surprising how much sympathy one gets as a grieving child.'

'Surely a small part of you must regret your actions? Do you not feel any degree of guilt all these years later? There can be no forgiveness without repentance. Penance follows remorse. You grew up a Catholic. You understand that! Seek forgiveness, or you'll face eternal damnation in the fires of hell.'

Heath crossed his legs, right over left. 'Now, let me think. Regrets, do I have any regrets? No, I can't claim that anything very much has changed a great deal since we last spoke all that time ago. I'm rather proud of what I did. I'd do the exact same thing again in the same circumstances. And why wouldn't I? Killing the little brat was a logical response to her unwelcome intrusion in my life. Survival of the fittest, red in tooth and claw, isn't that how creation works? Isn't that the world your God created?'

The priest felt his chest tighten. 'You seem to be forgetting peace, justice and love. We are nothing without love.'

'I killed my sister because I wanted to kill her. I killed her because it served a purpose. Because it amused me to do so. And I got away with it too, that's what matters. Why did your God let that happen? If it was such an abomination, why didn't He stop me? Ask yourself that. Has He no interest in your form of justice? Didn't He love my sister enough to save her from death at my hands? It seems that way to me.'

'God cares for all His children. He cares about your sister.'

'But not enough to save her.'

The priest opened his mouth as if to speak, but he couldn't find the words, anything adequate, nothing that seemed even remotely sufficient. He'd faced evil before, but never anything like this.

'Are you lost for words, Father? Don't tell me you've got nothing to say for yourself?'

'What can I say in the light of such evil?'

'Oh dear, I've just had the most terrible thought. Maybe you've wasted your entire adult life in-dulging a fantasy. Or perhaps it was the devil's work. That could be it. I could be the devil in human form, Beelzebub, The Lord of the Flies. You could be talking to the devil face to face right now. You have to admit it's a possibility. I have no concern for anyone but myself. Surely, that makes me evil personified? I'd be interested to know your thoughts.'

The priest winced as a sheen of sweat formed on his brow despite the cool temperature of the ancient building. 'Why would you say those terrible things? Why tell me all of this if you're not here to seek absolution for your sins?'

'I would have thought it was obvious. I'm telling you because I want to. I'm telling you because I can. The rules of the confessional bind you more effectively than any prison walls. You can't tell anyone, not a single soul. You can't unburden yourself however much you want to. Happy days! I find it rather amusing.'

'Don't forget about God! This is His house. There has to be a small part of you that feels guilt. I have to believe there's some good in you somewhere.'

'Are you referring to a small but distinctive voice in my head? A voice pointing out my many failings and encouraging me to change for the better, that sort of thing?'

The priest's eyes widened. 'Yes, a conscience, the knowledge of right and wrong, the voice of God.'

Heath was silent for several seconds as if considering his reply. As if it mattered. 'No, not really, not that I can think of. Maybe I haven't been listening closely enough. Or maybe there's no voice to hear.'

The elderly priest took a brown plastic medicine bottle from a trouser pocket. He unscrewed the white plastic cap, and urgently placed an angina pill under his tongue. 'Is there nothing positive you have to say for yourself before we bring this charade to an end?'

'Now let me think, positives... positives... are there any positives? Ah, yes, there is one thing which may interest you. I trained as a nurse and gained a degree. It made my dear mother so very proud.'

The priest's relief was evident. 'That's good to hear, Henry. Nursing is an admirable calling.'

'You'd think so, wouldn't you?'

'Sorry? What are you trying to say?'

'I worked for various overseas charities after qualifying, in war zones, famine areas, natural disasters, Asia, Africa and the Middle East. I've seen this world's suffering in all its infinite complexities. I've seen it up close and personal. And believe me, it's not a pretty sight, even for the likes of me. It's a terrible world when you think about it. Why does your God let so many people down?'

The priest wiped the sweat from his face. 'I sometimes think of life's challenges as an opportunity for learning. You did a good thing, a worthy thing. That's to your credit. It seems you're not entirely devoid of empathy or virtue. There is hope for you yet.'

'Do you really think so?'

'Yes, yes, I do, absolutely I do. God gave us free will. You chose to help others. That's to be celebrated. You put your dark past behind you.'

'Does that please you, Father? Does it give you hope for my ultimate redemption? Do such things reinforce your faith?'

'We all have the capacity to change for the better with God's good grace. You are no different.'

'What, even me?'

'Yes, you, even you.'

Heath laughed, head back, mouth wide open, his dark fillings in full view. 'You're assuming I helped all those victims of random circumstance in their times of great adversity. But you really couldn't be more wrong. Help? I don't know the meaning of the word. Nursing gives access to the vulnerable. Crisis work access to the desperate. Such work provided me with ideal opportunities to indulge my true nature to the ultimate degree. It served a purpose. Nursing facilitated my offences. I raped and killed with impunity. Do you hear what I said, Father? With impunity!'

The priest began panting now. His breathing laboured, his voice a whisper as he pulled his collar loose. 'How many?'

'How many? How many what exactly?'

'How many did you kill?'

'Oh, I'd say nineteen, or maybe twenty. Mainly young children but the odd adolescent too, when the opportunity arose and was simply too good to ignore. I'm not entirely certain what happened to one dark-haired boy I left hanging on to life when my activities were disturbed by a man, who stumbled on the scene of my crime at the worst possible time, before I left Syria. Now, that I do regret. If the police had taken the witness seriously, I wouldn't be sitting here now. I lost my job; I was encouraged to resign. But things could have been a lot worse. Maybe God was on my side.'

The priest threw a hand to his heart. 'All those children!'

Heath pressed his face to the screen. 'You could have stopped me, Father. I wanted you to know that. I want you to live with your guilt for however long you've got left as you approach death. Because you are guilty. You're as guilty as sin. If you'd chosen to speak out eighteen years ago, if you'd gone to the authorities when you had the chance, all those innocent children would still be alive. It's your responsibility. All those lost lives are down to you.'

The priest felt a sharp pain fire down one arm as the confessional booth became an unfocused blur. 'You are the devil!'

'I've been working as a teaching assistant at a primary school since returning to the UK. Did I mention that? The opportunity arose, and I thought, well, why the hell not? All those needy children, all those potential victims to target when the time feels right. I'm like a kiddie in a sweet shop. It was far too good a chance to miss.'

The priest coughed, clearing his throat, searching for a response he couldn't find.

'What, nothing more to say for yourself, Father? That's such a great shame. I thought you might be interested in my plans.'

'Oh, for God's sake, what now?'

'There's a particular young girl I've taken rather a liking to. She's staying over at my place for a week or two's entertainment, if you get my gist. I'll tire of her soon enough, but I'll allow her to live for a time. I've told my dear mother all about it. I had a special friend no-one else could see or hear as a child, and now I've got her. She's so very different since her death. She accepts and encourages my dark side. She's a far better mother now than she ever was.'

'You're ill, Henry. You need expert help. For God's sake, man, talk to your doctor.'

Heath shook his head. 'You hear the voice of God and I hear my mother. Is that so very different? I suspect mother's far more real.'

The priest reached for his tablets for a second time as his chest constricted, a sudden wave of nausea making him retch. He fumbled with the bottle and then dropped it to the floor. He reached out, but his fingers fell short. When he spoke, his words were whispered. 'You need help. You need treatment.'

'Killing is all the therapy I need.'

The searing pain spread to the priest's neck, jaw and back as a bright white tunnel of light gradually replaced his physical reality. His final words were barely audible. 'Help me, Henry. I need... I need...'

A face-stretching smile dominated Heath's otherwise unremarkable features as he rose slowly to his feet. 'Oh, I don't think so, Father. My work here is done. I'll be off now. She'll be waiting for me. It's time to meet your maker.'

13

Kesey hugged Janet, her best friend and partner in life, before turning away and switching on the kettle. 'Tea or coffee?'

'Tea please, you know how I like it.'

Kesey dropped fair trade teabags into two white porcelain mugs before pouring in the water. 'Fancy a biscuit?'

Janet patted her stomach, which was protruding slightly over the top of her jeans. 'No, you're all right, ta, I'm still trying to lose a bit of weight before the holiday. I'm going to look like a beached whale if I don't sort myself out. I can't get anywhere near that new bikini I bought. I should have got a bigger size.

Maybe a fourteen was always a bit on the ambitious side. Talk about rolls of fat. There are only three weeks to go. I'm running out of time.'

Kesey's face dropped as she added a splash of semi-skimmed milk to both mugs.

'What is it, Laura?'

Kesey handed Janet her hot drink before joining her at the kitchen table. 'What's what?'

'Oh, come on, you know what I'm talking about. You had a face like a slapped arse when I mentioned the holiday. I can read you like a large print book.'

Kesey averted her eyes to the wall. She stalled initially and then rushed her words. 'I... eh... I may not be able to go.'

Janet jerked her head back. 'What? Did I hear you right? We've been looking forward to it for months. And so has Edward. It's going to be his first proper trip away from home, our first foreign holiday as a family.'

Kesey sipped her tea, grimacing slightly when it burned her tongue. 'I'm so very sorry, Jan. It's this new case I'm dealing with. The missing girl I told you about. She's only a little bit older than Ed. I'm the divisional DI now. It's my responsibility to find her. It's not something I can avoid, however much I want to. I've got to see it through.'

'You've got three weeks. Surely you'll have found her before then.'

'It's eighteen days, Janet. We're supposed to be going away in eighteen days. I checked the calendar.'

Janet frowned hard. 'Okay, so it's eighteen days. Isn't that long enough? You've got an entire police force at your disposal. How hard can it be?'

'We've got nothing, Jan. No suspects, or at least none that look even remotely likely. The girl's mother did suggest one name. He looked like a possibility. But Ray spoke to him, and nothing came of it. We're starting at the beginning again.'

'There must be other things you can do.'

'House-to-house hasn't come up with anything. It's the same story with the search officers. And the forensic evidence is next to useless. I had the results rushed through. We've got a few interesting fingerprints on and around the kitchen window where we believe the perpetrator entered the property, but they're not on record. They can help rule a suspect in or out when we've actually got one, but as of now they don't help us at all.'

Janet rose to her feet, her mug in one hand. She reached for a packet of custard cream biscuits with the other. 'Have you finished?'

'What do you mean?'

'I would have thought it was obvious. You're a wife and mother as well as a police officer. Why do you always have to put your work first? Don't we matter to you?'

Kesey reached out to touch Janet's arm, but she withdrew her hand quickly when Janet pulled away. 'Oh, come on, Jan, be fair. We're talking about a young child's life. A missing five-year-old girl abducted from her home in the middle of the night by someone who'll likely do her harm. You know the score. It's my case, my responsibility. If I don't find her, then who?'

Janet took a bite of biscuit, chewed and swallowed. 'Surely there must be someone else who could do it. You're not the only detective in the force.'

Kesey sighed. 'Maybe I can rearrange the holiday. You know, move it on a few weeks. That wouldn't be too much of a problem, would it? We'd still be going. Just at a different time.'

'What about school?'

'We could talk to the head. She's not an unreasonable woman. I'm sure she'll give us her consent in the circumstances. We're only talking primary school, and travel's an educative experience in itself. It broadens the mind. Isn't that how the saying goes? Why wouldn't she agree?'

Janet took a slurp of tea, leaving a milky residue above her top lip. 'I was looking forward to some quality family time, that's all. It's been over two years since we've been away together, and that was to visit my sister in Scotland. There's always something more important. It seems your job always comes before we do. It rules our lives.'

'Oh, come on, be fair. I'm a copper. I've always been a copper. It's not like a civilian job. You knew the deal when you married me. There were no pretences. We talked about it. I made my situation perfectly clear.'

The phone rang out in the hall before Janet had the chance to comment.

'Sorry, I'm going to have to take that. It could be urgent.'

'Yeah, yeah, it's always urgent, no change there. I can't say I'm surprised.'

Kesey held the phone to her face. 'Oh, hello, Ray, I was about to give you a ring. Any news?'

'The press conference is arranged for half eleven tomorrow morning. I've got the local papers, radio, and someone from the BBC Wales news team. There's a lot of interest. I wouldn't be surprised if we even get a couple of nationals.'

'What about the parents?'

'Yeah, it's sorted, they'll both be there. I told them to meet you in reception half an hour before kick-off. I've explained that you need to speak to them in advance of meeting the press. They're keen to co-operate. There's no way they'll be late. They're investing a lot of hope in the event's success.'

'Aren't we all.'

Lewis laughed humourlessly. 'Yeah, we've got fuck all else.'

'Is there likely to be any friction?'

'Friction? What are you talking about?'

'The parents. Are they playing the blame game?'

Lewis paused before responding. 'No, I don't think they are. They both seem entirely focused on finding their daughter. I think it's brought them closer together if anything.'

'What, they're not having a go at each other? Not at all? Not even when the pressure gets to them?'

'Not that I've seen.'

'Okay, if you say so. It seems unlikely to me, but we'll see how things go in the morning. We need them presenting a united front, no distractions. You know what the press is like. We want them focused entirely on Lottie Weller.'

'I think it's going to be fine, boss. I can't see a problem.'

'Will I see you first thing? There's a couple of things I want to discuss.'

Lewis paused, then replied, 'I've got to call at the surgery on my way in. The old back's playing up again. Can't we talk now?'

Kesey glanced up to see Janet seated, cross-legged, in the lounge, munching her way through the packet of custard creams, a sour expression on her face. 'No, it's nothing urgent, nothing that can't wait until tomorrow. Just come in as soon as you can, and we'll take it from there. But I want you there for the press conference. That's not negotiable. I could do with a friendly face.'

'Yeah, no problem, I need a prescription for a few

pills, that's all. I'm going through them a bit quicker than usual.'

'Thanks, Ray, I'll see you tomorrow. It's going to be an interesting morning.'

Kesey re-joined Janet in the lounge only seconds after ending her call. The detective sat next to her partner on the sofa, nudging up close, their thighs touching. She patted Janet's knee and smiled. 'Okay, so this is what I suggest. I'll rearrange the holiday and we'll go the second this case is at an end, whatever the outcome. We'll go to the same hotel, the one you chose on the seafront, all-inclusive, but we'll go for two weeks instead of one. And I'll pay the additional cost, my treat. How does that sound?'

Janet's determined frown gradually became a smile as her mood softened. 'Well, I suppose it'll give me some more time to lose a few pounds. There's a new gym opened in town. They've got an introductory offer on, twenty quid a month including classes. Perhaps I should join. It couldn't do any harm.'

Kesey beamed, more relieved than anything else. 'There you go, that's the spirit. Not that I'm saying you need to diet. I like the curvy look. You're lovely as you are.'

'Yeah, yeah, I'm sure I am. You never were a very good liar... are you sure it will be okay to take Ed out of school? I saw something on the news about the government tightening up the rules. Some parents are getting fined.'

Kesey nodded enthusiastically. 'Yeah, it'll be all right. I said so, didn't I? I'll have a word with the head myself. I can give her a ring. We're on the local child protection committee together. She likes me. We get on. There won't be a problem.'

Janet began to relax. 'And we're definitely going this time? No more excuses. There's not going to be another case that gets in the way?'

'I'll speak to the chief super; I'll arrange cover well in advance. Everything will be okay.'

'Do you promise?'

Kesey squeezed Janet's hand. 'Yeah, I promise, of course I promise. I'm looking forward to it as much as you are. All that sun, sea and ouzo, what's not to like? It can't come quickly enough. I can't wait.'

'Well, I suppose it is a little girl you're looking for.'

'So, you understand?'

'Can you imagine if Ed was abducted? That poor

mother. Not knowing if her daughter is alive or dead. It doesn't bear thinking about. It must be the worst feeling in the world.'

Kesey nodded. 'Yeah, absolutely, the worst! There are some evil bastards out there. You've just got to hope they don't impact your life. Lottie drew the short straw. I just hope I can find her alive.'

'Lottie?'

'Yes, the little girl, Lottie, her name's Lottie.'

A look of recognition dawned on Janet's face. 'Oh, yes, I saw a poster in the Post Office now that I think about it.'

'The parents have been putting them up. They told Ray all about it. I think they said twenty in total.'

'Do you think it'll help?'

Kesey shrugged her shoulders. 'It could do, I suppose. Someone may see it and ring in. It can't do any harm, that's for sure. I think I'd be doing the same in their place.'

Janet shivered despite the room's warmth. 'Fancy another cuppa?'

'There's a bottle of Spanish red in the fridge if you fancy it? A glass or two wouldn't do us any harm. It may even help me sleep.'

'And a few crisps?'

Kesey nodded. 'Yeah, what the hell, why not? Cheese and onion if we've got them. I'll choose a film if you're up for it?'

'How about a rom-com? I don't think I can cope with anything scary. Real life is bad enough to deal with without seeing it on screen as well.'

Kesey picked up the TV remote as Janet headed towards the kitchen, her shapely backside wobbling like a moulded jelly with every step she took. 'Yeah, you've got that right. I'll find something funny. Something to make us laugh.'

Janet took a corkscrew from a kitchen drawer, speaking loudly enough for Kesey to hear in the adjoining room. 'I don't suppose Lottie's mum is doing much laughing. Life can change in the blink of an eye, and not always for the better.'

Kesey silently observed that Janet had never said a more valid word in her life. 'How about *Notting Hill*? I know we've seen it twice, but it always makes us smile.'

Janet appeared at the lounge door, the uncorked wine bottle in one hand, the crisp packet and two glasses in the other. 'Are you changing the subject?'

'Yeah, I suppose I am. Guilty as charged.'

'Everything will work out for the best, Laura. You're a good detective. You've just got to find her, that's all.'

Kesey pressed the play button. 'Yeah, I know, believe me, I know, but that's the problem. Where else do I look? I don't know where to start.'

Heath looked around the spacious attic of his recently inherited, large, and detached four-bedroom Victorian home and smiled contentedly. The space was almost perfect. What more could any young girl possibly want in the final weeks of her life? The pink wallpaper, the plastic dolls, the teddy bears, the black metal cage, the stainless steel feeding bowls, and the secured wooden hatch, reached only by a retractable ladder.

It was inspired, a work of undiluted genius. How else could one describe his creation? The space provided security, it provided comfort, and it offered total privacy from a misguided and judgemental

world that so misunderstood his needs and inclina-
tions. Just like the priest. That holier-than-thou fool.
What the hell was wrong with the man? He got exactly what he deserved. And not before time too. It
was such fun to watch him die.

Heath rose to his feet, humming a tune from
Carmen as he slowly circled the cage, balding head
tilted first to one side and then the other. He looked
in at his captive's sleeping form as he continued his
thought process. Yes, the room was perfect. It had all
the required elements precisely as he'd designed it
before the little brat's arrival in the darkness of the
night. Just as he'd fantasised. Just as he'd dreamed of
as he'd watched and he'd planned, biding his time
until the moment was exactly right for capture.

And he was there to care for her too, lucky girl,
if she behaved herself, if she didn't outlive her purpose sooner than expected. If she did exactly what
she was told without protest whenever he allowed
her to wake. Maybe he'd even remove her gag sometime soon if she acted correctly and stopped all that
pathetic whimpering she seemed so very keen on
every time the drug wore off; such an inconve-
nience, such an abuse of his care. So much to put up

with. That was worthy of punishment if anything
was.

Heath allowed the bars to support his weight as
he peered in at his prisoner, lying curled up in a
foetal position, back curved, head bowed, and limbs
bent and drawn up to her torso. He shook his head
and winced before continuing his rumination, all too
familiar feelings of frustration and inadequacy
threatening to become uncontrolled rage that could
erupt at any moment, exploding to the surface
without warning. The feeding tube did the basics; it
provided nourishment; it kept the little bitch alive for
as long as required without the use of the bowls. But
it was far from ideal.

How could she tell him she loved him or scream
out her dread with her mouth taped shut?

Heath began swaying to and fro as his anger in-
tensified, skin flushed and mottled, his limbs
shaking at the extremities. What was it with little
brats of her age? He'd gone to a great deal of effort
on her behalf. The little bitch! Why not show some
gratitude in her lucid moments? 'Mummy, Mummy,
Mummy,' was all the obnoxious little brat was capable of saying in her times of clarity.

This one had better shut her stupid mouth. She'd better not annoy him any more than she already had. She had to wake sometime. He couldn't sedate her forever. Where was the fun in that? What use was an unconscious child?

Heath began massaging the back of his neck before slumping to the floor, his hands moving in jerks as the young girl began to splutter in her sleep, her throat irritated by the tube. He reached out, touching her elbow through the bars, his mind still racing, darting from one thought to the next as was his custom. Maybe this one was different. She may understand him, learn to love him, unlike the others, the disappointments who'd let him down before death.

Heath jabbed a digit at his captive, nostrils flared, eyes wide, showing the whites. The little brat had better be different for her sake. He could tear her apart. Slice her to pieces. Feed her to the rats in the sewers. She would prove no less disposable than the rest. The brats he'd entertained in the war zones, the famine regions, the victims of natural disasters in need of charity. Before he was thrown on the scrap heap, his career in tatters, at a premature end. Before the bastards in charge forced his resignation for no good reason at all.

Heath raised a hand to his mouth, touching his lips as he searched his troubled mind for reassurance. Thank fuck for the inheritance, and for his father's timely death too. The one good thing the morale-sapping, supercilious old git ever did in his miserable life. It almost made up for the man's many failings, the constant criticisms, the total lack of any emotional warmth and worse, much worse.

It had destroyed his self-worth – the negative experience of his childhood. Yes, yes, that's what the psychiatrist had said in that know-it-all, self-important way of hers after the drowning of his needy little sister. Were all doctors so full of themselves? She was a stuck-up cow, with such a predictably unjustified sense of superiority. What a bitch, Dr know-it-all! Why not track her down? Why not destroy her life as his was destroyed? It wasn't too late. Maybe that would help alleviate his angst. Perhaps he should kill her too.

Heath crossed the room and studied the six-by-four-inch colour photo of his mother, pasted on the attic wall immediately next to a large gilt-framed mirror he'd taken from the parlour wall several days before. He pulled on a long black wig made from real human hair, tugging it first one way and then another, adjusting it repeatedly before taking a pair of stainless steel scissors and carefully trimming the fringe, ensuring it matched his mother's style as closely as possible.

Heath craned his neck, moving a little closer to the mirror, edging forward, once, then again, applying bright red lipstick, studying his reflection, his nose almost touching the glass. The lipstick wasn't too bad. It wasn't an exact match. It wasn't perfect. But it was probably the best he'd achieved up to that point. It was acceptable, wasn't it? He'd gone to a lot of effort, ruling out numerous other shades before deciding on the cherry-red. Surely it was good enough.

Heath looked in the mirror and saw his mother's face staring back at him, as if she was there in the room, reincarnated, as if she hadn't died. She was as real to him as she had been in life, as real as flesh and blood. She was staring at his lips with fixed, unblinking eyes, shaking her head with a look of unbridled disapproval on her face, that was all too familiar. When he heard her speak only seconds later, her tone was critical, as it often was in life.

'Cherry-red, what were you thinking, boy? It's nothing like my lipstick, not even close.'

Heath tore the wig from his head, flinging it to the floor in an attempt to silence her. But his overactive imagination wouldn't let up. The voice was still there, getting louder, reverberating around the room, filling the space with continuous sound that seemed all too real. 'You really are a stupid boy.'

He hit out, striking air. 'Shut up, shut the fuck up! I wonder why I bother with you sometimes.'

'Don't ever go thinking you can escape me that easily, you little shit. I know exactly what you did to Pamela. I'm going to haunt you for as long as you live. Did you hear me, Henry? You brought this on yourself. I'll never let you go.'

He looked away from the mirror, frantically wiping the lipstick from his mouth with a sleeve as he stamped down on the wig, grinding it into the floor with the heel of his brown leather shoe. 'I'm not Henry, don't use that name, not any more. I've got a new name now, a new identity.'

'*Henry, Henry, naughty Henry! Feeble, inadequate little Henry! You'll always be Henry to me.*'

Heath wrung his hands together and jumped as a dog barked somewhere outside the house. 'Be quiet, woman, you've said enough. What part of shut the fuck up didn't you understand?'

His mother's voice was quieter now, softer, more conciliatory. As if she cared. '*Why on earth have you brought the little brat into my house? I can't figure it out. I hope you're not assuming she can take Pamela's place. Don't go thinking you can kill her all over again. Your baby sister is here safe with me.*'

Heath dropped to his knees, clamping his hands over his ears as his head began to pound. He looked up to the ceiling as his mother's image drifted up-wards, visible only in his peripheral vision as he low-ered his gaze, pointing at the cage. 'Can you see any water, Mother? Does it look as if I'm going to drown the little bitch? I've got plans, exciting plans, impor-tant plans. I've gone to a great deal of trouble getting her here. Do you think I'd do that if I was going to kill her in an instant? I could do that anywhere, any time, with a lot less prior effort. This time is different. I'm biding my time and for a good reason too. Do you like casting doubts on my competence? Do you enjoy further crushing my fragile self-esteem? It seems so. It really seems so. You should be congratulating me on my magnificent self-control, not looking down on me with a frown on your supercilious face.'

Her voice was a little louder now, more insistent, ringing in his ears. '*Why bring her here, to my house, to Pamela's house, of all places? Why would you do that? It seems ill-advised at best. What if someone saw you? What if they tell the police what you've done? Are you incapable of reasoned thought?*'

'I was careful. I wore the wig, the make-up, your old clothes. I was more you than me.'

'*Oh, I'm well aware of that, Henry. I saw you. But why take the risk? Why gamble with your freedom?*'

Heath closed his eyes tight shut, a single tear running down his face as she came back into focus. 'Do I really need to explain myself?'

'*Oh, I think you do, Henry. Maybe then I'll allow you some rest. Best listen to Mother, don't you think? Mother knows best.*'

'Okay, okay, if it shuts you up, I'll tell you. I'll outline the entire project.'

She perched on the edge of the cage. '*All right, I'm*

listening. But don't disappoint me again. What have you got to say for yourself?'

'I need you to understand that abducting the little brat wasn't something I did on a whim. It's something that matters to me. Something I've given a great deal of thought.'

'Just get to the point, Henry, there's a good boy. I haven't got all day.'

Heath gritted his teeth and continued, resenting her more than he'd ever thought possible. 'The little brat is in my class at school, if you must know. I tried to talk to her mother a week or so ago at the end of the school term. I intended to share my observations regarding her little brat's recent emotional decline, because it amused me to do so. I so wanted to rub it in and watch the woman squirm. But would she listen? No, she would not. I smiled my best smile, I was polite, I was pleasant, but she looked down her nose at me as if I were nothing. She made some pathetic excuse about being in a rush to get the brat to a dental appointment. She even expressed regret and apologised before rushing away. But I knew what the bitch was really thinking. I'm just an assistant. I'm not a real teacher.

She didn't actually say it, not in so many words. But she may as well have.

'I hated her with a blazing intensity from that moment. I wanted to make her suffer more than anyone has ever suffered before. I've never felt so slighted. Did you hear me, Mother? Are you as outraged as I was? The stuck-up bitch walked away as if I hadn't said anything at all. As if I was a bit of dog shit on the sole of her overpriced shoe. As if I don't matter. I shouldn't have to put up with that. Nobody should. Who the fuck does the bitch think she is?'

'So, what's the problem? She was right. You are nothing, you stupid boy.'

He heard shrill female laugher that seemed to get louder, and penetrated his head like a drill.

He looked away, closing his eyes tight shut, but it didn't drive her image from his mind. 'Be quiet, Mother, please be quiet. I'm begging you. You've said enough.'

The laughter stopped as abruptly as it began. *'No, what was I thinking? You're worse than nothing. You did nothing but let your father and me down from the day you were born.'*

Heath opened his eyes. He jumped to his feet in

one adrenaline-fuelled bound, and rushed back to-wards the cage, shaking the bars. He could feel his mother's breath on his neck as she circled him. 'Can you see the little brat? Can you see her, Mother? I took her from her home, I imprisoned her, I drugged her, and when the time is right, I plan to kill her too. I've done all that by myself with no help from you or anybody else. That is true success, real power. The ability to decide who lives and who dies. Mark my words.

'The brat's bitch mother is going to notice me now! I'll be the centre of her world, the thorn in her flesh, her worst nightmare as I tear her life to shreds. Did you hear me, Mother? Megan Weller's going to suffer for ignoring me. The bitch, the total fucking bitch! She'll beg for my forgiveness before I finish with her. I'll be the demonic puppet master pulling her strings. She has no idea of the torment to come.'

15

'You let me take the lead and only speak when I indicate the time's right,' said Kesey to the Wellers. 'If you're asked any direct questions, take your time and think carefully before you answer. And don't be afraid to show your emotions. The public will understand and sympathise. They'll want to help. In my experience, they always do.'

Dale and Megan Weller nodded in unison, as Kesey shuffled her notes to little effect, more a means of stress control than anything else. 'Do either of you have any final questions before we go in?'

Megan wiped a tear from her cheek and said, 'I

think we're as ready as we'll ever be.' Her voice quivered, as anxiety threatened to overwhelm her.

Kesey rose to her feet, brushing a speck of white fluff from her black skirt. 'Right, come on, let's get this done. These things are never easy, but they are important. The media have a wide reach. When potential witnesses ring in – and they will – I'll have officers ready to take their calls. Not everything we're told is useful, but hopefully the publicity will give us the break we need.'

Dale took Megan's hand in his. He was both surprised and relieved when she didn't pull away. It seemed their mutual grief had united rather than further divided them, as he feared it might. Megan went to hug him, but she recoiled when his spirit-soaked breath filled her nostrils. She pushed him away, hissing her words, her face contorted as much from disappointment as rage. 'You have got to be kidding me. Now, of all times. What the hell were you thinking?'

Dale shuffled from one foot to the other, unable to settle as the two women looked on accusingly. 'I only had the one glass of whiskey. Honestly, it was just the one small tot to steady my nerves. I'm not

used to this media stuff. Being in the spotlight, questions, accusations, dirty looks from people in the
fucking street. It's the first drink I've had since all this
happened. I'm not pissed. It was just the one, like I
said. What's the fucking problem?'

Megan's face reddened. She wanted to slap him.
She wanted to yell in his face and keep yelling until
he understood how badly she felt he'd failed her. But
that would be futile, worse than useless. Now wasn't
the time. Not there in a public space, not with the
journalists just a few feet away on the other side of a
closed door. She spoke quietly rather than shout,
fearing the press may overhear. 'Do you know, I was
starting to trust you again. I really believed you'd
stopped drinking this time.'

'I'm sorry. It was only one. What more can I say?'

'Yes, so you keep saying. But one is one too many,
Dale. When are you going to get that into your thick
head?'

Kesey glared from one to the other. 'I need you
both to stop now. Remember why you're here, focus,
we're here for Lottie. We're here to help find her. And
believe me, you two arguing isn't going to aid the
process one little bit.'

Both parents offered their profuse apologies but Kesey could almost feel their mutual resentment quietly festering. The detective checked her watch for one final time. 'Right, it's time to get in there.' She took a packet of extra strong mints from her bag and handed one to Dale. 'Suck, chew and swallow. You don't want to be still eating when you sit yourself down. Have I made myself clear?'

Dale popped the sweet in his mouth, nodding his understanding as Kesey led them towards the door. She stopped before turning the handle, speaking in hushed tones for only them to hear. 'Right, this is it. Are you both ready? If you're going to argue, do it later. For now, I need you to present a united front. And Dale, I don't want you swearing – even once – while we're in there. We need the media on our side. Do you think you can do that for me?'

Both parents nodded but said nothing more.

Kesey pushed open the conference room's double doors, entering first with the estranged couple close behind, to be met by a barrage of clicking, flashing cameras and lively journalistic chatter, the members of the press baying for the next big story. All three stopped, steadying themselves, gaining their bearings before sitting behind two adjoined, white cloth topped tables at the front of the room, directly in front of a large West Wales Police logo.

DS Lewis, who was already seated and waiting, nodded his welcome. Lewis noted the recently applied sticking plaster covering the first two knuckles on Dale's slightly swollen right hand, and grinned knowingly, chuckling quietly to himself as he pictured the scene. Lewis suspected he knew exactly what had happened. The injury told its own story. But it wasn't anything the sergeant felt inclined to investigate.

Kesey checked her watch, letting the seconds tick by until the time was precisely right. She looked out on the three rows of seated journalists, some with cameras, some with notepads, and raised a hand in the air to silence them, half expecting them to continue talking.

You could have heard a pin drop as Kesey stood and spoke, the faint hint of a Welsh accent combining with her Midland nasal tones. 'Okay, it's time we made a start. I want to begin by welcoming you all to West Wales Police Headquarters. Thank you all for attending. I hope we have a productive morning.

For those of you who don't know me, my name is Detective Inspector Laura Kesey, the lead officer, or SIO, on the case.'

She paused to catch her breath. She was well outside her comfort zone, but she didn't let it show. 'I'd like to introduce you, firstly to Detective Sergeant Raymond Lewis, who is seated to my right, and to Lottie's parents, Dale and Megan Weller, who are seated to my left. I intend to update you all on the case, and then allow you the opportunity to ask any questions. I would advise you, however, that there may be some matters on which I am unable to comment for operational reasons.' This was a bluff. Kesey had very little to share. The briefing was a fishing exercise more than anything else. A fishing exercise with very little bait. But nobody needed to know that, not the parents, not the press, not the chief super, and especially not the perpetrator, should they be watching the Welsh evening news.

Kesey waited for what she considered the inevitable murmurs of discontent to gradually dissipate before continuing, her tone rising an octave, insistent, demanding to be heard. 'We're here to raise awareness of the disappearance of Lottie Weller, a five-year-old little girl who was taken from her mother's home address in Picton Street, Caerystwyth, sometime between the hours of 2.30 a.m. and 7.10 a.m. on the nineteenth of this month. She has now been missing for three days. A team of officers are actively conducting relevant investigations as we speak. It is imperative that we find Lottie sooner rather than later. I would ask that you assist me in achieving that outcome.'

A dishevelled local journalist with wild, receding hair tinged with grey, and wearing a badly creased cotton jacket with a flower in the lapel, raised a hand in the air like a child in a classroom. 'Okay, so how much progress have you made? As you said, three days have passed. That's a long time in investigative terms. Have you identified any suspects? Surely it's about time you did.'

Kesey shuffled her notes, buying time, gathering her thoughts. 'Investigations are ongoing. We're following several relevant leads. At this stage, I can't say any more than that.'

The journalist wasn't inclined to give up easily. 'What sort of enquiries?'

Kesey chose not to answer. What was the point of

responding when you had nothing worthwhile to say? She turned to Lewis and nodded. 'If you could switch the laptop on now, please, Ray.'

Lewis flicked a switch, projecting a large, ten-by-six-foot colour image of Lottie's smiling face on the white-painted wall to the side of the force logo. Kesey looked around the room, weighing up the photo's emotional impact. The attendant journalists were paying close attention. It seemed the picture had had the desired effect. It was time to drive home her advantage, time to gain their co-operation.

'As you can all see, Lottie has shoulder-length, slightly curly, pale-yellow hair, light-blue eyes and prominent freckles on both cheeks. She is of slim build, weighing approximately forty pounds or eighteen kilos, and is approximately forty-two inches or one hundred and seven centimetres tall. In summary, Lottie is an average, happy five-year-old girl with good communicative skills, who's going to be missing her mother. She speaks both English and Welsh.' Kesey paused to maximise the impact of her statement, and then continued, acutely aware that Megan had started crying into her hands, her head bowed.

'If you could display the second slide now, please, Ray.'

Lewis followed orders.

'This second slide shows the same type of outfit as that worn by Lottie at the time of her disappearance. As you can see, it comprises a light green pyjama top and trousers, decorated with images of smiling frogs seated on lily pads.'

Kesey walked around the table to the front, looking directly into the Welsh TV news camera as she spoke, clearly enunciating each word. 'I want to take this opportunity to appeal to any members of the public to contact the police as a matter of urgency if they have any information which may help us find Lottie Weller.'

Kesey nodded to her sergeant and then pointed to a phone number projected on the wall by the third and final image. 'Anyone with anything to share should ring this number to speak directly to a member of my team, who will be ready and waiting for your calls. You can also contact your local police station. I want to stress that you should ring us even if unsure if your information is relevant. Contact us, share your concerns, and let us decide if it's important. You can contact us twenty-four hours a day, seven days a week. As I said, please don't hesitate to call.'

Kesey turned away from the camera, returning to her original position. 'Are there any final questions before I ask Mr and Mrs Weller to share anything they wish to say.'

A middle-aged woman with brown hair cut in a bob raised herself to her feet. Kesey recognised her as a journalist she'd encountered before. A reporter on the local weekly paper. 'Can you tell my readers when an arrest is likely?'

Kesey exhaled slowly. 'That's not something I'm able to answer at this point.'

'Does that mean you haven't got any clue who took the child?'

Kesey knew that was precisely what it meant. But she was never going to admit that, not there, not now. 'That's not what I said. As I explained earlier, we are currently following several important leads. I expect to be able to inform you of further developments in the near future.'

The journalist appeared satisfied with Kesey's response as she scribbled some notes on a pad in black ink.

'Any last questions?'

No-one said a word.

'Would you like to say anything, Mr Weller?'

Dale rose to his feet, opening his mouth as if to speak, but he then slumped back into his seat, weeping into his hands when no words came.

Megan reached across, touching Dale's knee, feeling genuine sympathy for her ex as she stood herself. Like Kesey before her, Megan stared directly into the television camera. She swallowed her sadness before speaking, planting her feet wide for fear of collapse. 'As DI Kesey explained a little earlier, I'm here talking to you because my lovely little daughter was taken from our home in the darkness of the night by someone unknown. I want to appeal directly to that person. If you took Lottie, if you see this, I'm talking to you. I'm asking you not to hurt my lovely girl. She's done nothing to harm you. Nothing to justify what you've done even in the slightest. She's a child, just a small child who shouldn't have a care in the world. If you want to hurt somebody, then hurt me.'

Kesey jumped up, fully intending to interrupt Megan's impassioned plea. But the detective returned to her seat when Megan chose to ignore her.

Megan paused for the briefest of moments and then continued, 'I'll gladly swap places with my daughter if given the opportunity. I'll get down on my knees if you want me to. I'll beg if it pleases you. Contact me. My number is readily available. Just say the word. All I ask is that you free my lovely girl. If she's still alive...' Megan allowed the table to support her weight as her legs threatened to buckle under her. 'If...' Megan blew out a series of short breaths. 'If you haven't killed my little girl, if she's still alive, please release her, leave her somewhere safe. I'm begging you to let her go.'

16

Kesey approached Lewis as the various media professionals made their way towards the exit, allowing Megan and Dale a brief interlude, time to talk, time to compose themselves, before leaving to face the remains of the day. Kesey looked into her sergeant's tired eyes and smiled, more in relief that the press conference was over than any sense of achievement. She wished she'd had more to say, something positive to report. Something she could back up with action as opposed to merely words.

'Do you know, I hate dealing with the frigging media. It doesn't get any easier however many times I do it. I think I'm more introvert than extrovert. It's just not my style.'

'The chief super was conspicuous by his absence.'

Kesey laughed humourlessly. 'Yeah, I'm not sorry, to be honest. The investigation isn't actually covering us in glory. I might be back directing traffic at this rate. And he'd love it too. I bet he'd be creaming his pants.'

Lewis grinned. 'What, don't tell me the two of you aren't getting on again? I thought you'd have kissed and made up long before now.'

'Oh, yeah, like that's ever going to happen. We're chalk and cheese, oil and water. The twat's always banging on about his time in the smoke, the Met this, and the Met that. The man's a misogynist, he resents women in positions of responsibility. If he pissed off back to London, I'd be a very happy girl.'

Lewis adopted a more serious persona, his smile becoming a frown. 'How do you think the conference went? Any thoughts?'

Kesey shrugged her shoulders. 'As well as can be expected, I guess. Someone knows something. They always do. Let's hope they see one report or another and ring in. We've got sod all else. We need a break.'

Lewis touched her arm. 'It's going to be all right, boss. We're bound to get something.'

Kesey knew he was trying to stay positive, attempting to boost her confidence, and she decided not to comment. He was well-intentioned, and that's what mattered. 'There's going to be a report on the Welsh news at about half six this evening. A lot of people are going to see it. Let's meet up in the canteen in the morning to see what we've got. I've got a briefing with Halliday at nine, lucky me, so let's say ten o'clock sharp. We're going to get calls, most of them next to useless if past experience is anything to go by. But hopefully, there will be something significant.'

Lewis nodded. 'I'll keep my fingers crossed.'

'Fingers and everything else, Ray.'

Kesey called Lewis back as he went to walk away, touching his elbow. She lowered her voice, speaking in a whisper. 'Did you notice the plaster on Dale's knuckles?'

Lewis tensed but hid it well. 'Yeah, I'll have a quick word with him in the car park.'

Kesey had intended to speak to Dale herself, but she decided to let it go. 'Okay, I'll leave it with you.'

'I'm going to be out and about all day with the search teams if you need me.'

'Yeah, okay, no problem.'

'I'll see you in the morning, boss.'

'Give me a ring immediately if you come up with anything useful, yeah?'

He could see the anxiety in her eyes. 'Yes, of course.'

Kesey looked towards the parents as they prepared to leave, the last of the press having left the room, their conversations at an end. 'I wish Megan hadn't said quite as much as she did.'

'Oh, come off it. Fuck convention. The woman spoke with passion. That's what matters. And who can blame her? You never know, it may even do us some good.'

Kesey pressed her lips together, a slight shudder running down her spine. 'God knows how the poor sods must be feeling – not knowing if their daughter is alive or dead. I can't think of anything worse. It's every parent's worst nightmare. I'll give them a quick update on what's happening and send them on their way.'

17

Heath smirked as he recalled recent events, focusing on his positives, magnifying them in his mind. The case was all over the news. Ha! He was famous by association, covered in glory. And the bitch mother looked distraught. All that pathetic pleading, all that pitiful begging, appealing to his better nature as if such a thing had ever existed. The woman had disintegrated in front of his very eyes, right there on the television screen for all to see. Just as he'd hoped, precisely as he'd planned.

Now to turn up the pressure. The bitch solicitor would be begging for mercy by the time he'd finished with her. Her terrors had only just begun.

Heath looked across at Lottie's sleeping form with a pensive expression, bulbous eyes shining in the light of a naked bulb. *Drug the brat or kill her? Drug her or kill her?* The weight of decision-making could be heavy at times. How could one little girl be so utterly infuriating? She'd only come around for a few miserable minutes since her enforced arrival. All that weeping, all that screeching, as if she didn't appreciate him taking the gag off.

The ungrateful little mare didn't realise how lucky she was. He could have dispatched her right there and then, rather than give her a secure home behind bars. Weren't the dolls good enough, and the teddy bears, what about the teddy bears? She didn't seem interested in them either. What a strange and unappreciative little creature he'd brought into his life. As if the little monsters in school weren't burdensome enough to deal with. Now he had one ensconced in his personal space too. But at least there was no school for another couple of weeks.

Yes, focus on his plans, on making the bitch lawyer's life a complete misery. Oh, what the hell, drug the little brat. Give her some more medication. It would at least give him time to think. He reached through the bars, clutching Lottie's left arm and pulling her increasingly emaciated, unconscious body towards him. 'Right, you little brat, you're going to live another day. Aren't you the fortunate one? My deceased father's drug it is. There's plenty left if we need it. He had a rather generous supply.'

Heath glared in at Lottie again as he prepared to administer the tranquillising chemical. She was lying curled up on the hard, soiled floor of the cage, blissfully oblivious to the realities of her new existence. Lost to the welcome oblivion of drug-induced sleep.

He spoke to her again with animated passion, as if she could hear and understand every word he uttered. 'What the fuck you've done to deserve such mercy is a complete mystery to me. I'm too nice for my own good sometimes, that's my problem. But don't get too comfortable, you little bitch. There's only so long I'll look after you. The temptation to harm is too strong.'

Heath tore open the paper packaging covering the needle and picked up a syringe, fixing the needle carefully in place. While holding the injection in one hand, he took a glass vial containing a potent sedative drug from his pocket and broke off its top with a distinctive snap that made him jump. He inserted the needle through the mouth of the vial, and slowly drew the clear liquid into the syringe chamber. Finally, he pressed the black rubber plunger gently with his thumb, forcing out the air, until a tiny drop of the liquid squirted from the tip. There, done.

The ready availability of his father's medication was fortuitous. Thank you, lung cancer! And at least the old git served a purpose. *Rot in hell, you hypercritical old bastard.* Heath smiled coldly as childhood memories resonated in his mind.

Heath plunged the needle deep into Lottie's upper arm, administering the drug with well-practised speed and efficiency, before discarding the syringe in a wicker wastepaper basket he'd brought into the attic for the purpose.

He pulled on the dark wig again before approaching the mirror, studying his image in the light of a single, bare 100-watt bulb, which highlighted every flaw in his eyes, every blemish, every wrinkle. It seemed time and gravity were taking their inevitable toll despite his relative youth. Maybe he should change the bulb. Perhaps it was too bright. A sixty maybe, or even a forty, something a little more sympathetic.

Another burst of inspiration. Just pop to the shops. Find the time, wear a suitable disguise. And keep a low profile too, something he was good at, head bowed, collar up, eyes focused on the pavement. That's all he had to do. Not get spotted. Keep his purpose secret from a judgemental world.

Heath applied that same cherry-red lipstick, pouting, taking his time, and then black mascara, removing the wand from the white plastic tube by twisting back and forth, wiping off the excess cosmetic on a paper tissue, and then looking up to lift the lashes. He studied his reflection again once satisfied with his efforts, taking a backward step as his image was gradually replaced by that of his mother, whose face filled the mirror.

'What do you want now, Mother? Will you never leave me alone?'

'*Why is she still alive, Henry? You killed your poor little baby sister quickly enough. You had no qualms about dispatching her at the first opportunity. So, why not the brat? She's not even family.*'

Heath looked away from the mirror and sighed,

emitting a slow, deep, audible breath before speaking in a well-practised, high-pitched voice that hurt his throat. 'Oh, for fuck's sake, not this again! It's a simple enough plan. I've told you all about it more than once. You're too much to cope with sometimes, a burden rather than a help. I'm tired, Mother. How many times do I have to explain myself?'

'For goodness' sake, calm down, boy. What on earth is wrong with you? I'd wash your mouth out with soap and water if I could get my hands on you. Is there really a need to swear?'

Heath dropped his head, turning away from the mirror, avoiding her accusing gaze. 'Do you want me to explain again, or not?'

He heard her snort loudly before she spoke again. *'I'm all ears, Henry. You've got my attention. But come on, get a move on, start talking. Get on with it.'*

Heath lowered himself to the floor, his legs crossed under him, and looked up at the beamed ceiling, as he pictured his mother hovering. 'I targeted the brat because her bitch mother dismissed me without a thought in the worst possible way. That, I'm sure you'll agree, is worthy of punishment. If I kill the brat now, it will all be over far too quickly.

Don't you get it? The brat's bitch mother could begin the grieving process. I don't want that. I want to drag her suffering out for as long as feasibly possible.' He smiled coldly. 'Sometimes, the anticipation of pain can be infinitely worse than the pain itself. I learnt that over the years. I sometimes used to bring a victim close to death and then resuscitate them, re-peating the process multiple times, before killing them when the anticipation of death became too much for me.

'I want to give the bitch mother hope and then snatch it away again. I plan to taunt her time and again until she can't take any more. Until she's craving death's dark release, the welcome oblivion of the grave. I want to crush her emotionally. I want to facilitate her psychological destruction, minute by minute, hour by hour, one slow day at a time. Now, do you get the message, Mother? Was that clear enough for spirit ears?'

His mother's image merged with the dark beams and white-painted boards of the ceiling, swirling, fading, and then coming back into sharper focus. *'Oh dear, Henry, you really do worry me sometimes. I can't help but question your judgement. Why not kill the brat now and be done with it? That's what you've always done in the past. Why change a successful protocol? Do you really think it's a good idea to keep her alive?'*

Heath yelled up at her whirling image, muscles taut, altering the shape of his face. 'Yes, I do, I absolutely do. Why wouldn't I? Caging her isn't something I'm doing on a whim. Why do you always feel the need to undermine me?'

His mother's face suddenly increased in size, rushing towards him, filling almost the entire one side of the attic. *'You haven't exactly got a history of good decision-making, have you, Henry? Your plans seem ill-advised at best. Keeping the brat here is risky. You could be caught. Have you truly thought through the potential consequences? You wouldn't cope well in prison. The other prisoners wouldn't like you. Nobody likes you. You'd be eaten alive.'*

He clamped his hands over his ears. 'I don't want to kill her yet, not yet. Restraint is hard enough without you weakening my resolve. What part of that don't you understand?'

Her image retreated now, reducing to the approximate size she'd been in life. *'Why not take her to the cabin in the woods? Your father and I used to love it there.*

The isolation, the peace and quiet. There's a lake. You could drown the brat in that.'

Heath shook his head frantically. 'Stop making ridiculous suggestions. It's too far from the bitch mother's house. I want to stay close, keep an eye on her, witness her decline.'

'You could put the brat in the boot of the car. Wrap her in a blanket. Take her to the cabin. That would be far more sensible. It's yours now. Why not take advantage of your father's generosity? You haven't been there for years.'

'No! I've made my reasoning perfectly clear. And you may recall my memories of the cabin are far less pleasant than yours are.'

'Why keep the girl in the house? Here in this street of all places? You always were such an impetuous child. I don't know what to do with you sometimes.'

Heath tore the wig from his head, flinging it aside. 'Shut up, shut the fuck up! I've already ex-plained my reasons. Why do you always feel the need to undermine me?'

'Someone's got to keep a close eye on you, Henry. You're my cross to bear.'

Heath was frothing at the mouth as he yelled his reply. 'You never change, always with the criticisms.

Always the little jibes. I hope you rot in hell. Have you no concern for my self-esteem?'

His mother's familiar voice became a high-pitched whisper, hissing in his ears as if lost on the wind. *'I'm your voice of reason, Henry. A purveyor of advisory caution to keep you on track as you stumble your way through life in that ineffectual way of yours. If you'd let the priest live, you could have talked to him. He'd have told you the same thing. You even got that wrong.'*

Heath threw his hands out wide. 'The bastard deserved to die. I should have done it long ago. Am I supposed to know what the fuck you're talking about?'

She hissed again, first in one ear and then the other, her image leaping from one side to the other in the blink of an eye. *'Don't keep the brat for too long, Henry, that's all I'm saying. Kill her if you receive even the slightest hint of police attention. Kill her and dispose of the body somewhere it can't be found.'*

Heath nodded. 'Like the woods? A grave in the woods? Somewhere we could spend time together after her death. I've taken rather a liking to her in some strange way. Maybe it's because she's unconscious. It's not unlike death. I wouldn't want to lose her forever.'

His mother sounded impatient now, as if she'd tired of their interaction. '*Yes, Henry, somewhere like the woods. Or the river. You could cut her up, weigh her down. Just like that boy in India who took such a liking to you before you showed your true colours. Do you remember? Surely you remember? The nine-year-old lad with the limp that you strangled when he threatened to say too much. Dismember the body, bag it, and add some suitably heavy stones. It's a simple and effective method of disposal. I wouldn't rule it out if I were you.*'

'I'd rather keep her if at all possible. I like the company of corpses, their unquestioning compliance. I like the way they look, the way they feel, the way they taste, and even the way they smell. Living people bore me. Unless they're suffering, of course. Unless they provide some fun. The dead are far more loyal. They don't let you down.'

'*Living people reject you, Henry, that's the truth of it. People don't like you. They never have. The dead suit you well.*'

His eyes flashed. 'Like the brat's snooty mother. She treated me with utter disdain.'

She sighed. *'Yes, Henry, as you say, just like her...*
don't rule the river out completely without very good rea-
son. You don't always consider all the complexities of any
situation with sufficient rigour. I'm not saying you're in-
capable of rational thought, not completely, you're not
totally inept. It's just that Mother knows best.'

Heath began nodding, time and again, as if he
was incapable of stopping. 'I hear you, I hear you,
you've said enough. Now, leave me alone. There are
things I need to do. The feeding tube needs adjusting. I need to replace the intravenous fluid. I need to
attach it to the drip stand. Keeping the brat alive involves effort. You don't give me nearly enough credit
for that. I've got a lot to do and very little time to do
it. Keeping a pet is an onerous responsibility.'

Her frown became a glower as she drifted away,
and then came back into focus. *'Get on with it, boy.*
You're all talk and no action, that's your problem. I'm only
glad your poor father can't see you now, sitting there,
pontificating, wasting my valuable time when I've got
better things to do up here in the spirit world. If you're
going to be a sadist, at least be a good one, that's my ad-
vice. You're such a disappointment! Torment? Torment?
You don't even know the meaning of the word. Inflicting

pain and humiliation on others for sexual pleasure is an art. You need to up your game, my boy. No half measures. Be the best killer you can possibly be.'

Heath rose to his feet and laughed, head back, crazed, cackling like a demented hyena. 'Didn't you see the early evening news, Mother? Weren't you watching the report? The police were there, and the parents, the bitch mother spoke directly to me. How could you not know that? I thought you knew everything. It seems you're not nearly as clever as you like to make out.'

She wagged a finger at him. *'What are you talking about now, you ridiculous boy?'*

Heath began pounding the wall, wishing it was her, raining down one blow after another until his hands were swollen and his knuckles bled. 'The police are looking for witnesses, Mother. They're searching for evidence. And that provides an opportunity. I'm sure they'll be fascinated by what I have to tell them. They'll lap it up like the fools they are.' He threw his arms in the air, spraying blood everywhere. 'Misdirection, smoke and mirrors, cat and mouse. I'll show you precisely what torment means.'

'Are you sure, Henry? Are you man enough to see it

through to the end? Or are you still that same inadequate little boy who failed your dear father and me so very badly?'

Heath smeared warm blood across his face as he glared at her. 'I'll show you exactly what I'm capable of, you infuriating shrew. You watch me tear their lives to pieces. I'll inflict infinitely worse horrors than you could ever imagine. And it all begins right here and now, my creation, my achievement, and mine alone. Just you wait and see. Megan and her interfering porcine helpers won't know what hit them. There's a foul and raging tempest coming their way. A tsunami of pain and destruction. A storm they can't hope to survive.'

18

Lewis was sitting alone in the notoriously terrible police headquarters canteen, enthusiastically tucking into a full English breakfast swimming in cholesterol-laden grease, when Kesey called out his name from the door. 'All right, Ray. I'll be with you in a minute.'

'Have I got time to finish eating?'

Kesey nodded as she approached the serving counter. 'Yeah, no problem, knock yourself out, there's a bacon roll with my name on it.'

Kesey ordered, paid and waited, before joining Lewis at the table a few minutes later, her food in one hand and a cup of strong coffee in the other.

'You're looking tired, boss.'

Kesey yawned, closing her eyes for a beat before speaking. 'Yeah, Edward didn't have a great night. I'm feeling like shit.'

Lewis chewed and swallowed a chunk of gristle, washing it down with a slurp of excessively sweet tea. 'What's up with him?'

'Jan thinks it's croup. The poor little bugger couldn't stop coughing. He emits a slight rattle every time he exhales. It was horrendous. I've never seen him in such a state. We tried steam inhalation, but it didn't seem to help a great deal. Jan's taking him along to see the GP. Hopefully, some medication can sort him out.'

'My youngest had the same thing years back. It's not nice.

There's nothing worse than watching your kids suffer.'

Kesey dropped a sweetener into her coffee and stirred vigorously, spilling a few drops of the hot liquid onto the table. 'Tell me about it. It always makes me feel so helpless. If I could have had it instead of him, I'd have done it in a heartbeat.'

'He's going to be fine. A few days of the right treatment and he'll be as good as new again.'

Kesey sipped her coffee, relaxing slightly as the rising vapour warmed her face. She asked her questions more in hope than expectation. 'Is there any news after the press conference? Anything significant I need to know about?'

Lewis grinned, happy to keep her waiting, taking pleasure in anticipation of what was to come. 'Well, we had the usual nutters ringing in confessing to assassinating Kennedy, causing global warming, that sort of thing.'

Kesey shook her head slowly and deliberately. 'Come on, Ray. Stop pissing me about. I can see it in your eyes. I know you've got something for me.'

'We had two possible sightings of Lottie, one in Cardiff and one in Exeter in the West Country.'

Kesey took a small bite of the roll before returning it to her plate, losing her appetite. Maybe a bit of brown sauce would help. 'Have you followed either of both leads up?'

'Yeah, I've had a word with the South Wales and Devon and Cornwall forces. They're going to check it out.'

'Did you stress the urgency?'

Lewis scratched the back of his neck, disappointed she felt the need to ask. 'Well, yeah, of course.'

'Don't get all defensive on me. It's just my way. I was only asking.'

He gave her a knowing look.

'Come on now, what else have you got for me? I know there's more.'

Lewis cocked an eyebrow, tilting his balding head at a slight angle, running a hand through what was left of his hair. 'You're not going to like it.'

Kesey sighed, tiring of his drip-drip approach to sharing information. She knew exactly what he was up to. He'd done it before, building to a climax like a showman on a stage. 'For fuck's sake, Ray, tell me what you've got. I'm tired of waiting.'

'We've got a witness. A witness who rang in claiming he saw someone leave Megan's Picton Street address in the early hours of that morning. A person carrying what looked like a young child. A person who walked out of the gate leading from the back garden, down the path at the side of the house, and along the pavement towards Steele Avenue.'

'Wow, that's more than I was expecting. At what sort of time did the witness claim to see all this happening?'

'It was about 4 a.m. Or at least, that's what he claimed.'

Kesey chose to ignore the implied element of doubt in Lewis's prior comment. 'And it was definitely that same night? The night Lottie went missing?'

'The witness said so, yes. I've read the transcript of the call. The nineteenth of this month, it seems he was certain of the date. He claimed it was his mother's birthday. They'd been celebrating. He said there was no doubt in his mind.'

Kesey felt a sinking feeling deep in the pit of her stomach. He's reused the word claimed, and that wasn't good. 'Okay, that sounds hopeful, so, who did he say he saw?'

Lewis paused for a second before answering, resting his large forearms on the table, his empty plate pushed aside. 'This is where it gets interesting.'

'Interesting how?'

'He claimed he saw a woman. A woman meeting Megan's description, same height, same hairstyle and colour, similar age, and of average build. And he said he thought the child she was carrying might have been dressed in green. But that's been all over the papers and TV news, so I don't think we should necessarily read too much into it. He could simply have been repeating publicly available information.'

Kesey jerked her head back, her pulse quickening. 'Who's the witness?' She guessed what the answer was going to be long before Lewis replied. Some things were too good to be true.

'It was an anonymous call. We know it was made somewhere in the Caerystwyth area, but that's as good as it gets. I'm guessing he was using a pay-as-you-go bought for cash. I'll make some enquiries, but I wouldn't hold your breath. I can't see me tracking him down anytime soon.'

Kesey's eyes narrowed, her disappointment almost crushing. 'Do you think it's genuine?'

'I've got my doubts, to be honest, boss. I'd be willing to wager he's a wind-up merchant, some headcase pulling our strings to make himself feel big. Call it copper's intuition, a gut feeling.'

Kesey blew the air from her mouth with a hiss. She wasn't ready to give up on hope. 'Yeah, maybe, but maybe not; I took everything Megan said at face value. I didn't even consider the possibility she was lying, not for a single second. It was stupid, unprofessional. She could have taken Lottie from the house herself. It's not inconceivable. What the hell was I thinking?'

'Oh, come on, give me a break. There is no way Megan Weller did anything to that child. No fucking way! I'd bet my house on it.'

'Stranger things have happened, Ray. No assumptions, that's what Grav used to tell me. Consider all the possibilities. Keep an open mind. I just saw Megan as a grieving mother, and that was it. I put myself in her place, I over-identified. I got too close, that's the truth of it.'

'Don't be too hard on yourself. I still think it's something and nothing.'

Kesey sat in silence, pondering her next step. 'Yeah, but what if it's not?'

Lewis pointed at her food, still sitting on its plate. 'Do you mind me having that if you're not going to eat it?' He patted his gut. 'I'm a growing boy.'

Kesey pushed her plate across the table. 'We're going to have to pull her in. She's got to be interviewed. There's no avoiding it.' Lewis stuffed half her bacon roll into his open mouth, pushing it to the side with his tongue, hamster-like, cheek bulging, before replying. 'Are you sure? It seems like a lot of crap to me.'

'It's got to be checked out. There's no alternative.'

Lewis sighed, resigned to the inevitable. 'Do you want me to do it? I've got a couple of hours free today if that's any good to you? I'm sure I can clarify matters without too much trouble.'

'No, I know you've got your doubts, that's obvious. It's something I want us to do together. But before we do, I want you to speak to Megan's doctor, and check out her bank records too. I'm going to have a chat with social services and the head at Lottie's school. Let's see if there's anything we need to be aware of before we approach her. If we're going to do this, we're going to do it properly. No half measures.'

'I guess we'd better search the house as well then, attic and all if we're going to go that far. You seem to want to go the whole hog.'

'Yeah, you're right, we will. Better safe than sorry.'

'Do you want another coffee? I'm buying if you fancy one.'

Kesey rose to her feet, twisting the silver ring on the middle finger of one hand with the fingers and thumb of the other. 'No, you're all right, thanks, mate. I'm going to get on with those calls. I'll meet you in reception at eleven o'clock sharp. I don't want to leave it any longer than we have to. We can talk on the way. You can do the driving. I'm too knackered to be safe.'

'Are you planning to update the chief super? You know, just in case I bump into him in the corridor. I wouldn't want to speak out of turn.'

Kesey screwed up her face. 'You have got to be kidding me. When we've got something concrete, I'll let him know. Until then, we keep it to ourselves. The less he finds out, the better. If I never had to speak to him again, it would make my year.'

19

Lewis knocked on Kesey's office door at 10.40 a.m., opening it and walking in without waiting to be invited.

Kesey looked up at him and then at her watch. 'I thought we agreed on eleven o'clock?'

The DS pushed a pile of crime files aside before resting his weight on the edge of Kesey's cluttered desk. 'I've had a word with Megan's GP, a Dr Potter. She was reluctant to talk to me at first. You know, medical confidentiality and all that, but she opened up when I stressed the urgency of the investigation.'

'Oh, shit, here we go. Tell me the worst.'

Lewis adjusted his position, unable to make himself comfortable. 'Megan suffered PND, postnatal depression. It was bad. She was in one hell of a state, apparently.'

Kesey didn't exactly have her head in her hands. But she may as well have. Her body language told its own story. 'How bad are we talking?'

'She was feeling low very soon after the birth, difficulty sleeping and even thoughts of suicide. She needed a lot of help with Lottie's care. It seems Dale stepped up big time. It was long before he started drinking. It seems he hasn't always been the waste of space piss artist he's become. He offered Megan a lot of support, along with her mother, Doreen Jones, who stayed at the house for a few weeks while she was at her lowest. They kept up a suicide watch for a week or two, day and night.'

'Oh, crap, that was the last thing I was expecting to hear. Is the depression still an issue?'

Lewis shook his head. 'No, and it hasn't been for over four years. And I think that's important. I'm not sure it's of any significance to the case at all.'

'Yeah, but it could be, Ray, it could be. Psychiatric conditions can be deceptively complex. It's like addictions. People can sometimes hide them surprisingly well.'

Lewis lifted his bulk off the desk, settling in the only available chair. He sighed as he sat himself down, crossing his legs one over the other, his knees complaining with the effort of it all. 'I've been giving it some more thought. The bloke who rang in when the case went public refused to give a name. He insisted on remaining anonymous despite several requests to identify himself. Ask yourself why? And how many people do you know that don't use a smartphone these days? Put those two things together, and it rings alarm bells for me. I don't know why he contacted us, not with any certainty, but I don't like it. If we focus on Megan, we're looking in the wrong direction. It's a distraction and nothing more. We've still got a good many nonces to look at. We should be concentrating on them. This whole business with Megan is a waste of our time.'

Kesey pressed her lips together in a slight grimace. She seemed quieter and less animated than usual. 'Have you heard of Meadow's syndrome?'

Lewis shook his head. 'I can't say I have.'

'It's a psychological disorder marked by attention-seeking behaviour. I came across it a few years back when I was with the West Midlands force. A young mother, a nurse, was lacing her toddler's food with small amounts of household bleach, making him ill, and then gaining attention by seeking medical help. She'd taken him to the family GP numerous times, and to several different casualty departments over a period of months. Her partner reported her to social services in the end. He suspected what was going on and set up tiny surveillance cameras when no-one would take his concerns seriously. He caught her in the act. If he hadn't, the child might well have died. He very nearly did.'

'What are you getting at, Laura? What's the relevance?'

'I'm saying that things aren't always as they seem. Don't jump to conclusions. If someone claims he saw a woman matching Megan's description carrying a child from the house that night, we can't rule it out without very good reason. Things can be infinitely more complex than they first seem. The bleach investigation taught me that. We could be dealing with one of those complicated cases.'

Lewis turned his body, speaking in a steady, lower-pitched voice. 'Why would this so-called witness be out and about at that time of the fucking morning? It's bullshit. He's full of crap, a wind-up merchant. We shouldn't get drawn in.'

'Did you run a credit check?'

'Yeah, she's fine, no significant money worries. I wish I were half as well off.'

'It's the same with social services, Megan's not known to them.'

'What about the school?'

Kesey smiled thinly. 'I spoke to the head, Sheena Aldridge. I know her pretty well. She's down to earth. I feel I can trust her judgement.'

'What did she tell you, any concerns?'

'No, she had nothing but nice things to say, nothing but positives. Sheena's known Megan since they were both kids and says she's a devoted parent. She feels nothing but sympathy for her situation.'

'There you go. What does that tell you? The woman's a victim, not a suspect. It couldn't be more obvious.'

Kesey opened and closed her mouth, collecting her thoughts, struggling to find the right words. 'I know what you're saying, Ray. But we still can't ignore the call. If we do nothing and it turns out that Megan was involved, however remote the possibility, where does that leave us? And that's a rhetorical question, by the way. I'd be hung out to dry. Right up shit creek.'

'Okay, I'll run with it. But if Megan did take Lottie into the street at four in the morning, what did she do with her? It's bullshit, utter crap. We've searched the entire area. If Megan hurt Lottie, or even killed her, and then dumped her, we'd have found the body. How far could she carry a child of that age, and without being seen by anyone else? I'm telling you it didn't happen. The caller wants to cause disruption. He's a troll who wants a reaction. And I say fuck him. He's got nothing to offer us.'

Kesey frowned hard. 'We've had this conversation. We've got to follow it up, simple as. I'm not any happier about it than you are. But that's the way it is. I'm not going to change my mind however long you bang on for.'

Lewis met her eyes with a look of resigned acceptance. 'Okay, you're the boss, we'll do it your way. But let's tread carefully. We'll have a good look around the house, talk to Megan, and then we can put it to bed and forget it. We'll have done our duty, and hopefully, we won't have caused the unfortunate woman any more distress than we have to. She's got enough shit to deal with without us trampling all over her life. Can you imagine how she's going to feel when we turn up at her door? If she's innocent, which I'm telling you she is, it's going to be the worst feeling in the world. And even worse than that, she's never going to trust us again.'

'What did I say? Do you think I like it? Not one little bit! But we asked the public for information, and now we've got it. We've got procedures to follow, standing orders. Suck it up. We've got to do things by the book.'

'What, like Grav used to do, you mean?'

'That was different. He was different. Times have changed.'

'Yeah, things have changed all right, and not for the better.'

Kesey rose to her feet, pulling in and then slowly releasing a deep breath. 'Okay, you've said enough. Let's get this done. The quicker we can get it over with, the happier I'll be.'

20

Heath stood watching, partially hidden behind the dark-blue velvet curtains in the master bedroom of his home on Picton Street, as Megan was led through her front door to the waiting police car. A female officer took the lead and a male held their prisoner's arm just above the elbow.

'Look! Can you see her, Mother? Can you see? They're putting the bitch in the back of the car. It's the same two pigs who were on the evening news, oink, oink, the stupid, ineffectual morons. And look at the bitch mother's demeanour. Ha! What a state she's in, the tears, the morose expression on her stupid face. What a triumph! I did that, me, that's my achievement. Mine and nobody else's. The shrew's destruction continues, and there's a great deal more to come.'

His mother's image gradually came into sharper focus, emerging through the wall initially, and then sitting on the bed, resting her chin on one hand, and looking only mildly interested in anything he had to say or do. She sighed and then spoke, the sound of her voice filling his head as if projected loud and clear from every part of the room. It came from every direction at once, bombarding him with noise. *'What on earth am I supposed to be looking at, Henry? All I can see is this bedroom, the four walls, the fading furniture, and the double bed, covered in its familiar quilt. I mustn't forget the bed. It's the one I shared with your dear father. The one in which you were conceived all those years ago. Maybe it would have been better if he hadn't touched me at all.'*

Heath flinched at the mere mention of his deceased father, but he drove the man from his mind. 'Quickly, Mother, quickly, come to the window, come and see. They'll be driving away soon.'

'What on earth are you making such a fuss about now?'

'There, there, look, there, the bitch mother's been weeping. She looks close to collapse. Come to the window, look, the male pig's helping her into the car. What are you waiting for? Hurry before they go. For goodness' sake, get up, it's well worth seeing. Please, Mother, come and see.'

But she didn't look. She just lay back on the bed, hugging a feather pillow, pulling it close, brushing it with her lips, as she sometimes had in life. *'I shared this bed with your dear father for over twenty long years. I can still smell his cologne on the sheets. It's quite a turn-on in some strange way. He was a very sexual man, your father, but then you claim to know that as well as I do. His memory stains the sheets. Why don't you have a sniff?'*

Heath screwed up his face, screaming, turning away from the window as Lewis started the car's engine and drove off. 'Will you give me some credit? Just this once, will you admit I've done well? And don't talk about that man. He brought nothing but stress and destruction into my life. The bastard! I fucking hate him. Focus on my accomplishments for once. Come and look before they leave the street.' He dropped his chin to his chest. 'Oh, for fuck's sake, they're out of sight. You're my mother. Is a bit of support too much to ask for?'

Her image drifted towards the window in his mind's-eye. *'Credit? Is that some kind of joke? You can't even be sure the woman's been arrested. She could simply be helping the police with their enquiries as a witness. Or they could be updating her on the case. She is the brat's mother, after all. They could be telling her they've got a suspect. They could be talking about you, Henry. Have you considered that very real possibility? I've told you to move the brat. Either that or kill her and be done with it once and for all. Maybe next time there's a police car in our street, they'll be coming for you.'*

'I used an old phone. I bought a sim card for cash, and well away from here. I used it once, only once before binning it at the other end of town. There is no way they can find out I made that call.'

'Are you sure, Henry? Maybe they're cleverer than you think. Are you really sure?'

He continued the one-sided conversation, snarling his words as he tore the sheets from the bed, flinging them to the floor followed by the pillows. 'Yes, I'm sure, I couldn't be surer.'

'What on earth are you doing now, you ridiculous boy?'

Heath bared his teeth, snarling, as he gathered the bedclothes together, rushing towards the stairs, loathing the feel of the material on his skin. He was breathing through his mouth for fear of smelling his father's scent. 'You have ruined this morning for me, Mother. It should have been a triumph, my moment in the sun. But no, you had to mention that poisonous man.'

'He's still your father, Henry. You can't change that fact, whatever you think of him. The facts are the facts. It's simple biology.'

Heath descended the staircase at speed, two or three steps at a time. 'Do you remember what he did to me? Don't you think I'd forget the utterly odious bastard if I could? He's a stain on my life, and I loathe his memory.'

'Such a silly fuss about nothing.'

Heath took a three-quarter full bottle of turps from a kitchen cupboard and searched for the matches. 'I was six, Mother, just six years old. I tried to tell you what he'd done at the time. But you closed your ears to me. You wouldn't listen to a single word I said. If you had listened, it might have changed everything. It may have set me on a different path. Perhaps I wouldn't have murdered your baby daughter. Have you thought about that? Maybe I wouldn't have become the man I am.'

She followed him out into the well-tended, high-walled garden at the back of the house. *'Your father went to confession. He sought absolution. He was forgiven. You are such a drama queen. You're looking for attention now, just as you were then.'*

Heath approached a large metal refuse bin, throwing the lid aside and stamping down on it, before turning the bin upside down, shaking it until empty. 'Oh, I know he made a confession, Mother. Because that's what good Catholics do. But it didn't stop him. He did it again. He always did it again.'

'Can't I keep the sheets, Henry? Or maybe a pillow, just one pillow. The scent is all I have left of the man. It still means so much to me.'

'No! A thousand times, no!'

'You can be so very cruel sometimes, so inconsiderate, such a bad son.'

'Look on, Mother. Watch them burn.' Heath stuffed the bedclothes into the metal receptacle, lifting a leg high and then stamping them down. He unscrewed the white plastic top from the turps bottle, and then poured the entire contents over the bedding, dousing it before striking a match, carefully shielding the flickering yellow flame with a cupped hand. Heath danced in a tight circle, smiling as the flames burst into enthusiastic life, sending plumes of black, acrid smoke spiralling high into the warm summer air.

'*Now, are you happy? Are you pleased with yourself, Henry? Was there really a need to upset me like that?*'

'Please be quiet, Mother. You've said enough.'

She looked around her, jabbing a bony digit at one window or another without the need for words.

Heath was suddenly acutely aware of the various overlooking houses. He imagined neighbours looking down at him, watching, non-existent curtain-twitchers suspicious of his actions, attempting to read his thoughts. He stood watching the dancing flames, shifting his weight from one foot to the other, willing the roaring fire to consume the contents of the bin and the memories they engendered as quickly as feasibly possible.

'*Think things through before acting, you ridiculous boy. People will see exactly what you're doing. They'll stick their noses in. Interfere in your business. Look around you, Henry. They're watching you right now.*'

Heath placed the lid back on the bin, starving the fire of oxygen. He hurried back towards the kitchen door, speaking without looking back. 'Be quiet, Mother, shut your mouth and keep it shut. You've already disrupted my plans more than enough for one day. There are things I need to do before the bitch mother returns to the house. Because she will, she definitely will. And when she does, I'll have something waiting for her. Not a nice surprise, but definitely a surprise. Something which will tear her heart to pieces.'

'*Get on with it, Henry, whatever it is, there's a good lad. If your plans are delayed, that's your fault, not mine. You've got no-one to blame but yourself.*'

He chose to ignore her latest put down as he opened the cutlery drawer next to the gas cooker, taking out a pair of all-purpose scissors, the same ones he'd used to trim the wig. He ran the cutting edges across a finger. Surely it was sharp enough. He held up his finger and licked it, as a small drop of blood oozed from his cut.

It was time to head back to the attic – time to implement the next stage of his plan. It was time to have some fun.

21

Megan stared into Kesey's tired eyes, fixating on the source of her anguish. There was apparent nervous tension in her voice and tone when she spoke. 'How many times do I have to say it? If someone insists that they saw a woman leaving my home address in the early hours of that awful night, there are two possibilities. Either the witness was lying through their teeth, or they saw someone else entirely.'

Kesey was inclined to believe Megan's impassioned plea, but she continued nonetheless. The detective had once made assumptions in a previous case. A case in which a woman seen only as a victim had gone on to stab and kill an officer under Kesey's command. 'Our witness claims that the woman he saw matched your description almost exactly.'

Megan's professional legal instincts came to the fore as she struggled to control her emotions, a desperate sense of injustice beating her down a little further with every question. 'You said "claims", and that's significant. He can claim whatever he wants to. That doesn't make it true.'

'He says he saw what he saw.'

Megan adopted a challenging tone, forcing a laugh. 'I'm assuming you've interviewed this mystery man you referred to? I'm assuming you've confirmed that he's a credible witness. Because if he's not, if he's provided you with misinformation for whatever reason, which I can assure you he most certainly has, you're wasting your damned time talking to me when you should be out looking for my daughter. You've let me down, Laura. And much worse than that, you've let my poor Lottie down.'

'All you've got to do is answer my questions.'

'I thought you were better than this. More fool me, I trusted you. You told me that you're a mother yourself. You told me you understood my predicament. How do you sleep nights? I don't think I could in your place. I'm beginning to think you didn't believe a single word I said.'

'Have you ever suffered from depression, Megan?'

Megan blinked away her tears. 'What?'

'I asked you if you've experienced depression?'

'What's the relevance?'

'Answer the question, please, Ms Weller.'

Megan took a deep breath in through her nose and then exhaled slowly through her open mouth. 'Yes, I have, after giving birth. But then you're already well aware of that. That's why you asked. It was several years ago. Surely you're not suggesting it could be of any relevance?'

'Do you still suffer symptoms? A great deal has happened in your life in recent months, the separation, Dale's excessive drinking, the injunction and the events leading to it. It wouldn't be surprising if all that misfortune got you down. It wouldn't reflect badly on you. People have broken down when faced with far less.'

'Postnatal depression and reactive depression are two very different things. I did have a hard time after Lottie's birth, and I'd be the first one to acknowledge that. But I received the help I needed at the time. What happened then has no relevance whatsoever to current events. Someone broke into my home, exactly as I told you. Someone took Lottie from the bed as I said. Your investigation is way off track. If you truly think I've got anything at all to do with my daughter's disappearance, you've got this horribly wrong. I'm asking myself if you're the right person for the job. I very much hope your superiors are doing the same.'

'We're obliged to pursue all leads. I'm following procedures, and nothing more.'

Megan's entire body was trembling uncontrollably as she wiped a tear from her left cheek. 'Isn't it strange that you never mentioned arresting me when you shook my hand not so very long ago. You looked me in the eye and assured me then that you'd do all you could to save my daughter, whatever the danger she faced. And I believed you. I actually believed you.'

Kesey resisted the impulse to look away. 'I said I'd find Lottie and I will.'

Megan gripped the sides of her seat, fearing the mounting stress may cause her to pass out and fall to the floor. 'Well, in that case, I strongly suggest you get on with it. If something happens to Lottie, something awful, something that's too terrible even to contemplate, I'm going to hold you personally responsible. I'll sue this incompetent joke of a police force for every penny it's got.'

Kesey found her mind wandering to the well-being of her own child, as she rose to her feet, keen to get out of there at the earliest opportunity. 'Thank you for your time, Ms Weller. I appreciate you answering my questions.'

Megan looked across at her incredulously. 'So, now you're happy? Are you pleased with yourself, Inspector? All this is hard enough to deal with without the very people who are supposed to be helping me making things infinitely worse.'

This time Kesey did look away, averting her eyes to the wall. 'Switch the tape off, Ray. I've heard enough. This interview is at an end.'

22

Heath was experiencing a heady mix of expectation and nervousness, as he hurried along the narrow, tree-lined path at the rear of Megan's home, and running past the adjoining properties towards the nearby park. He checked to the right and left, searching for non-existent witnesses with quick darting eyes for a full thirty seconds, before scrambling up and over the six-foot-high wall, which separated the stone-strewn path from Megan's back garden. Heath rushed across the overgrown lawn, his pack on his back, unable to believe his luck when a sleek, jet-black tomcat crossed his path, the same, diamond-bright eyed feline creature he'd seen when entering the house only days before. He took the sighting as a positive sign. A sign that both Lady Luck and destiny were on his side and cheering him on. All of a sudden, his nerves had gone.

Heath's confidence was soaring as he approached the back of the house. He wasn't expecting to find a partially open window this time. But he'd planned accordingly. He took a steel claw hammer and six-inch masonry nail from his backpack before slowly approaching the double-glazed door. He briefly considered attempting to enter that way, but then decided to break the same window through which he previously entered, simply because it amused him to do so. He was keen to give both Megan and the police the clear message that a closed window was no obstacle to him, because of his almost infinite predatory powers. A closed window didn't keep Megan safe. Nothing kept her safe. She was in terrible danger, potentially fatal danger. And he wanted her to know it. He could do whatever the hell he wanted to and nobody could stop him. He thought it and believed it.

Now it was time to show the world.

Heath placed the point of the nail in the bottom

right-hand corner of the windowpane before striking the top with a single sharp blow of the hammer. The double-glazed unit shattered immediately, allowing him to reach through the gap, turn the handle and open the white plastic frame wide. He returned both the hammer and nail to his backpack before glancing behind him.

Was that the sound of someone in an adjoining garden? He flinched.

He listened intently, straining his ears, waiting until reassured by the silence, before scrambling through the open frame head first, and then lowering himself to the kitchen floor with a muted call of triumph. He drank water at the tap, strode across the red-tiled kitchen, through the comfortably furnished lounge, and into the hallway.

Heath laughed on seeing a twelve-by-eight-inch framed colour photo of Lottie's smiling face hanging on the wall, in pride of place next to the door. He studied the picture for a few seconds, thinking how different his captive now looked, without that yellow hair, and behind the bars. He edged a few inches closer to the photo and then repeatedly spat on the glass, masking the image in saliva, before climbing the stairs.

Heath went straight to Lottie's room. He congratulated himself on his success as he walked through the door. It was obviously the brat's room, being so typical of the style chosen by, or for, any number of little girls of her age, with its pink bedclothes, sparkling unicorn wallpaper, and age and gender-specific toys.

Heath unzipped his black corduroy trousers and emptied his bursting bladder onto the bed, spraying yellow urine over almost every inch of the summer quilt and feather pillow, before eventually refastening his trousers with a grin. He stood back, admiring his work with a look of unbridled satisfaction. The experience wasn't quite orgasmic, but it wasn't far off, as adrenaline flooded his body and his emotions danced. He pictured Megan's reaction to seeing for the first time the results of his efforts. He imagined her disgust, her horror, her rage and despair. His cock swelled, pressing against the tight cloth of his pants, as hard as he'd ever been.

He briefly considered unfastening his trousers for a second time and masturbating, right there and then, but what if his mother saw? She'd mock him for his lack of focus. Criticise him for his failure to concentrate on the task at hand. And so he refocused, fixating on what he was there to achieve. Distractions weren't helpful, whatever the potential physical pay-off, not at such a critical juncture. Megan's psychological destruction was everything. It's what he lived for.

Heath searched three dressing table drawers and then a white-painted wardrobe, gathering several items of Lottie's clothing, which he thought suited his purpose. Yes, they'd be ideal, absolutely ideal. His actions were inspired. They were works of unbridled genius to be applauded, worthy of note in the annals of criminal history. His oh so critical mother had been wrong all along.

Heath held the various items of clothing out in front of him in turn, taking full advantage of the light of the window. 'Can you see them, Mother? Come look, they're almost perfect, don't you think? I've done well, haven't I? That's worthy of a pat on the back if anything is. Three cheers for me. Your boy has become a man.'

Her face appeared to his right, emerging from the

same wardrobe from which he'd taken the clothes, its image gaining in dark intensity and size, contrasting dramatically against the brightly coloured wallpaper, scowling. *'Get on with it, boy. You don't want the bitch coming home and ruining everything before you've finished, do you? That wouldn't do. It wouldn't do it at all.'*

'I could kill her.'

She shook her head and sighed. *'Yes, you could. I'm very well aware of that, Henry. But that's not part of your plan, or, at least, not yet. Surely, she should suffer a great deal more first. Isn't that your intention? You've crowed about it often enough. I suggest you stop standing there preening like an overexcited peacock on heat and get on with doing what you're here to do.'*

Heath looked into his mother's eyes and knew she was right. He didn't appreciate her wording, but he understood her point of view. He had a plan and needed to stick to it.

He descended the stairs with a rekindled determination to maximise the emotional impact of his visit. He winced on hearing a car slow almost to a stop in the street outside, his mother's accusing, cautionary voice whispering in his ear. But he relaxed almost immediately as the driver travelled on by. Now, nothing could stop him; he said it and believed it. Everything was just as it should be, exactly as he'd pictured it in his mind.

Heath sat himself down on the thick woollen carpet at the centre of the lounge floor. He took care to lay out Lottie's clothes in the shape of a young girl's body, a bright-orange top, purple leggings and white leather trainers, the heels of which lit up and flashed when moved even slightly. Heath studied his new creation, happy with his progress, and then took a folded piece of paper from the inside pocket of his thin, dark cotton jacket.

The paper was cut in the shape of an oval and had a dour girl's face crudely drawn on it in black marker pen, large eyes, teardrops, a button nose, and the thin line of a mouth with a slight downward curve. He took a clear plastic bag from a side pocket of his backpack and began laying out Lottie's pale blonde hair, taking his time to create as close a representation of her as he could achieve with the available materials. Heath stood, looking down and frowning for a second or two, before lowering himself back to the floor, balancing on his knees and adjusting the position of the fringe, first one way and then the other until he thought it was precisely right.

'Come and take a look, Mother. It's almost as if the little brat is here with us in the room.' He began jumping up and down on the spot, as excited as a child on a birthday morning. 'Look, Mother, look, it's truly wonderful. I'm such a clever boy.'

'For goodness' sake, calm yourself down, Henry. Take a breath. It's time to get out of here.'

'Never a word of praise from your mouth, not a single one.'

'Oh, come on, stop feeling sorry for yourself, you needy boy. It's time to leave back the way you came. And stay close to the wall as soon as you're back on the path. Keep your head down. Focus on the ground. You'll avoid being seen and identified that way, and that's important. You don't want to be a jailbird. Being caught isn't a part of the plan.'

He looked back at her with a contemptuous sneer. 'I know that, Mother, I know. Weren't you watching? What do you think I did on my way here?'

Heath was about to leave the lounge to make his way home when he suddenly remembered the tube of cherry-red lipstick in his trouser pocket. He removed the top, strode purposefully towards an area of the white wall directly above a coal-effect gas fire, and began writing, taking pride in creating the words in well-practised, one-inch high capital letters.

DEAR BITCH,

I HOPE YOU ENJOYED THE SURPRISE I LEFT FOR YOU. IT CERTAINLY AMUSED ME. THERE'S ANOTHER SMALL GIFT IN THE HALL AND YET ANOTHER IN THE BRAT'S BEDROOM, WHICH I'M SURE YOU'LL FIND INTERESTING. SHE'S STILL CLINGING ON TO LIFE FOR THE MOMENT, BUT YOU'LL NEVER SEE HER AGAIN. I PLAN TO HAVE SOME FUN WITH HER BEFORE SHE DIES. THINK ABOUT THAT AND WEEP. I'LL KEEP YOU UPDATED IF THE MOOD TAKES ME. YOU'VE BROUGHT THIS ON YOURSELF.

LOVE AND KISSES,

YOUR WORST NIGHTMARE X

23

'Well, that went well.'

Kesey glared at Lewis with a look that said a thousand words. 'Yes, thanks very much for the sarcasm, Ray. It was frigging horrendous. I'm well aware of that.'

'I was just saying, that's all.'

'Well, don't. It wouldn't be a bad idea to keep your opinions to yourself.'

'The fingerprints on the window tell us all we need to know.' Kesey was quick to reply. 'They could have been there for any length of time. They point us towards a potential suspect, I'll accept that much, but they're not definitive, not in themselves.'

Lewis shook his head. 'Give me a break. They were on the frame. They were on the glass. They tell their own story. Who else left them? Follow the evidence. Every word Megan said was true.'

Kesey sighed. 'Where is she now?'

'She's still sitting waiting in reception, as far as I know. I told her I'd run her home.'

'We're not a taxi service.'

'Oh, come on, boss, it's the least we can do.'

Kesey folded her arms. 'Do you think I don't know that? Really? Is that what you're suggesting? I'm not made of stone, you know.'

Lewis blew the air from his mouth, avoiding direct eye contact. 'How's Ed doing?'

Kesey relaxed slightly, lowering her arms to her sides. 'The medicine seems to be working quicker than expected. Or maybe he's getting better by himself. I was seriously worried for a while. Thanks for asking.'

'That is good news. Glad to hear it.'

'Yeah, it's great.'

He reached for his car keys. 'Right, I'd better make a move. Hopefully, I can build some bridges with Megan on the way back to her place. God knows, the woman can do with all the support she can get.'

Kesey forced a thin smile. 'No-one said police work is easy.'

'You've got that right.'

'I'll see you later, Ray. There's a couple of nonces I want to discuss. One with links to Peter Davies. Davies was out of the country, but his contact wasn't.'

'The scumbags network, that's the problem.'

'Yeah, I know. We can talk about it later.'

The big man nodded. 'Anything you need while I'm out and about?'

She reached into a pocket, retrieving a folded five-pound note. 'A bag of toffees, if you're passing the supermarket. Or a bar of dark chocolate, a big one, either would be fine.'

'Okay, no problem, I was planning to call in that new place by the garden centre, I could do with some fags.'

'I thought you'd given up.'

He laughed humourlessly. 'Yeah, so did I.'

She reached out, offering him the money, but withdrew her hand when he didn't accept it, waving it away. 'We are going to find Lottie, Ray. We'll get the break we need. Just you wait and see.'

'Let's hope so, time's passing. If any of the dirty bastards we're looking at have got her, it doesn't bear thinking about. I'd nail the filthy cunts to a tree by their balls if it were up to me. And leave them there to rot.'

Kesey grinned, despite the tension, conflicted memories of her mentor flooding back and surrounding her. 'Grav used to say much the same thing back in the day.'

Lewis glanced back on approaching the door. 'Yeah, and he meant it too. Now, there was a DI who knew what he was talking about. I'll see you later, it's time for me to go.'

24

Lewis was profusely apologetic as he drove Megan from Caerystwyth Police Station to her Picton Street home. He apologised that she'd been arrested in the first place; he apologised that she'd been detained for over two miserable hours; but most of all, he apologised for the fact that she'd been released on pre-charge police bail pending further enquiries.

He explained that all of this had been done contrary to his advice, stressing that he didn't suspect her of any crime, let alone harming her own daughter. He said it and meant it.

But none of this seemed to make Megan feel any better. It was often more comfortable to talk sitting alongside an interviewee, rather than opposite them, eye to eye, and Lewis tried to take full advantage of his opportunity.

He tried sharing personal information regarding his family, his ex-wife, his grown-up kids, the curse of his arthritic knee, attempting to encourage Megan to open up and talk, but with only limited success.

Megan wasn't inclined to share. She'd said enough and heard enough too. But that didn't stop Lewis trying. The more he said, the more she clammed up, right up to the time she couldn't swallow her sense of betrayal for another moment when she told him exactly where he could stick his apologies. Lewis took it on the chin, knowing he'd have said a great deal worse in her place. It was surprising she was talking to him at all.

'Tell me about Lottie.'

For the first time during the journey, Megan turned in her seat to face him. Most friends and acquaintances wanted to avoid asking about Lottie. They seemed awkward, tongue-tied, as people often were following the death of a loved one. Some had even crossed the street on seeing her, keen to avoid contact.

Megan wanted people to talk of Lottie. She wanted them to acknowledge her existence. To express their grief and hope. To offer their prayers to whatever God they believed in. And so, Megan welcomed Lewis's question, whatever his motives. Whether he was merely making conversation, asking in the interests of the case, or if he were actually interested as he'd claimed, didn't matter a great deal. Megan was just pleased that he'd asked at all. She smiled for the first time that day. Not a warm smile, not a happy smile, but, a smile nonetheless. A smile that told its own story. 'What do you want to know?'

Lewis signalled to turn right, lifting his foot off the accelerator and touching the brake as the traffic slowed almost to a stop. 'Tell me all about her, her personality, her hobbies, her likes and dislikes. She seems like a lovely little girl. I'd like to know more about her. It sometimes helps to build up a picture of a missing person, whatever their age. I like to know who I'm looking for.'

Megan thought that if she began weeping again, she might never stop. She feared she might cry for eternity, floods of tears flowing until she was old, wrung out and dry. And so she resisted her grief, talking of happier times, telling Lewis about Lottie's maternal grandmother, her school friends, her love of books, dancing, and gymnastics. And the frogs too.

As Megan spoke, she clung on to hope. She also prayed, pleading, bargaining, offering herself as a sacrifice, anything at all to potentially aid Lottie's rescue. In truth, Megan had no idea if God was listening. But what else could she do? She'd distributed the posters. She'd walked around the town for hour after hour in the forlorn hope that she may see Lottie, or gain some hint as to her location. She'd talked to the police; she'd pleaded her case, and appeared at the press conference. Now, all that was left was hope.

As Lewis pulled up outside Megan's semi-detached Victorian home, he offered her his business card, taking it from an old, brown leather wallet that looked almost as time-worn as he did.

Megan stuffed it into a trouser pocket with trembling fingers before unfastening her seat belt. She still wasn't entirely sure if Lewis was simply playing her, or sincere in his expressed concern. But there was something about the big man that she couldn't help but like. And there was some comfort in that.

'Okay, here we are, love. Pick up the phone if there's anything you want to discuss, day or night, don't hesitate. I'll always be glad to hear from you.'

Megan rested her hand on the door handle. 'I was wondering if anything came of the name I gave DI Kesey? Is it something you've looked into?'

Lewis puffed out his cheeks, spitting his words as if the mere mention of the man was an affront to his day. 'Are you talking about Peter Davies?'

'Yes, it was just a thought, that's all. He's a risk to children, that's obvious, and I thought... well, you know what I'm saying. Did anything come of it? I'd hate to think...'

'I had a quiet word with him. He was out of the country at the time of Lottie's disappearance. It wasn't him. That's one hundred per cent certain, no room for doubt.'

Megan opened the car door. 'Okay, it was just a thought... I'll err, I'll tell Dale.'

Lewis gave her a knowing look. 'Oh, I wouldn't worry about that, love. I'm sure he already knows.

And you needn't worry about Davies. He won't be bothering you.'

So, it seemed the detective was on their side. 'Thank you, Ray. It is all right if I call you Ray, isn't it?'

He smiled warmly, revealing nicotine-yellowed teeth, the remnants of a habit left in the past until today. 'Of course it is, love. You know where I am. You've got my number. Ring me if you need me.'

Megan nodded, thinking she'd made a useful connection, maybe even found someone she could trust, not exactly a friend, but a confidante. 'Yes, yes, I will. And thank you again. Please find my daughter. Don't leave any stone unturned. It means everything to me. Any words seem inadequate. Nothing else matters. I couldn't go on without her.'

'I won't rest till I find her. That I can promise you. You have my word.'

She looked the big man in the eye and believed his every word. 'Thank you again. I'm relying on you. Your help means a lot.'

25

Megan saw the crude representation of her daughter laid out on the floor as soon as she entered her lounge. She walked slowly towards it, unable to look away. Megan stared at the familiar clothes, the bright-orange top, the purple leggings, the nearly new trainers. Then at the paper face, and at the fine blonde hair that had so recently framed her daughter's pretty face. Megan sank to her knees next to Heath's creation, not wanting to accept it was real.

But as she reached out, picking up a length of pale-yellow hair and raising it close to her eyes, she knew the colour; she knew the feel of it, and she knew the scent of it too. There was no room for denial, however tempting. The hair had been sheared from Lottie's head recently.

Megan knew it with total, unrelenting certainty, and she understood that some unseen person was playing with her sanity. Somebody with absolutely no concerns for society's usual conventions of decency. Someone who would go to any lengths to make her life even more of a misery than it had already become. Who would do such a terrible thing? She searched her mind but without resolution. Whoever it was must hate her so very much.

Megan was weeping as she looked up to see the writing on the wall. She crept towards it, one cautious step at a time, asking herself how she hadn't seen it as soon as she entered the room. As she began reading, she became acutely aware that the writer of those awful words may still be in the house. He may be watching her. Feeding on her vulnerability and ready to pounce. A small part of her hoped that he was. That she'd have the opportunity to confront him, to see his face. She felt ready to fight despite her fear. Prepared to do whatever it took to overcome her oppressor in the name of her daughter, do or die, life or the grave.

Megan rushed to the kitchen, where she picked up a ten-inch bread knife, clutching it tightly in her right hand. She returned to the lounge to continue reading, willing him to appear. She read one line after another, stopping briefly and then starting again when the emotional impact of the written words became too much to bear. She'd read the entire message twice before she could fully take it in, feeling more hate for its author than she'd ever thought possible.

Megan pictured the mystery man of her worst nightmare at her feet, hog-tied and at her mercy to do with whatever she wished. She imagined herself unleashing untold suffering upon him without pity until he revealed Lottie's whereabouts to set her free. Megan saw it all in her mind's eye and willed it to become true, manifested by thought and heightened emotion alone.

She studied the writing style, asking herself if it were in any way familiar.

Megan thought of Lottie, vulnerable, innocent, lovely Lottie, in the hands of such a man, a monster capable of scribing such vile and ruthless words. The burden was too terrible to bear.

The reality too awful to contemplate. Megan gagged, swallowed, and gagged again as she hurried across the lounge, stumbling towards the downstairs toilet, where she threw up until her gut ached and there was nothing left but bile.

Megan still had the knife clutched tightly in her hand as she climbed the stairs one slow step at a time, urging herself on. *One step, two steps, come on, Megan, you can do it, keep going, one more step, do it for Lottie, for your little girl.*

She feared what she might find when she opened Lottie's bedroom door. And in some strange way, it was something of a relief when she was met by the unmistakable stink of urine assaulting her nostrils. She stared at the soiled bedclothes and pillow, reassuring herself that she hadn't found a body, Lottie's body... or blood, there could have been blood. Things were bad, but they could have been worse. Things could always be worse.

Megan briefly considered searching the other first-floor rooms before rushing from the house, but her resolve had reached its limits, as her own bladder threatened to evacuate where she stood. It was time to get out of there. Time to phone the police. Time to seek help. There were clues, evidence, that was obvious even to her. Maybe the monster man had blown it this time.

Perhaps he'd revealed his identity, without ever realising his mistake. Megan reached into a pocket for Lewis's card as she descended the stairs, dropping the knife to the hall floor as she reached the bottom. She was holding her smartphone in her hand as she opened the front door, gagging again on seeing the spittle covering Lottie's photo. What sort of madman was she dealing with? What kind of animal? Megan stood outside on the uneven pavement and dialled, only having to wait a matter of seconds before hearing Lewis's reassuringly gruff Welsh voice at the other end of the line.

'You need to come back. You need to come back now. He's been here. He's been in my house.'

Lewis hit the brake hard, performing an expertly efficient U-turn despite the heavy traffic. 'Are you sure, love?'

Megan spoke through her tears. 'Yes, he's... eh, oh God... he's left Lottie's hair on the lounge carpet.'

'Where are you now?'

'I'm outside, on... on the pavement, outside the house. What shall I... what... what shall I do?'

Lewis switched on the blue light, pressing the accelerator to the floor, signalling and passing two cars at speed despite the 30 mph limit. 'I'm on my way, love. Do not go back into the house. Do you hear me? I'll be with you in two minutes. Stay exactly where you are.'

26

Kesey sat on the three-seater settee with Edward sleeping next to her. She was drinking a cup of strong coffee sweetened with two heaped teaspoonfuls of cold-pressed Carmarthenshire honey, which she considered a justifiable treat at a difficult time. An iconic early Joan Armatrading album of which both she and Janet were particularly fond of was playing in the background.

'Do you know, I actually told that poor woman that I suspected her of harming her daughter. She needs my support. I should be there for her. Holding her hand every step of the way. What the hell was I thinking?'

Janet set her latest chick-lit paperback aside, carefully folding the page. 'Are you certain she didn't play any part in her child's disappearance?'

Kesey nodded. 'Oh, I'm certain all right. Whoever took Lottie went back to her house while I was wasting my time interviewing her mother under caution. The bastard must be laughing his frigging head off. He took full advantage. He's playing me for a mug.'

'Do you think he was watching? Do you think he knew the house was empty? Maybe he was waiting for you to take the poor woman away.'

'Yeah, it was a set-up all right. I think that's exactly what happened.'

'That must have taken some nerve.'

'We've got the bastard's fingerprints, we've got his DNA, and we know he's either living locally or knows the area well. He's operating within what Grav used to call a zone of comfort. We know all that, but we still haven't got the slightest clue who he is. And he's gaining confidence now, more full of himself. He's running rings around us, and he knows it. I think it's a game to him. He's enjoying every frigging moment.'

Janet made a face. 'You keep saying "he". Are you certain it's a man? You've always said you never make assumptions. Isn't that what you're doing?'

'The perverted bastard pissed all over the little girl's bed. He hasn't only abducted her. He's now taunting the mother, playing with her sanity like a cat with a mouse. There is no way we're looking for a woman. This has got male scrote written all over it.'

Janet shuddered. 'Oh, for goodness' sake, I couldn't do your job however much they paid me.'

'It gets worse. You don't know the half of it.'

'What are you talking about?'

'Do you really want to know? You can't unhear this stuff once I've told you.'

'I asked, didn't I?'

'Okay, if you're sure. The psycho cut the little girl's hair off. He laid it out on the lounge floor for Megan to find along with some of her clothes. Can you imagine how horrendous that must have been for the poor woman when she walked in? Firstly, I give her a hard time for no good reason at all, and then she finds that vile abomination after Ray drives her home. It's like something out of horror film. Worse than a horror film, it's real life.'

'Oh my God, that's ghastly. He must be some kind of psycho.' Kesey sipped her coffee.

'And as if that wasn't bad enough, he'd left the poor woman a message scrawled on the lounge wall in what looks like bright red lipstick.'

'What sort of message?'

'Threats and implied threats. Trying to scare her, trying to hurt, and succeeding too. She's traumatised, terrified, and fearing the worst. I'm beginning to think this is all about Megan. That this isn't some random crime. Whoever took Lottie targeted her because she's Megan's daughter. It's someone with a grudge. He wants her to suffer worse than she's ever suffered before. And I think he's capable of doing almost anything to make that happen.'

Janet looked across at Edward, as he slept, adjusting his position on the sofa, pressing himself against Kesey's warm thigh. 'Whoever it was, went back to the house in broad daylight. It's a residential area. Someone must have seen something. Not everyone would have been in work. Not even you're that unlucky.'

'There's a quiet path at the back of the house. It's likely the perpetrator came in that way.'

'So, where's Megan now?'

Kesey's brow furrowed. 'She spent last night at her mum's place while the SOCOs did their bit, but then she insisted on going back to her house this morning.'

'What? That's the last place I'd want to be. I'd feel like a sitting target. If he's broken in twice, why not again? She's at risk. It seems insane to me.'

'Yeah, I said much the same thing to Ray. He tried to talk her out of it. She had other options. She could have carried on staying at her mum's place or gone to stay with her ex. They both offered. But she's got it into her head that she needs to be there in case Lottie comes back.'

'That doesn't make a lot of sense.'

Kesey was quick to reply. 'It doesn't make any sense at all, Jan. But try telling her that. Ray said he'd tried every angle, but she wasn't having any of it. She was staying put, and that was it.'

'Can't you put an officer in the house to look after the poor woman until the maniac's caught and locked up? You know, someone who can keep her safe? You could have someone with her twenty-four hours a day. I think that's what I'd do in your place.'

Kesey sucked in her cheeks. 'Yeah, you'd think so, wouldn't you? But Halliday won't agree to it. We can't justify the cost, apparently. Megan's chosen to stay there rather than having to, or at least, that's his rationalisation. I've had a panic alarm fitted, linked directly to the police station. That's the best I can do. If Megan presses it, there'll be an immediate emergency response. There are covert cameras covering both gardens, front and back. They were set up by the tech team this afternoon. And I've told the patrol cars to drive past the house whenever they're in the area. Resources are limited. I'd like to do more, but I can't. You can shake your head as much as you want to. It's the best I can do.'

27

'Is that your father's camera?'

Heath spun on the ball of his right foot, looking directly at his mother's unreal image as she appeared, materialising from the mirror, becoming ever more vivid, the colours brighter with each second that passed. Heath was dressed from head to foot in her old clothes, dark tights, a skirt let out at the waist and a blouse with floral lace decoration around the collar. The blouse was at least a size too small. He was in full make-up, but not wearing the wig, due to the warmth of the day.

'Yes, Mother, it is my father's camera, as you well know, the German one, his favourite SLR. I feel sure you recall what he used to do with it. All the photos he took of me in various states of undress. The ones he shared with the priest and his other like-minded predatory friends. I was quite the star.'

She flashed a cold smile. *'I hope you're not trying to excuse your particular peculiarities, Henry. We're all responsible for our actions in this life. Blaming the long-gone past is rather a lame excuse if that's what you're up to. The vast majority of abuse victims don't go on to become abusers.'*

'But I did, Mother, I did. Cause and effect. Those formative events set me on a path. And now look at me. Look where it got me. Those events defined my life.'

Her eyes widened. *'Don't tell me that's the hint of a conscience raising its ugly head? Are you feeling guilty, Henry? Is that where this is going? I never thought I'd see the day.'*

He clawed at his scalp. 'Ha! Don't be so absurd. I was born evil; I was rotten from day one. Daddy would be so very proud. I'm wicked to the core.'

She pointed at the camera. *'That old thing seems a little dated now, don't you think? Surely there's something more up to date you could use, something digital, some-*

thing that produces images you could upload directly to that computer you seem so very fond of.'

He pulled his lips back, baring his teeth, snarling. 'I need actual photographs, Mother. Pictures I can develop myself – pictures I can hold in my hand. You can't put digital images in an envelope. You can't put them in a post box. I would have thought that was blatantly obvious.'

He heard her sigh in an exaggerated, dramatic way as if she was performing on a stage, signalling her disdain, as she had so many times in life. And then she spoke again. As he knew she inevitably would. *'What on earth have you got planned now, you ridiculous boy?'*

Heath held up the local weekly newspaper in clear view, pointing to a bold headline announcing Lottie's disappearance, emblazoned on the front page in two-inch high capital letters. Lottie's smiling face filled two-thirds of the page, with only two bold words above it:

'The powers that be are looking for the obnoxious little brat, Mother. And they're looking for me too – the ineffectual pigs with their criticisms and judgements. I'm a mystery man, a monster that haunts their dreams, the talk of the town. The investigation is in full flow.'

She wagged a finger. '*I told you to move her, either that or kill her. When will you ever listen? You can't target the brat's mother effectively if you're languishing in a cell. Think about that, my boy. You were incredibly fortunate to avoid prison in Syria. Why gamble with your freedom yet again? It's ill-advised at best.*'

Heath winced at the mere mention of incarceration. But he remained confident in his ability to outwit the authorities. He always was when anticipating the end game. The doubts came later. 'Watch and learn, Mother. The potential pay-off entirely justifies the risks.' He walked towards the cage, the newspaper still clutched tightly in one hand. He began shaking the cage with his free hand, pulling the entire structure first one way and then pushing it the other, the metal base rattling against the floorboards. He continued shaking it more and more vigorously until Lottie partially woke from her drug-induced stupor, opening one eye and then closing it again moments later.

Heath placed the newspaper on the filthy floor of the attic room, positioning it so that the top half rested against the bars at an angle, the headline and date in clear view. He picked up the camera, checking the various technical settings for one final time. And then he began taking photos, one after another, using the entire thirty-six shot film, as Lottie stared through the metal bars. The young child was lost somewhere in a dreamworld, drifting between semi-consciousness and sleep, her experience a blur of partial reality and a nightmare she couldn't begin to understand.

Lottie called for her mother only the once, shouting out the word, eyes tight shut, and then she began screeching, high-pitched, piercing, as the sedative effects of the drug gradually wore off. Heath placed the camera aside before rushing forward, grabbing Lottie's right hand, dragging her arm through the steel bars, and plunging the needle of a prepared injection deep into her bicep, administrating the adult dose of the sedative drug to ensure rapid effectiveness. Heath slumped to the wooden floor, panting hard as Lottie rolled up in a tight ball, clutching her knees to her chest. He fought the almost overwhelming urge to harm her further. To act out his deviant, unreflective impulses to throw all semblances of self-control aside.

But he somehow succeeded in focusing on the long game, rather than grasp the glorious but all too short-lived pay-off immediate violence would bring. In time he planned to kill her. To inflict terrible suffering as he had on all those who'd died at his hands. But the time had not yet come. Like it or not, that pleasure would have to wait.

Heath suddenly jumped to his feet in one athletic bound, picking up the SLR and walking slowly towards the attic's hatch, as his dead mother's image came back into sharp focus, lingering close to the opening, unavoidable, obstructive, getting in his way.

'Do you know how to use the darkroom, Henry? Come to that, do you even know where it is? It was your father's private space, after all, his sanctuary. You never ventured down those grey concrete steps, not as a child, and neither did I, for that matter. Such things were forbidden, out of bounds to all but him.'

Heath's smirk became a sneer. 'It's in the cellar, Mother. Where else would the steps lead? And, yes, I know how to use it.' He thrust the camera towards her, holding it only inches from her non-existent face. 'It's all there online. I've done my research. I've had to. I can hardly send the film to a lab.'

'*No, quite so, for once I can appreciate your point of view.*'

He clapped his hands in glee, hopping up and down on the spot. 'They'll be black and white photos, arty, creative, and large for maximum impact. A brilliant idea, don't you think?'

She looked back at him with a scowl. '*Are you up to it, Henry. Do you really know what you're doing? Or is it all talk?*'

His face fell as he stopped his impulsive jig. 'Yes, Mother, yes, it's simple enough. The photos' development will take me an hour at most, nothing more. And I plan to make good use of them as soon as they've had sufficient time to dry. They'll be the next nail in the bitch mother's psychological coffin. I cannot wait; it will tear what little's left of her peace of mind to shreds.' He laughed, close to hysteria. 'You said, be the best sadist I can be. Well, that's precisely what I'm doing. My plans are coming to fruition better than I could ever have hoped. Stand back and admire my accomplishments, Mother. Watch the bitch crash and burn.'

28

Heath was busy in his deceased father's darkroom, developing large, black and white photos of Lottie imprisoned behind the steel bars, when he heard a sharp, rapid knocking on his front door. Following a shower he was wearing nothing but a blood-red silk dressing gown, a garment bought by his father years before on one of his regular solo visits to the Far East in pursuit of his deviant interests. It was an item of clothing of which Heath was fond of, despite its associations with a man he despised.

Heath swore crudely as the caller knocked again. He shuffled from one barefoot to the other, hoping for silence, but there it was again, bang, the sound of intrusion as if to taunt him at a most inconvenient time.

'He's not going to go away, you know. You should have worked that out by now.'

'Do you have to interfere again, Mother? I know what I'm doing. Just leave me alone.'

'I told you to move her. I told you. I told you. But would you listen? No, you always think you know best. You saw the police car in the street. You saw the plain clothes pig getting out in his creased suit and shoes in need of polish. He's snooping, Henry. He's sticking his piggy snout in. Who else would it be knocking on your door at this time of day?'

Heath froze as the caller knocked again, harder this time, the sound louder, even in the cellar, which didn't have the benefit of the attic's soundproofing. 'Be quiet, Mother, as quiet as a mouse. He may go away if he thinks we're out.'

She shook her head somewhere in the darkness. 'Answer the door, Henry, there's a good boy. He'll only come back. They always come back. You'll have to see him sometime. Best get it over with, don't you think?'

'What if he knows something?'

'There's only one way to find out. Get up those stairs and answer the door.'

Lewis peered through the brass letterbox, assuming the house was empty as most others had been. He was preparing to walk away when he suddenly saw wet footprints on the hall tiles. He pushed the letterbox open, holding it wide and shouting 'Police', at the top of his abrupt voice. Within seconds he saw a man wearing a silk kimono walking down the hallway towards him. The man opened the front door reticently with the security chain still attached.

'Sorry to keep you waiting, officer. I was in the shower. Have you got some form of identification? I take my safety precautions seriously.'

Lewis took an immediate dislike to the man nervously peeping through the gap. The detective took his warrant card from the inside pocket of his summer jacket, handing it to the man, who looked at it closely, raising it close to his eyes for what seemed like an age before handing it back.

'Right, I think that's satisfactory, although the photo could do with an update. You had more hair in those days. And fewer lines on your face.'

Lewis quietly seethed. 'Just open the door, please,

sir. I'm hoping you may be able to help me with my enquiries.'

Heath fought to stop his hand shaking as he reached for the chain.

'You seem a little nervous if you don't mind me saying so, sir.' The man opened the door, but didn't invite the detective into the house, or stand aside to allow him to pass. 'I'm cold after my shower. I didn't have the time to dry myself properly. You called at a most inconvenient time.'

There was something about the man that made Lewis suspicious. He seemed on edge. He was worried about something, but what? Lewis had conducted his previous interviews on the doorstep, knocking at one house after another, hoping for and sometimes receiving a reply from those who weren't in work. But this time seemed different. There was a tension in the air. 'My name's Detective Sergeant Raymond Lewis, I'm part of a team investigating the disappearance of a little girl named Lottie Weller. She's a neighbour living across the street. Do you know her?'

The man nodded his acknowledgement. There seemed little purpose in lying. Placate the pig, that was best. Show no fear. He wanted him gone, and quickly too. 'Yes, I know her family well, lovely people. My name's Martin Heath; I'm a teaching assistant at Lottie's school. It's a terrible business. I think of little else. I'm having difficulty sleeping nights. It's awful to think that such things happen in a quiet town like ours.'

Lewis weighed up the response. He was a teaching assistant for sure, but the rest of it? The man was clearly on edge. Maybe it was nerves. Contact with the police sometimes did that, even to the innocent. 'Can I come in, please, Mr Heath? I can see you're shivering. It would be more comfortable than speaking on the doorstep.'

Heath mumbled under his breath as if talking to somebody else entirely, before eventually saying, 'Is that really necessary?'

Lewis studied him closely. 'I really would appreciate your help. As you said, you know Lottie. I'm sure you'd want to assist me if you can.'

Heath thought of refusing. But what would that achieve? Best let the pig in. Best get it over with. He turned and walked down the hall. 'If you'd follow me, Sergeant, we can speak in the lounge. If there's anything I can do to help, I'll be only too delighted. Lottie is an innocent in a dangerous world.'

Lewis thought Heath odd, or perhaps eccentric. And the house appeared dated as if owned by a much older person. Not suited to a relatively young man at all. The detective paused on reaching the foot of the staircase. 'Is it all right if I use your bathroom? Too many cups of tea. It's the copper's curse.'

Heath looked at Lewis with eyes that didn't seem to blink at all, like beads of glass planted in a doll's face. 'There's a toilet down here, the first door on the left. It's at your disposal. My mother's asleep upstairs. She's not a well woman. She wouldn't want to be disturbed.'

Lewis didn't need the toilet; he wanted to look around. But what choice did he have? He closed the door behind him, flushing after a few seconds, and then running the tap as if washing his hands. He wasn't surprised to find Heath still standing in the hallway, waiting for him when he exited the small, white-tiled room.

'If you follow me, Sergeant, we'll be comfortable in here.' Heath led Lewis into a dank sitting room full of brown furniture, fashionable in a long-gone era. The curtains were partially closed, casting the room in shadows. 'Take a seat; make yourself comfortable.'

The chair felt slightly damp when Lewis sat himself down.

As if the house had been left empty for a time. The whole place felt unkempt and unloved.

Taking the sofa directly opposite Lewis, Heath sat and crossed his legs, revealing a little more than the detective found comfortable. 'As I said, I work at Lottie's school. It's so very sad. She's such a wonderful little girl. It breaks my heart that she's still missing.'

'We're doing all we can to find her.'

'Just so, Sergeant, just so... now, what do you need to know? Mother will need her medication soon. I don't like to neglect her for very long.'

'Is the house yours, Mr Heath?'

'Yes, it belonged to my dear father. He was such a thoughtful man. He left it to me in his will.'

'To you rather than your mother?'

'*Shut him up, Henry. It's none of his business. He's a bully. Don't let him push you around. Listen to your mother. Stand up to him like a man.*'

'I thought you wanted to ask me about Lottie?'

He regretted the question almost as soon as it left his mouth.

The detective wasn't ready to let it go. 'It would be helpful if you could tell me a little about your background.'

'Why? I don't understand the relevance.'

Lewis held his gaze, knowing full well that he was pushing his luck. 'I like to know who I'm talking to.'

Tell the pig about your charity work, Henry. Knock him off track.

'I worked abroad for several years after completing a nursing degree at Swansea University. I returned to Wales when father died a short time ago. Mother needed me. I'm an only child. There was no-one else to help.'

'Who were you working for?'

You're saying too much, Henry. Keep it simple.

'Several international charities, the last of which was in Syria.'

'But you're not nursing any more?'

'I fancied a change.'

'When did you last see Lottie?'

Heath's left eye began to twitch. 'Well, I see her

on a daily basis in school, of course, but far less so during the holidays. I do occasionally see her out and about with her lovely mother. They are neighbours, after all. Megan's such a friendly woman, and she never fails to say hello.'

'When was the last time you saw Lottie? Try to be as specific as you can.'

'Be careful, Henry. He's suspicious, he's asking too much. Give nothing away.'

'Um, now let me think, it was a day or two before I saw the report relating to her abduction on the Welsh evening news. It was such a terrible shock. I couldn't believe what I was seeing. It left me heartbroken. I really thought you'd have found the poor girl long before now.'

'You saw the news of the press conference?'

'Yes, I did.'

'In that case, you'll be aware that Lottie disappeared from her home in the early hours of the nineteenth of this month.'

'As I said, I saw the report.'

'Did you see or hear anything that was in any way suspicious on either the night of the abduction or in the days leading up to it?'

'Not that I can think of, but I did see a middle-aged woman hanging about outside the Wellers' house yesterday, very shortly after Megan was taken away in the police car. I think you were one of the two officers accompanying her, weren't you? I'm not someone who's naturally curious. I like to keep myself to myself. But I happened to be returning home after a visit to town.'

All of a sudden Lewis was interested. 'You say "hanging about", can you be more specific?'

'She was standing outside on the pavement staring at the house, as if trying to see through the lounge window. I didn't think anything of it at the time, but now that you ask...'

'Had you ever seen the woman before?'

'Be careful, Henry, don't say too much. Mum's the word.'

'No, never, but strangely enough, she looked like a younger version of my mother.'

Lewis thought it an unlikely coincidence, but he decided to go with it. 'And you're sure of the timing? It was definitely yesterday?'

'Oh, yes, I'm certain of it, there's no doubt in my mind.'

Lewis took out his pocketbook. 'Can you describe her for me?'

'That's it, Henry, smoke and mirrors, misdirection. He's not the brightest spark. It shouldn't be difficult to confuse him.'

Heath was beginning to feel more confident now, keen to drive home what he saw as his advantage. Maybe the pig's visit wasn't such a bad thing after all. He went on to provide a full description, basing it on his mother's clothes and appearance. He was careful to describe a person of a very different height to himself.

'That's very helpful, Mr Heath, it's appreciated.'

Heath rose to his feet, his fragile ego temporarily boosted. He began walking back to the front door, increasing his pace more than once when his mother urged him on. 'I'm sorry I didn't contact you myself. I would have, had I thought it important.'

Lewis reached out and shook Heath's hand firmly. 'If you do think of anything else, don't hesitate to contact me.'

'That's it, Henry, get rid of him. Out he goes.'

'I will, Sergeant, I'm very glad you called. It's been good to meet you.'

Lewis didn't like Heath any more than when he'd first arrived as he stepped out of the house into the warmth of the day. He asked himself if the information he'd gleaned was useful. Maybe his visit was worthwhile, after all. Or were his gut instincts more accurate? There was something about Heath. Something that didn't fit. The big detective turned back and waved on reaching the pavement, still wracked with doubts, as Heath closed the door.

29

Kesey drained her coffee cup, resisting the desire to take another chocolate eclair from her almost empty packet. She picked up her office phone on the third demanding ring. 'CID, how can I help you?'

'Hello, ma'am, it's Sandra on the front desk.'

Kesey grinned, asking herself why the long-serving receptionist with her efficient and friendly persona, always felt the need to state the obvious. 'What can I do for you, Sandra?'

'I've got a Mr Michael Gavin here with me, who says he has some information relating to the Lottie Weller abduction.'

Kesey was on full alert in that instant. 'Get someone to bring him up. I'll see him in my office.'

Sandra responded in hushed tones the detective could barely hear, almost a whisper. 'The lift's playing up again. He's in a wheelchair.'

'Haven't they fixed the damn thing yet?'

'A technician is coming this afternoon, apparently. I'll believe it when I see it.'

Kesey sighed. 'Okay, put him in whatever interview room's the most convenient. Keep an eye on him and don't let him leave. This could be important. I'm on my way.'

'I'll put him in room two. There's more space.'

Kesey entered the sparsely furnished, brightly lit interview room to be met by a somewhat overweight, middle-aged man with shoulder-length brown hair swept back in a ponytail, who looked up and forced an unconvincing smile that seemed strangely out of place. One of his legs was amputated at the knee. Kesey noted the military tattoo on his lower arm, the parachute, the wings, the crowned lion, all of which told their own story. She wondered if his time in the elite Parachute Regiment explained the disability as she reached down, shook his hand and introduced herself. He looked tired, worn down by life.

'It's good to meet you, Mr Gavin, my father served with the Royal Airforce. I was a military child. I've got a great deal of respect for veterans. I know how much dedication service involves.'

Gavin nodded but didn't say anything in response, as he sat in silence, slowly massaging his stump with his left hand.

Kesey sat herself down with her interviewee on the other side of the table. 'Can I get you a tea or coffee before we make a start? It's no bother if you fancy one. The kitchen's only a couple of doors down.'

He shook his head stiffly, wincing slightly with each movement of his body. 'I'm good, thanks, I'd rather get this over with.'

The detective smiled warmly, opening her pocketbook at the appropriate page. 'Okay, straight to the point, I like that. Let's start with your full name, address and contact details.' Gavin provided the information as requested.

Kesey tapped the tip of her biro on the table. She felt sure this broken man wouldn't be there if his information weren't important. She was desperately hoping that he may provide the break she so badly needed. 'Right, Sandra on the front desk tells me you have some information relating to Lottie Weller, the missing child. I'd be pleased to hear anything you have to tell me.'

Gavin continued massaging what was left of his right leg, as if he hoped the physical stimulation might help it grow back, returning him to the adventures of his youth before time blunted his edges. 'As I said, I live in Picton Street; I bought the place after my discharge. I had a few quid compensation after a medical cock-up.'

Kesey nodded her understanding as she waited for him to continue.

'I don't know the Wellers personally, but I've seen them about. The little girl always smiles and says hello when she sees me in the street. And the mother's friendly enough for an office type, she's not like some of the stuck-up tossers I've got as neighbours. At least she speaks to me. That's more than some of them do.'

'Are you aware that Lottie hasn't been seen since the nineteenth of this month?'

He frowned hard and stopped massaging his knee for a moment before starting again. 'Yeah, a mate of mine told me all about it when he visited me in hospital. I'd have been in touch sooner, but I was out of it for most of my stay and couldn't have given you a helpful account. I was only discharged this morning. I think they must have needed the bed.'

'So, what have you got to tell me?'

'I was awake that night, the nineteenth. I'm in a lot of pain a lot of the time. I take a great many pain killers, morphine, oxycontin, and the like, enough to kill most people. Even diamorphine on occasions when things are particularly bad.' He pointed to the stump. 'Your body gets used to that shit, that's the problem. It's all the doctors can offer me, and it seems to do fuck all.'

'Did you see something that night? Something I need to be aware of?'

He nodded, focusing back on the case. 'Yeah, I did. After the police drove off, I couldn't sleep so I was just sitting in a chair looking out of the bedroom window at the front of the house, listening to Bowie on my CD player and smoking a few fags. It's something I do to pass the time. I see foxes sometimes poking about in the bins. The cheeky bastards think they own the place. It's amazing how nature can adapt.'

Kesey raised one eyebrow, willing him to get to the point. His mind seemed to wander. Maybe it was the opioids. 'You were going to tell me what you saw.'

He looked back at her with haunted eyes that had seen too much death and destruction in the name of queen and country. 'I saw a woman walking up the street. Someone I hadn't seen before. She walked up the Wellers' driveway, through the gate at the side of the house, and into the back garden. That was it, and I didn't see her again. And I didn't think much about it at the time. I'd just taken a swig of temazepam syrup to take the edge off. It doesn't help me sleep much any more. Too many memories, too many flashbacks, but it stops the pain for a time. That's the best I can hope for these days. We take so much for granted until it's taken away. I know I did.'

'Are you certain you saw this woman enter the Wellers' back garden that same night? I need you to think very carefully before answering. Your information could be crucial.'

He took a deep breath, filling his lungs, casting

his mind back to that night, picturing events behind his tired eyes, a part of him doubting his capacity for accurate recollection. 'Yeah, some idiot was shouting in the street, banging on the Wellers' door, and then the police turned up. I saw the woman about half an hour or so after that. I can't be certain of the time. Memories don't always come in straight lines any more. Pain medication can do that for you. It fucks up your thinking.'

Kesey tilted her head to the ceiling. 'But you are certain it was that night, yes?'

'Yeah, it was. It stuck in my mind. I wondered what she was doing out and about at that time. I can remember that much, her and the foxes.'

'You said you hadn't seen her before. Is there any way it could have been Megan Weller?'

His reply was immediate. 'No, no way. It wasn't her, no way at all.'

'But you are sure it was a woman you saw, yes?'

He hesitated before answering. 'Yeah, I think so.'

Kesey dropped her chin to her chest. 'You said, "I think so", not "I know so". That suggests you're less than certain.'

'Yeah, that's the thing, it's strange, fuck knows, to be honest.'

'Take your time, Mr Gavin. Can I get you that hot drink I offered? Maybe take a break before we continue?'

He shifted his position in the chair, trying to get comfortable. 'A glass of water would be appreciated.'

'I'll be back with you in two minutes.'

Gavin accepted the glass gratefully on Kesey's return, washing down two strong painkillers before placing the empty glass on the small table in front of him.

'You were telling me about the person you saw.'

'They looked like a woman, they were dressed like a woman, but there was something about them that made me think it may have been a man in drag.'

'Okay, tell me more.'

'Well, if it was a woman, she was unusually tall. And the shoes, they looked like a bloke's shoes. And she walked like a bloke too. She had no grace, no sway of the hips. It could have been a dyke, I suppose. Some of them look more like blokes than most blokes do.'

Kesey hid her annoyance surprisingly well. On

another day, in other circumstances, she'd have ripped into him, old soldier or not, but now was not the time. 'Okay, let me see if I've got this right. You're telling me that the person you saw was tall, they may have been wearing men's shoes, and in your opinion, they walked like a male. I need you to focus. Are you saying it was a man, or that it could have been a man?'

'It could have been, that's what I'm saying. It could have been, that's all. Or it may have been a woman too.'

The detective tried to stay patient. 'Can you put a percentage on it for me?'

'I'd say fifty-fifty, it was one or the other. The hair looked feminine, the make-up looked feminine, and the clothes, but the rest not so much. And whoever it was seemed to be talking to themselves. That's the best I can offer. I'd opened a bottle of whiskey by that point. Between that and the meds, I was pretty far gone.'

Kesey struggled to maintain her composure. She doubted the value of his evidence. She was asking herself if it was evidence at all. 'But you are certain you hadn't seen the person before? Is that correct?'

'Yeah, I'd put money on that one.'

'And you haven't seen them since?'

'No, I was taken away in an ambulance later that morning. I'm diabetic. My carer found me in a coma. Lucky really, if she hadn't turned up when she did I would have died. Although, that may not have been such a bad thing, now that I think about it. My best days are long gone.'

Kesey picked up her pen. 'I want you to give me as full a description of the person you saw as you possibly can. Do you think you can do that for me?'

His expression hardened. 'If you think I'm wasting your time, I'll piss off now. You only have to say the word.'

Kesey leant towards him, admonishing herself for her agitation. 'I'm sorry. It's been a tough week. Take your time. This matters. I've got as long as it takes.'

'White Caucasian, shoulder-length dark hair, brown or maybe black, it was hard to say in the moonlight. And I'd say somewhere between five foot ten inches and six feet tall, slim build. Is that any good to you?'

'That seems very specific if you don't mind me saying so.'

'I notice people. It goes with the territory. Watching strangers, weighing up risks. It's ingrained in me. I couldn't stop even if I wanted to. As I said, she stuck in my mind.'

'You said, she, not he, not they, she.'

He nodded twice. 'Yeah, I guess I did. First impressions count. Maybe it was a woman, after all.'

30

Lewis handed Kesey a half-pint glass of weak lager shandy and joined her at a table for two in a quiet corner of Caerystwyth Rugby Club's lounge bar. 'There you go, boss, that should take the edge off.'

Kesey accepted her drink with an outstretched hand, smiling as he took his seat opposite her. 'This is the same table me and Grav used to sit at. Right opposite the dartboard. Every time I come here, I feel surrounded by his memory. He took me under his wing when I first arrived in Wales. I'll always be grateful for that.'

Lewis emptied almost half his pint glass of best bitter down his throat in one greedy swallow. He wasn't in the mood for reminiscences. 'Yeah, I know what you are saying, good bloke and all that... now, tell me, what did you make of the soldier's statement? Is it something we should be taking seriously?'

Kesey slurped her shandy, spilling a few drops of the golden liquid onto her blouse before placing her glass down on a sodden beermat. 'He's not the world's most reliable witness. I can tell you that much. Everything about our perpetrator's MO screams bloke for me.'

'Yeah, I've been thinking along the same lines. But now we've got the anonymous caller, Heath and the soldier all talking about a woman. And the various descriptions are a pretty good match for each other. Maybe Heath or the soldier was the anonymous caller. That would make sense of it. My money would be on Heath. The soldier came in of his own volition, up front and honest. Ringing in incognito doesn't seem his style.'

Kesey shook her head. 'Maybe, it's a possibility, but it's a big leap. You called at Heath's house, and he gave you a statement. It seems he tried to help as best he could. There's nothing to suggest he'd spoken to us previously. You're making assumptions we're not entitled to make.'

Lewis felt sure it was an argument he couldn't win. 'If there is a woman involved, she's an accomplice. There is no way in the world it's a woman acting on her own. The facts don't fit. I'd bet my pension on it.'

The possibility of two offenders acting in unison wasn't something Kesey had considered up to that point. But there were cases, well-known cases, that told her it wasn't something she could rule out without very good reason. 'We've got three potential witnesses, one of whom's anonymous and of dubious value. Add to that the fact that the soldier was seriously pissed, up to his eyeballs on prescription drugs, and it was dark, doesn't fill me with confidence. He can't even say if he saw a man or a woman with any certainty. And that's if he saw anyone at all. That leaves Heath's evidence. He does at least know what he saw, but that's as good as it gets. All he's saying is that he saw a woman of similar description standing outside the Wellers' house on the pavement on the day of Megan's interview. She wasn't going into the house. She wasn't coming out of the house. I don't like coincidences any more than you do, but I don't think we should read too much into it. There are significant differences in the descriptions despite some similarities. It's dubious at best.'

Lewis drained his glass as he rose to his feet. 'Do you want another one of those?'

Kesey handed him a ten-pound note taken from her bag. 'Get me a coffee, white, one sugar. I could do with cheering up. Oh, and a bag of crisps, cheese and onion if they've got them, plain if they haven't.'

Lewis returned to the table with her order a couple of minutes later, still deep in thought. 'I hear what you're saying, boss. The soldier's a shit witness, okay, I get it. The legal system doesn't allow for weaknesses. But none of that means he didn't see exactly what he says he saw. His house is no more than a couple of hundred feet away from the crime scene. He'd have had a clear view of the street from his bedroom, however dark it was. The street lamps are on all night, I've checked with the council. The man says he saw someone and I believe him. It's just a matter of who.'

Kesey stirred her coffee, pushing her plain crisps aside unopened. 'I'm not convinced he didn't dream or hallucinate the entire thing. Most people would be unconscious after what he'd taken.'

'I've got to disagree with you, Laura. He didn't make it up, not a chance. I've got mates who are ex-services. They're serious people. I don't think there's even the slightest chance he'd have come anywhere near the station if he had any doubts his information was useful.'

'Yeah, fair point, it can't have been easy for the man. Not in the physical state he's in.'

Lewis nodded. 'Now that I think about it, there was a serial rapist a few years back who cycled to and from his assaults dressed in women's clothes and a wig. And the MO worked well for the cunt too. Catching him took a lot longer than it otherwise would have. Maybe that explains the soldier's confusion. Our abductor could be doing the same thing. It would be one way of confusing the evidence. You could well be right. Heath's statement could mean nothing at all.'

Kesey blew her coffee before sipping it, uncomfortable with his regular use of the c-word, interested in his proposition, but far from persuaded. 'How's the house-to-house going, Heath apart, any joy? Our offender went back to the Wellers' place in broad daylight. Surely someone else must have seen something. Unless he's the invisible man.'

'We've got nothing else, just like before. Most people were at work. And those that weren't didn't see a fucking thing. Or at least nothing that they're telling me about.'

She sat back and studied him. 'What is it, Ray? I know you too well by now. There's something you're not telling me. I can see it in your face.'

He wiped the beer from his mouth with a shirt-sleeve. 'Oh, it's probably something and nothing.'

'Come on, spit it out, tell your Aunty Laura all about it. I don't bite.'

Lewis grinned, glad she'd lightened the mood. 'It's Martin Heath. He lives in number sixty-six on the opposite side of Picton Street to the Wellers' place. About fifty yards down the street in the opposite direction from the park.'

'Okay, I'm listening.'

'I know you said he was trying to help, but I've still got my doubts. There was something about the bloke that set my teeth on edge. I can't tell you what it was exactly, but I didn't like him. It was a gut feeling more than anything else. I left his house, thinking we needed to know a lot more about him.'

Kesey leant in towards her sergeant. 'Okay, so what have you found out?'

'Nothing that helps.'

'Come on. I need more than that. Start talking.'

Lewis cradled his pint glass in both hands. 'He's a qualified nurse. He was working overseas for some charity in Syria before coming back to this area for his father's funeral a few months back when he inherited the house. I knew of the father. He was suspected of being part of a paedophile ring offending against multiple kids years back.'

'Was he done for it?'

'No, sadly not, he was only named by the one young child, with no corroboration. Nothing came of it. I don't think he was even arrested in the end. They concentrated their efforts on other key suspects.'

Kesey looked back with a thoughtful expression. 'Okay, that may or may not be relevant. You said Heath was a nurse in Syria. What's he doing now?'

'He's a teaching assistant at a primary school. St Mary's, the same one attended by Lottie Weller.'

Kesey's eyes narrowed. 'Okay, I know where

you're coming from on this, but it's not much of a co-incidence if you think about it. It's a small town. There are only so many schools in the area.'

'I'm not so sure, boss. It's too much of a coinci-dence for me.'

'Oh, come on, if Heath's working as a teaching assistant, he must have been DBS checked. It's an es-sential part of the application process. If he had any sort of relevant record, he wouldn't have been al-lowed near the job, let alone appointed. That's the way the system works.'

Lewis lowered his eyes. 'Yeah, he was checked, and, no, he hasn't got a record. It's the first thing I looked at.'

Kesey sighed. 'So, basically, you're telling me that Heath's a model citizen who was only too ready to help us.'

Lewis frowned dejectedly. 'On the face of it, yeah, I'll give you that much. But I would love to have a good look around his place. If I thought I could get a warrant, I'd be there now. The bloke's got nonce written all over him.'

Kesey shook her head. 'We'd need one hell of a lot more than a gut feeling before getting a warrant.'

He nodded. 'Yeah, I know. More's the pity.'

'On a positive note, we've had a few more alleged sightings of Lottie in various parts of the country. Nothing solid, nothing that gives me any real hope of finding her, but at least the press coverage has got people talking. She's in the news, that's what matters. Maybe it would be worth me doing another radio interview to keep her at the forefront of people's minds. The soldier wouldn't have come in without the publicity. There may be another witness out there who hasn't contacted us yet. Someone knows something. They always do.'

'It's all over social media. Photos of Lottie, people discussing who could have taken her, one nutter was even suggesting it's a case of alien abduction. What the fuck's that about?'

'Are you saying I should leave the radio for a bit?'

'I'll leave that stuff to you and the top brass, boss. It's well above my pay grade.'

She pointed towards his empty pint. 'Do you want another one before we head off?'

He pushed his glass across the table. 'Is the Pope Catholic?'

'I'll have a quiet word with the head teacher. Let's

see what she makes of this Heath character. It can't do any harm to ask.'

Lewis nodded. 'Cheers, Laura, that makes me feel a little better. As I said, there's something about the bloke that rings alarm bells. If he gives me even the slightest excuse, I'll be all over him like a rash. My nonce radar's doing somersaults.'

'Don't get fixated on the man, Ray. You've been wrong before. None of us are infallible, not even you.'

His expression darkened. 'Okay, so I've fucked up once or twice. I'll give you that much. But I'm right this time. And I'll prove it too. You wait and see.'

31

Megan screamed when she first opened the large brown envelope. She emitted a long piercing cry and then collapsed to the hall tiles as her legs gave way. She sat, panting hard, allowing the wall to support her weight, with the photographs held tightly in a trembling hand. She looked at them in turn, choking on her tears, filled with dejected horror, but unable to look away.

There were five photos. Five large, black and white images of Lottie prone on a wooden floor stained with intermingling bodily fluids. The bars, those dark metal bars, a clear plastic tube inserted into Lottie's mouth, and held in place by metallic plastic tape wrapped around her poor head and face. Each photo was no less awful than the other. They were taken from different angles, as if the photographer had repositioned himself for each terrible shot.

Megan wept as she forced herself to study them, searching for even the slightest clue as to the location, looking for something familiar. But there was nothing that stood out. Nothing that gave her even the slightest hope.

Megan threw up as she dragged herself to her feet. She bent over, spitting acidic vomit, before standing. She hurried to the kitchen on unsteady legs, to where her mobile was charging on a shelf. She placed the photographs face down on the oak table, washed her mouth out at the sink, and then dialled Raymond Lewis's number, which was stored in her phone from the last time she'd called him.

Megan tapped a foot against the floor as she waited, seconds seeming like minutes. *Come on, Ray. Answer the damned thing, come on, come on. You said ring any time, any time at all. Come on, detective, where the hell are you?*

'DS Lewis, how can I help you?'

Megan swallowed hard before speaking. 'Hello,

Ray, it's Megan, Megan Weller. He's sent... he's sent me photographs in the post. Photos of Lottie imprisoned in some terrible place. I've never seen such awful images. They're like something out of a fright film, but real. That's the thing I can't get my head around. My little girl is trapped in a cage. The photos are actually real.' She sat down on the nearest chair for fear of fainting. 'What should I do, Ray? Tell me what to do.'

'Where are you now?'

Megan resisted the urge to vomit again as her gut spasmed. 'I'm... I'm at the house, in the kitchen. Is, is that okay? I don't know what... I don't know what to do for the best. Should I be somewhere else?'

'Take a breath, love. Where are the photographs now? Let's take this one step at a time.'

'They're on the table next to me.'

'And the envelope they came in?'

'What?'

'The envelope. Where's the envelope?'

'It's on the hall tiles. I was s-sick. I need... I need to clean up.'

'Okay, now listen to me. I don't want you to touch the photographs again, or the envelope. I want you to leave them exactly where they are until I get there. We can worry about cleaning up the hall after that.'

Megan glanced down at the photos and then quickly looked away. 'Are you coming now?'

'Just stay where you are. I'm on my way.'

'Please hurry.'

'I will, love, promise. I'm heading towards my car as we speak. And I'll come in through the back. Don't worry when you hear the gate opening. Keep the door locked until I knock. You'll see my face through the glass.'

Lewis was wearing thin blue nitrile gloves when he picked up the photographs from the kitchen table about twenty minutes later.

Megan watched him closely, unsure of what to do or say as he studied each image in turn, the haunted expression in his eyes telling its own story. Lewis placed the photos into an evidence bag, searching his mind for something positive to say. Anything that may relieve Megan's trepidation even slightly. He steadied himself, looking her in the face as she continued to fall apart in front of him. 'I'm sorry you had to see those. It can't have been easy. But at least they suggest whoever's got Lottie is keeping her alive.

That gives us hope. And the photos may give us some ideas as to the type of property she's being held in. We can have them looked at by a property expert, someone who can comment on the features in the room, the floorboards, the wall in the background. As terrible as the photos are, they may help us find her.'

'And we know they were posted in Swansea.'

'Yeah, that's right, we do. The postmark couldn't be clearer.'

Megan clutched her arms to her chest. 'Who'd do such a wicked thing? To keep my little girl in a cage with conditions worse than an animal?'

Lewis struggled for an answer. 'Whoever it is, we're going to catch the bastard.'

'Lottie's looking thin; she's lost weight, and... and did you see the tube?'

'Yes, love, I saw it. I've seen something like that once before. I'm guessing it's a feeding tube. He's using it to keep her alive.'

'It's stuffed in Lottie's mouth, taped to her head. The monster cut her lovely hair off and now this. I wouldn't treat my worst enemy like that. Let alone a child. I can't get the pictures out of my head. You've got to find her, Ray, you've got to find her.'

Lewis was lost for words. What could he say in the light of such evil? 'Can I get you a cup of tea, love? You look as if you need one.' He silently admonished himself. *Oh, for fuck's sake, was that really the best I could do?* Any words, however well-intentioned, seemed entirely inadequate.

Megan shook her head. 'I couldn't keep it down.'

He nodded his understanding. 'I'll get the envelope assessed by a handwriting expert. It's an additional piece of the investigative jigsaw. Every new piece of information takes us nearer success.'

'Do you really think so?'

He didn't, but he was never going to admit that, not to her, not now. 'Yeah, that's how these things work.'

'I was sick in the hall. When I saw the photos, I... err... I...' She stopped speaking mid-sentence, looking into the distance but seeing nothing at all.

'I know, love, you told me. Don't worry about it. It's not a big deal. There are more important things to think about.'

'Do you think he lives in Swansea?'

Lewis shrugged his big shoulders. 'Maybe yes or maybe no. Does anyone come to mind, a client maybe?'

Megan shook her head. 'No, no-one I can think of.'

'Right, I'm going to need a plastic bag, a bucket and a cloth.'

'There's no need for you to do it. I can clean up later.'

He forced a brittle smile. 'You stay where you are. You've had enough to deal with. Now, where will I find them?'

She pointed to her right. 'They're all in the cupboard under the sink.'

'Is there anyone I can call for you before I make a start? Your mother maybe, or Dale, I'm sure both would be pleased to help. I'd be a lot happier if you agreed to stay somewhere else. But if you are determined to stay put, I'd rather you not be on your own.'

'I'll give my mum a ring in a minute or two when I get my head together.'

Lewis bent down, opening the cupboard door and peering in. 'I'm going to have to tell Dale about the photos. And he'll have to see them. He's Lottie's father. He has the right to know.'

'Yes, I understand. But I don't want him coming here. I don't want him in the house. Not to stay, anyway. It may give him the wrong idea.'

Lewis began filling the bucket with warm water. 'It wouldn't be a bad idea to have a bloke around the house for a while. You know, until we catch the bastard. I can't see him coming back again, but it could happen, nothing's impossible.'

'I said no, and I meant no.'

'Okay, love, have it your way. I was just saying. I couldn't force you even if I wanted to.'

Megan picked up her phone. 'I appreciate your understanding.'

He winked once, regretting it immediately. 'Right, you ring your mum, and I'll do my household duties. I'll stay with you until she arrives. How does that sound?'

'Thank you, Ray, I'm glad of your support. You've been brilliant in truly horrendous circumstances. I don't know what I'd do without you. Now, all you've got to do is find my daughter.'

32

Heath felt his cock swell in his pants as he pictured Megan's traumatised face, making the image big and bright. 'Can you imagine the horror she felt, Mother? Can you imagine the sinking feeling deep in the pit of her stomach?'

'*What on earth are you talking about now, Henry?*'

His cock returned to its flaccid state in the blink of an eye. 'The photos, the photos! What the hell else did you think I was talking about?'

She shook her head. '*You and that camera, click, click. You're as bad as your father.*'

Heath slowly approached the cage, kneading his genitals through his trouser pocket. 'The waiting is getting harder. I have to acknowledge that. The anticipation of death isn't going to sustain me for very much longer. I need to get my hands on the little brat. I need to feel the warmth of her skin before her life-force drains away.'

His mother swept past him in one direction, and then the other, coming in and out of focus before taking on an apparently solid form. *'Why wait? I've told you to kill her.'*

He flung his arms wide. 'You told me to move the brat. That's what you told me, to move her.'

'Well, why don't you do that then?'

He dropped his head. 'Do you always have to suck the joy out of everything?'

'Kill her or move her, make your mind up. But either way, stop bothering me about it. You're a grown-up now, an adult with adult responsibilities. Someone of your age shouldn't be suckling at his mother's teat.'

Heath looked into the mirror and saw his mother's face glaring back at him. 'Sending the photos should have been a triumph, one of the greatest achievements of my life. And yet you can't even congratulate me on my accomplishments. Are a few kind words too much to ask for?'

He heard her sniggering before she spoke again, her tone rising in pitch. *'You've got rather an inflated opinion of yourself, don't you think?'*

Heath punched the mirror hard, smashing the glass with his second blow, cutting a knuckle down to the bone. 'Now look what you've made me do, you vicious witch.'

And then a line she'd used before. *'Such a silly fuss about nothing.'*

Heath began waving his wounded hand in the air, showering small droplets of blood, as he had only days before, over the floor, the walls, and even the ceiling, like a Jackson Pollock painting exclusively in red. A few drops fell on Lottie's virtually bald head.

'What on earth are you doing now, you ungrateful boy? Do you have to make such an awful mess? You haven't even cleaned up after the last time.'

'I'll get around to it.'

'And look at the terrible state of the cage. What were you thinking? You should have bought sufficiently large nappies. The brat's unconscious, it's not rocket science.'

Heath snarled at first, growling, spraying spittle, but then he smiled as his thought process took him off in another direction. 'I've been thinking of ways to kill the brat when the time comes. Fantasy is enjoyable enough, but it can't sustain me indefinitely.'

'That's all very well, Henry. But why delay? It would be a lot safer to get on with it.'

'It will be soon, very soon, but not quite yet. The bitch mother hasn't suffered nearly enough. There's more to come. I've explained all this. I want to get to know her better. I want to witness her ultimate decline up close and personal. I'll hold on for as long as I can. And then they'll both die a horrible death.'

33

'Take a seat, Laura. I've got precisely twenty minutes. I want you to summarise your progress as succinctly as possible.'

Kesey looked up at Halliday, perched on his higher seat behind his excessively large desk. 'What do you want to know?'

'It's now been over a week since Lottie Weller was last seen. I'm asking myself if you're up to finding her. I hope appointing you as the senior investigating officer wasn't an error of judgement on my part.'

Kesey gritted her teeth. 'I'm doing everything I can. And my team are too. If you want to reallocate the case, that's up to you, but nobody could do more.'

He checked his watch. 'If you say so, Laura, if you say so.'

Kesey leant forwards in her seat, holding his gaze as her anger boiled to the surface. 'What is your problem?'

'I beg your pardon?'

She raised herself upright in her seat. 'You know exactly what's happening with the case. I've briefed you on a regular basis. And you've read the paperwork. You know what's going on as well as I do.'

Halliday's expression darkened. 'I'd remember who you're talking to, if I were you, Inspector.'

Kesey bit the inside of her lower lip hard. 'Okay, have it your way. We've been through the list of nonces. Eight have been interviewed to date, and there's another five worth looking at. They'll all be brought in and interviewed over the next few days in priority order. We've had the photos looked at. They're genuine; it's definitely Lottie in the pictures. And it's highly likely the abductor developed them himself. Each image has the perpetrator's fingerprints all over it. Those fingerprints are a match for those found in the Wellers' home. The offender made no effort to hide them because he knows they're not on record. He's gaining confidence. He thinks he's cleverer than we are. And when that happens, offenders sometimes get careless. The way things are going, that may well be our best chance of catching him.'

The chief superintendent smiled thinly. 'It's good to see some passion on your part, Laura. I very much approve. Let's hope that enthusiasm engenders positive results sooner rather than later.'

'I've had an architect assess the photos from a building perspective.'

His eyes widened. 'And?'

'She couldn't help us as much as I'd hoped she would.' Halliday sighed, exhaling with a groan.

'Why the hell not?'

'She thought the pictures were likely taken in an attic room, and that the room has been adapted at some time in the last thirty years or so. We can say that there's been a conversion, but it's not possible to identify the age or type of property. In short, we know it's not a new build, but that's about it.'

'That is extremely disappointing. Is it worth asking someone else to look at them for us?

Someone with a greater degree of experience or se-
niority, perhaps?'

'Have you actually seen the photos?'

Halliday checked his watch for a second time,
pushing up his sleeve. 'No, I can't claim that I have.
That's your job; I have other responsibilities. I can't
concern myself with the minutiae.'

'Well, if you had seen them, you'd know they're
all focused on Lottie and the cage she's imprisoned
in, taken from different angles. We only get glimpses
of the room, nothing more.'

'Well, in that case, what about the cage? Can't we
find out where it was sourced? It seems an obvious
enquiry. There can't be many places selling that type
of thing.'

Kesey shifted uneasily in her seat. 'Do you really
think I haven't thought of that?'

'Just focus on the facts, Laura. I asked you for an
update, not a discussion.'

Kesey shook her head slowly, first one way and
then the other. 'It could be an animal cage, for large
dogs, for example. Or there's a number of companies
based mainly in Germany and The Netherlands that
produce metal cages for bondage enthusiasts. I'm of

the view that our cage is more likely to be in that second category. We've undertaken extensive enquiries, and those enquiries are ongoing. Some firms are reluctant to share information; others claim not to keep records. As of now, we have been unable to identify any orders delivered to this area. If we do succeed in finding any purchases that match that in the photographs taken by the abductor, you'll be the first to know.'

'Anything else?'

'We've installed motion-sensitive cameras at the Wellers' property. I still think we should have an officer at the house full time. But the cameras are a second-best given your refusal.'

'The abductor has accessed the house twice already. I can't imagine he'd be stupid enough to visit again.'

'But he could do. Isn't that the point?'

'Budgets are tight, as I've already told you. Difficult decisions are a burden of senior rank. We can't do everything. You may learn that one day if you ever get that far.'

'Austerity? You sound like a politician You'll be blaming Brexit next.'

'Leave it there, Laura. You've said too much already.'

Kesey thought better of further escalating an argument she couldn't hope to win. 'Well, if he does return for the third time, he'll be photographed. We'll know who he is.'

Halliday made that same strange humming sound with which Kesey was becoming increasingly familiar. 'That all sounds somewhat desperate. I was hoping for more. We can't rely on luck.'

Kesey raised her voice, back in the fight. 'I can only repeat myself. We're doing all we can.'

'The case is receiving a good deal of interest thanks to your efforts with the media. That has its advantages, but also its disadvantages. The chief constable has had the local MP on the phone demanding results. Even the Home Secretary is taking an interest. I've backed you. I've said you're the right person for the job. But there's only so long the boss will tolerate continued failure. It doesn't reflect well on the force.'

Kesey's exasperation was as plain as the nose on her face. 'I want to catch the bastard as much as anyone.'

Halliday looked down at her with a dismissive scowl. 'It's results that matter in today's world, not good intentions. Mediocrity is simply not good enough. I want Lottie Weller rescued alive, and I want her abductor arrested, charged, convicted and imprisoned for a very long time. I want him locked up and rotting. Nothing less is acceptable. This case will define your future, Laura. It's make or break. Failure is not an option. Make it a success, for you, for me, for the force, but most of all, for that little girl. Her life is in your hands.'

34

'Is he drunk?'

Megan peered around a lounge curtain, partially hidden.

'Um, no, I don't think he is.'

Her mother's eyes widened. 'Well, that's a first.'

'The abduction's hit Dale as hard as it's hit me. We should probably let him in.'

'Are you sure?'

'He helped me after the birth. Maybe we should be there for each other now. What harm could it do?'

'You put the kettle on, and I'll see what he wants.'

Doreen Jones opened the front door to find her ex-son-in-law dabbing at his eyes with a black cotton sleeve. He hurriedly lowered his arm before speaking, not wanting to lose face any more than he already had. 'Oh, hello, Doreen, I'm glad Meg's not on her own.'

'What can we do for you, Dale?'

'I'm hoping you've heard something. The police are telling me fuck all. I don't know how much more of this I can take.'

She stood to one side to allow him to pass. 'Come on in, come and sit in the lounge, Meg's making coffee.'

'Is she all right about me being here?'

She nodded. 'Yes, I think so. As long as you're sober.'

Dale slumped onto the sofa, asking his questions more in hope than expectation. 'Is there any news? Anything at all?'

Doreen shook her head, lost for words, as Megan re-entered the room, carrying a tray of hot drinks in unmatched mugs. She placed the tray on a low table before approaching Dale, who stood to greet her. They hugged each other, awkwardly at first, but then more warmly when their shared adversity overcame their initial reticence. Megan withdrew from their embrace first, pointing to the wall above the fireplace. 'The police arranged for a workman to paint over the bastard's message once they'd taken care of all their evidential needs. They took measurements, samples and plenty of photos. That's what DS Lewis told me. I couldn't stand looking at the damned thing for a second longer than I had to.'

Dale cracked his knuckles. 'Whoever wrote that shit must be a right nutter. I would really like to get my hands on the bastard.'

Megan sat in the nearest chair, actively avoiding the settee. 'The fact that someone who's capable of writing such a thing has our Lottie is too awful to think about. We're agreed on that. But, what are we going to do about it? I feel so useless, sitting here, waiting for hour after hour. We've got to do some-thing, but what?'

Doreen picked up her mug from the tray. 'I'm going to head upstairs and give you two some time to speak alone. Is that okay with you, Meg? I can stay if you want me to.'

'It's fine, Mum, you're looking tired. And it will be good for me and Dale to talk.'

Doreen climbed the stairs to the guest bedroom and closed the door against the world.

Dale raised a hand to his face. 'The police showed me the fucking photos. Oh my God! What sort of sicko does something like that?'

Megan's shoulders slumped as her tears began to flow. 'I can't get those pictures out of my head. They keep appearing behind my eyes. I think they're imprinted on my brain for however long I live.'

'What are you doing here, Meg? Why not stay at my place? Or a hotel. Why not book into a hotel? It's not as if you're short of a few quid. What if the bastard comes back?'

Megan moved forwards in her seat, reaching out and gripping Dale's hand. 'This is my home, and it's Lottie's home too. This may sound crazy, but I feel close to her here. I'm not giving up on that, not for anyone, and especially not for the shit stain that took her. He's not taking that away from me. It may be the only thing I've got left.'

'We've got to hold on to hope.'

'I'm trying, believe me, I'm trying.'

'Will you least let me move back in until this is over.'

Megan shook her head. 'I don't think that's a good idea.'

'But what use is your mum going to be if the bastard comes back for a third visit? I want to protect you. I can't do that if I'm not here.'

'I've got knives hidden all around the house. If he does come back, I'll be ready for him. He'll be begging to tell me where Lottie is before I finish with him.'

'That's not the best idea you've ever had.'

She snapped back at him. 'What the hell else am I supposed to do?'

'Okay, I hear you. I'm just worried about you, that's all.'

Megan stood, crossing the room to where a three-quarter full bottle of brandy was sitting on the light-oak sideboard. She returned to her seat, pouring a generous tot into her coffee. 'Are you going to have one?'

He shook his head, desperately resisting the golden spirit's allure. 'No, I haven't touched the stuff since, well, you know, since the morning of the press conference. I can't have the one, that's my problem.

Start, and I'll finish the bottle. Although oblivion doesn't seem like such a bad idea.'

Megan picked up the bottle, carrying it to the kitchen, where she poured the entire contents down the sink, before returning. 'Do you want a sandwich or something.'

'I can't face eating.'

'You've lost weight. You're looking thin.'

Dale forced a brittle smile. 'When we get our lovely girl back we're going to give her the best time of her life, a party with all her friends, no expense spared. You wait and see. It's going to be brilliant.'

Megan's face was ashen. 'Don't you mean "if" we get her back? The police don't s-seem to be getting anywhere.'

'There may be things they're not telling us.'

She nodded twice. 'I could ask DS Lewis off the record. He s-seems like a decent enough man. It's got to be worth a try.'

'What about Kesey?'

'The woman arrested me. And all because of some ridiculous anonymous phone call. I don't feel I can trust her any more. She let me down.'

He sipped his coffee. 'She's doing her job, that's

all. You know how the system works.'

Megan made a face. 'Maybe you're right.'

'I've made some more posters.'

'We could put them up tomorrow.'

He rose to his feet. 'Okay, I'll be back first thing. At least we'll be doing something. Sitting and waiting achieves fuck all.'

Megan looked out of the window as the rain began to fall. 'You can sleep on the sofa if you like, just for tonight. I'm on compassionate leave. We could head into town straight after breakfast.'

'Um, yeah, if you're sure?'

'I'm not sure about very much at all any more. But I need to sleep. If I know you're here, I'll feel safe to take a tablet. But it's only for tonight. I wouldn't want you getting the wrong idea.'

'Okay, thanks, Meg, it's appreciated.'

'You do realise this isn't us getting back together, don't you? It's a matter of convenience, nothing more.'

He broke eye contact, shoulders slumped. 'Yeah, you've made that perfectly clear. Let's just focus on getting Lottie back. Until that's achieved, nothing else matters.'

She went to close the curtains, looking out as Heath walked past carrying a black umbrella. He was glancing at the house. She waved as he hurried along the wet pavement.

'Who was that?'

'Oh, it's just Martin, he walks past most evenings. He's a teaching assistant at Lottie's school.'

'Ah, yeah, I met him at the sports day. He seemed like an all right sort of bloke from the little I saw of him.'

Megan nodded. 'Yes, he is, I've spoken to him a few times now. I like him, and Lottie does too. He's always friendly, always interested, and never dismissive. I had to rush away the last time I saw him at school. He seemed disappointed for some reason I still can't quite understand. I guess he must be the sensitive sort.'

Dale rolled his eyes. 'Maybe he's gay. Some blokes are too soft for their own good.'

Megan pecked Dale on the cheek, barely touching his skin. She was thinking that a bit of sensitivity on his part wouldn't go amiss. A bit of yin to go with his yang. 'Goodnight, Dale, please say a prayer for Lottie. I'll see you in the morning.'

35

'Did you speak to that headmistress you mentioned?'

Kesey pushed her paperwork aside and looked up at Lewis, who'd just entered her office for the first time that day. 'And a good morning to you, Ray, it's nice to chat.'

He shook his head and frowned. 'Yeah, yeah, lovely to see you too. So, did you talk to her, or not?'

'Sheena? Yeah, I did, as it happens, at home. The school's still shut for the holidays.'

His eyes widened. 'So, come on, what did she say?'

'Nothing you were hoping to hear.'

Lewis switched on the kettle, located on the floor to the side of Kesey's desk. 'This is a bit like getting blood from a fucking stone. Are you going to tell me what she said, or what?'

The DI handed him two mugs, one a gift from Janet, emblazoned with a large, capital L, red on blue. 'She had nothing but positives to say about Heath. He's good with the kids, he's a hard worker, he's reliable, and there is nothing about his conduct or personality that causes her even the slightest concern. I asked her more than once, and she said the exact same thing. He's covering maternity leave, but she's hoping he'll agree to stay on when a suitable vacancy arises.'

The sergeant's brow furrowed. 'Okay, that's all very well on the face of it. But why isn't he still nursing? Why's he at the school at all? It doesn't make a lot of sense to me.'

'Heath wants a career change. What's wrong with that? He's planning to go back to university at some point to qualify as a special needs teacher. The head said he's one of the most intelligent staff members she's ever had the pleasure to employ. And that's a direct quote. She rates him highly.'

'Maybe he's a good actor. He wouldn't be the first psycho to hide in plain sight. There's any number of killers who've conned all those around them with consummate ease. Only their victims see the monster behind the mask.'

'Not this time, Ray. You're getting fixated again. There is nothing to suggest Heath's a suspect. You asked me to talk to the head, and I've done it. She likes the man. She's even agreed to be introduced to his mother at some future date.'

Lewis handed Kesey her coffee, the mug filled almost to the brim. 'I hear what you're saying, but I'm not so sure.'

She groaned theatrically. 'Think about it. It was always a long shot. Heath's a professionally qualified nurse who put himself in danger by helping the vulnerable in some of the world's most dangerous places. And now he's back in Wales, a popular, well respected teaching assistant at a church school, who spends his free time looking after his elderly mother. And he's got no record, nothing. You've said that yourself. He's not a known abuser and he's not a suspected abuser. There's a long list of nonces we need to consider but he's not one of them. We've got nothing to suggest he's anything other than a nice guy. You're barking up the wrong tree on this one. He's not our man. We're looking for somebody else.'

Lewis scrunched up his face, still not ready to let it go. 'There was no sign of an old woman from what I could see.'

'Does it matter? It's not like you searched the place. She could have been in another room or upstairs.'

'Yeah, that's what he said.'

'There you go then. Is it of any relevance at all?'

He sipped his coffee. 'No, probably not.'

Kesey opened a desk drawer, taking out a packet of individually wrapped chocolate biscuits. She took one herself before handing Lewis another. 'There is one other thing I need to discuss with you.'

He sat himself down, mug in one hand, biscuit in the other. 'Okay, I'm listening.'

'I've had a DI Lee on the phone from the South Wales force.'

'Arthur Lee?'

'Yeah, that's right, do you know him?'

Lewis nodded. 'He grew up in this area. We

played for the same rugby team back in the day as young men. He's a good bloke and a good copper.'

'He's got a suspect for us.'

Lewis moved to the edge of his seat. 'Does it sound hopeful?'

'Um, yeah, it may do, or maybe not. They've arrested a delivery driver who attempted to abduct a seven-year-old boy from a public park in Cwmbran a couple of days back. His name's Jerry Bridges, a thirty-three-year-old married man with a long history of child porn offences, but this one's a first. It seems his offending has escalated. Fantasy isn't enough for him any more.'

'There's any number of nasty little nonces out there. His MO isn't a good fit for our case. Is there more to it?'

'He's remanded in Cardiff nick following a confession. He talked to his cellmate about Lottie's abduction. He seemed excited by the idea, apparently. He said abducting and imprisoning a child was his greatest fantasy – something he'd like to make reality someday. The cellmate informed a guard, and it went from there. Arthur thought Bridges might be talking about something he's already done. If he has, it likely means Lottie's either already dead or alone. If he's our man, we need to get him talking. If Lottie is alive, she's not going to last for very long without food and water.'

Lewis took a second biscuit from the packet. 'Is this Bridges character familiar with our patch?'

'He was travelling through our area to and from Pembroke Dock at the relevant time. I had a quick word with his employer. He's made the same journey numerous times in the past three years. He could have made a quick detour into Picton Street without any problem at all.'

He studied her. 'Having said all that, you still don't look convinced.'

Kesey shook her head, a forlorn expression on her face. 'The fingerprints don't match.'

'What about DNA?'

'We're waiting on results. But I'm guessing it's not going to be a match either.'

Lewis's shoulders slumped. 'Is it even worth me talking to the scrote?'

Kesey tried to look more positive than she felt. 'He could be working with an accomplice. You know, two paedophiles offending together. It's not unheard of. We can't rule it out without checking.'

Lewis rose to his feet. 'Okay, give Cardiff nick a ring and tell them to expect me. And I may well pay Heath another visit on my way back.'

'Oh, come off it, Ray. On what grounds?'

He drained his coffee cup. 'I'll think of something.'

'You need to let it go.'

'Is that an order?'

Kesey nodded once. 'Come up with some evidence and we'll look at him. Until then it's not happening.'

'What about the feeding tube?'

'What about it?'

'Heath's a qualified nurse. He'd know how to use one.'

'So would all the other doctors and nurses in the area, and the vets too. And quite a few other people who could work it out for themselves. Are you going to visit them all?'

'Thanks for the sarcasm, much appreciated.'

Kesey folded her arms in front of her. 'What is it

with you and Heath? I can't understand your obsession with the man. He's just a man who happens to live in the same street. There's no evidence against him, nothing to suggest he's involved in any way at all. Do some further background checks if you have to. Ask around. See if there's anything at all to support your suspicions. But do it subtly. You can't afford another complaint, not after the last one. The force has changed. It's not like the old days when you could get away with just about anything. You've got to take the final written warning seriously. If you're not careful, you'll be out of a job.'

'So, you'll take a look at him if I come up with something, yeah?'

'If there's good reason, yes, of course we'll look at him. But it has to be factual. I'm talking about actual evidence, not blind suspicion that could be interpreted as harassment.'

Lewis smiled despite the conversation's emotive nature. 'So, am I right in thinking you don't want me to arrest Martin Heath today?'

'Yeah, hilarious as always, now, piss off to Cardiff and stay clear of Heath unless new evidence emerges. Something solid that actually suggests he should be treated as a genuine suspect. And you taking a dislike to him doesn't qualify. Are we clear?'

He bowed and curtseyed in mock salute. 'Anything you say, ma'am. Your wish is my command.'

As Lewis left her office, Kesey doubted he'd listened to a word she'd said.

36

'*Where are you going all dressed up in your father's clothes?*'

Heath stared at his mother's image in the kitchen window and sighed. 'I'm going out. I would have thought that was obvious.'

'*But where to, Henry, where to? I'm not a mind reader.*'

Heath pictured his dead mother following him as he entered the garden at the back of the house. He picked various multi-coloured summer flowers, taking care to make the resulting bouquet as attractive as possible. 'I'm planning to call on the brat's mourning mother. I saw her peeping out at me the other night when I went for my walk. Maybe I can find out what the bitch was snooping at.'

'Your father planted those flowers.'

Heath glared at her non-existent face. 'I'm very well aware of that, thank you, Mother. He wanted his ashes sprinkled amongst them. Or at least, so father's solicitor told me when he read the will. I threw them in the rubbish. It seemed more appropriate.'

'You're such a silly boy.'

'I'm going out now, and I don't want you coming with me. I need you to keep an eye on the brat. Will you do that much for me?'

'Will you sing to me when you get back? One of the arias I'm so very fond of, from Madam Butterfly, possibly, or Carmen. Something rousing, something that stirs the blood.'

'Very well, as long as you do what I ask.'

Heath checked his appearance in the ground floor shower room before exiting the house. Within a few minutes he was knocking on Megan's front door, holding the flowers in clear view.

Megan looked surprised when she opened the door. She was haggard, exhausted, with dark shadows around her eyes. 'Oh, hello, Mr Heath. I thought I saw you coming up the path. I've only recently got home.'

He imagined himself gouging out her eyes with his thumbs and felt slightly aroused. 'It's Martin. I've told you before. There's no need for formality.'

'Okay, Martin, what can I do for you?'

You could cut your throat and die, that would be amusing. 'I saw what happened to poor Lottie on the news. I feel so very sorry. I wanted to call and offer my condolences. How are you coping?'

Megan resisted the urge to cry. 'I'm err... I'm as good as can be expected in the circumstances, thank you.'

The bitch looks thin, broken, close to tears. What a beautiful sight to behold. 'I've brought you some flowers.'

Megan reached out to accept the bouquet, thinking it a most inappropriate gift. It reminded her of funerals. 'That's very kind of you, thank you.'

'I've been thinking a lot about Lottie. I was hoping to come in and talk.'

Megan was surprised he'd called. But a part of her was glad he had. She silently acknowledged that she was fond of Heath. And now here he was accepting of her grief. It may feel good to share. 'Yes, of course, please come in. We can talk in the lounge. Give me a second. I'll put the flowers in some water.'

'Have you been doing some painting?'

'Sorry?'

Like the bitch didn't know exactly what he was talking about. 'The area of wall above the fire seems somewhat fresher than the rest of the room.'

Megan thought it an odd observation, but she didn't read anything into it. He was trying to be friendly, making conversation, nothing more. 'I'll sort out the flowers.'

Heath looked to the floor, honing in on a single strand of Lottie's yellow hair, and smiling as Megan re-entered the lounge. 'Is there any news? Are the police any nearer to finding her? I'm worried sick. I've been thinking of little else. Lottie is such a lovely little girl, one of the nicest in the class.'

'There's only so much I can tell you.'

He so wanted to laugh. *Who are you trying to kid? The pigs haven't got a fucking clue.* 'A young boy I'd come to know was the victim of a vicious assault while I was working as a nurse for an international charity in Syria. The law enforcement agencies were next to useless. I very much hope the police here are a great deal more effective in your case. I'd hate to think of Lottie's safety being compromised by incompetence.'

Megan felt much the same way. 'I err... I believe they're doing all they can.'

Heath stifled a laugh. The moronic bitch was such a poor liar. The woman was shitting herself. It couldn't be more obvious. It was written all over her stupid face. 'But is it enough? That's what you've got to ask yourself, is it enough? You must be so very worried that they'll let you down.'

Megan was desperate to change the subject. 'Can I get you something to drink, a tea or coffee?'

Heath reached out, patting her knee. 'You stay exactly where you are, and I'll fetch us some refreshments. The house has much the same layout as mine. It shouldn't be a problem. What are we going to have?'

Megan felt inclined to say no, but he was already on his feet, striding towards the kitchen like he owned the place. 'I'll have a cup of tea, thanks. Help yourself to whatever you fancy.'

I've already done that, bitch. She's lying bound and

gagged in a cage in my attic. You saw the photographs. Ha! There may be more to follow. 'Do you take milk and sugar?'

'Just milk, please. It's in the fridge.'

Heath noticed that the window had been re-paired, as he switched on the kettle. He called out, loud enough to be heard. 'How many days is it now?'

'It's been nine days. Lottie's been missing for nine days.'

He reappeared at the lounge door with a full cup in each hand. 'And what have the police actually done to help you in that time?'

Megan accepted her cup but didn't drink. 'They're making the usual enquiries, and they've put cameras outside the house in case he comes back.'

Heath's eyes widened. *The devious bastards! Cameras, fucking cameras!* 'Oh, really, where?'

Lewis had advised her not to share the locations of the cameras with anyone, not even her mother, but she asked herself what harm it could possibly do? Heath was such a nice guy. A caring man who knew Lottie well and was concerned for her welfare. Someone who'd stepped up when she needed sup-port the most. 'There's a wide-angle one in the back garden and another high in a corner of the porch overlooking the front door. They're only tiny. You'd never spot them unless you knew they were there.' So, it seemed a change of plans was necessary unless he wore a convincing disguise, of course. A black stocking, maybe, or a mask, something covering his face. 'Don't you think that seems rather inadequate? I'd have thought they'd have officers doing twenty-four hour surveillance by now.'

Megan frowned. 'They're short of resources.'

Well, that was good news. Fate was smiling on him. 'That's completely ridiculous; what does money matter? What's more important than a little girl's survival?'

'I think it's a matter of priorities. They don't think he's coming back.'

Well, the cretins got that wrong. 'I pray that he doesn't. But what if he does? Have you considered that possibility? What if he does?'

Megan's muscles jumped under her skin. 'A part of me hopes that's exactly what happens. I want to know who he is. I want to see his face, look into his eyes. I want the opportunity to force him to talk.'

Be careful what you wish for, bitch. I'll pay you an-

other visit soon enough. 'I have to say that you're wonderfully stoic in the circumstances. If there's ever anything I can do to help, anything at all, you only have to ask. I'm very fond of Lottie. She reminds me of my sister.'

Megan looked him in the eye and thought he meant it. That they weren't just empty words as uttered by so many. He appeared sincere. As if he really cared. 'Thank you. I'm doing all I can to stay strong for Lottie's sake. My falling apart isn't going to help her.'

'You've never said a truer word, and it's to your credit. I don't know if I could be nearly so brave in your place.'

'Thank you again. I'm glad someone understands.'

'Are you a woman of faith, Megan?'

Megan replied in a soft, halting voice, 'Why do you ask?'

'I was brought up a Catholic. My dear father used to trust in prayer. He believed in miracles. He was such a good and worthy man. I like to think I share his virtues.'

Megan took a sip of her fast cooling tea, glad of

the time to think, however briefly. 'I never thought I'd hear myself saying this, but I've been doing a lot of praying in recent days. If there is a God, I'm very much hoping He's listening.'

Heath smiled. *And now here you are entertaining the devil's disciple. If only you knew the truth, if only you understood the horror you faced.* 'Would you like to pray with me now? We could kneel together.'

Megan was well and truly outside her comfort zone, but that was never going to stop her, not if there was even the slightest possibility that prayer would help save her little girl from whatever dangers she faced at the hands of an unseen monster. The two knelt alongside each other. Eyes closed tight shut and heads bowed.

'Shall we link hands, my dear girl?'

Megan thought it a strange choice of phrase, but she reached out anyway, holding his hand in hers with a firm grip, as he started quietly chanting in Latin. She listened in contemplative silence for almost three minutes before he stopped and spoke, 'Hopefully that's got the Almighty's undivided attention. My father taught me the words and phrasing as a boy when we were alone together. Would you like to pray now, or would you like me to take the lead? I'm no expert, I can't guarantee results, but it's something I've done many times in the past with good outcomes. Often in times of great adversity. I've spent a great deal of time with children in need of help.'

Megan choked back her tears, her eyes still shut, as he turned his head to watch her, taking pleasure in her obvious distress, wallowing in her suffering, amused by her forlorn hope. 'You... err... you take the lead. I'd be grateful if you would.'

'Very well, my new friend, I'll make a start.' Heath spent the next few minutes pleading for Lottie's safe return. When he moved on to ask God to care for her, should she die at the abductor's hands, Megan was inconsolable. Heath hugged her tightly, pulling her close and picturing himself tearing off her clothes, as she lay in a blood-soaked and battered heap.

'Thank you, Martin. I'm glad of your help.'

'I'm here for you whenever you need me. I want you to remember that. And you know where I live. Call on me any time if you need to talk. We can pray together again any time you wish. I'm at your disposal. All you have to do is ask. My door is always open. I'd like to think this is the start of a long and fruitful friendship.'

'Thank you, it's appreciated.'

Such a stupid woman, so gullible, so desperate for comfort. He looked into her eyes, resisting the almost overwhelming desire to place his hands around her throat and squeeze. 'I'm glad to be of assistance. If Lottie lives, I'll help you celebrate. And when she dies... I'm sorry, I meant to say if, if she dies, I'll help you mourn.' He closed his eyes for one last time, pressing his palms together. 'Hear our prayer, God Almighty on high. No little girl should be alone, terrified and desperate for her mother's touch. Have mercy on Lottie and her dear mother too. Let their misery come to a rapid end one way or another.'

37

'What the fuck happened to your face?'

Kesey touched her right cheek. 'Kick-boxing, I took a class last evening. A student caught me with a turning-kick when I was trying to spar and teach at the same time. Distractions aren't a good idea if you're fighting.'

Lewis grimaced. 'Ah, yeah, I remember Grav saying something about your extracurricular activities, now that I think about it. There must be easier ways to keep fit.'

'Hitting things keeps me sane. I've been doing it since I was a kid. It helps to work through my frustrations.'

'Yeah, I get that. Rugby used to do the same thing for me.' He patted his overhanging beer belly. 'I have to rely on the booze these days.'

'How did it go in Cardiff?'

'If it's him, I'll eat my fucking hat. And yours too, if you've got one.'

Kesey blew the air from her mouth. 'Can you expand on that for me?'

'The scrote grabbed the boy, panicked, and then actually shat himself. He was humming, crap running down the inside of his trousers, when the South Wales boys stopped his van about ten minutes later. The man's a nervous wreck. I thought he was going to puke at one point when I put a bit of pressure on. And he cried twice, more with concern for himself than anyone else. I've never wanted to slap a man more. There is no way he broke into the Wellers' house, climbed the stairs in the dark, and took Lottie from the bed while Megan slept next to her. He's enough of a pervert, I've no doubt on that score, but he hasn't got the bottle. He'll be shitting himself a few more times before the penal system's done with him. Prisoners don't like nonces. They'll punch his teeth out and use his gob as an arsehole. And good enough for the cunt, the world would be a better place without him.'

Kesey was struck by the intensity of her sergeant's statement. She asked herself if he'd ever encountered such a man in his youth. Was he a survivor? 'I wasn't expecting you to say anything different, but we had to check it out. We've had the DNA results through. They're not a match, but then you'd already guessed that. I'd have been amazed if they were.'

Lewis nodded his agreement. 'I've had Megan on the phone.'

'Oh, really, what did she want?'

'Just a catch-up. I wish I could have told her something more positive. And she's had Heath at the house. He did the good neighbour routine. He was very supportive, apparently.'

'There you go, I told you he's a decent bloke.'

Lewis grinned. 'The Pope will be making him a saint at this rate.'

'You still don't look convinced.'

'I don't like the man. It's as simple as that.'

'Fancy a coffee?'

He shook his head. 'No, Ben picked up that ex-music teacher we're looking at. The nonce who's been giving private piano lessons since his sacking. I want to sit in on the interview.'

'I had an expert look at the photographic paper.'

Lewis raised an eyebrow. 'Anything that helps us?'

'It's the sort of stuff that was commonly available years back before digital took hold. There's no way of identifying where or when it was bought.'

'Another dead end. It doesn't get any better.'

'It's ten days, Ray, ten days today. That's ten days too long.'

His expression darkened. 'Yeah, I know, it's not good. I'm beginning to think we're not going to find Lottie alive. I hope I'm wrong, but we're not getting anywhere. It's one blind alley after another.'

'We've got to keep our heads up for the troops. We don't want their enthusiasm flagging. We can't show even the slightest sign of losing hope. We're going to find her. It's just a matter of when and if she's alive when we do.'

Lewis grimaced. 'You've seen the photos. She's in the hands of a total psycho. Maybe she'd be better off dead. Can you imagine what that poor kid's going through?'

Kesey swallowed hard. 'I'm trying not to think about it. We've got to focus on the job, follow the evidence, or at least the little evidence we've got. If we keep plugging away, we'll get a break. Lottie's out there somewhere, and so's the bastard who took her.'

38

Heath was wearing one of his mother's black stockings, pulled down tightly over his head, as he crept along the path at the back of the Wellers' home in the early hours of the morning. He glanced in every direction, satisfying himself that no-one was watching, before scrambling over the wall and lowering himself to the grassy ground. He had no intention of entering the house, but he wanted Megan to know he could any time he wanted to. That, he assured himself, would increase her fear, introducing a crushing panic that wouldn't let go.

It took Heath almost twenty minutes to find the small camera in the semi-darkness, despite his prior knowledge. When he did find it, he held it close to his face, surprised by the tiny lens. He knew his disguise masked his identity. He was wearing his mother's clothes, full make-up and dark wig, which when complemented by the tight nylon stocking made him totally unrecognisable. He was confident in and amused by the likely future impact of his deception, and so he returned the camera to its original position as if he hadn't found it at all.

Heath strolled casually across the lawn, which was badly in need of cutting. He took Lottie's pyjama top from his backpack, pulled up his skirt and his pants down, and shat on it, using a comparatively clean sleeve to wipe himself before repositioning his clothing to their original position. He then hung the stinking top at the centre of the clothesline, taking care to maximise its impact when it was first seen in the light of day. He stifled a laugh as he stood back and admired the results of his efforts. And then congratulated himself on his achievements as he walked away, resisting the impulse to invade the house, drag Megan from her bed and show her exactly what he'd done.

Heath approached the wall, glancing back at the

soiled top for one final time before climbing the structure with relative ease. As he dropped back onto the stony path, his adrenaline-fuelled elation was already slowly subsiding, to be replaced by the desire to inflict greater suffering and ultimately death. He knew that he was approaching the end game. There was only so long he could refrain from murder, however hard he tried and whatever the pay-off. Maybe he'd give it another week. Could he manage a week? *Yes, why not kill the brat first and then the bitch mother?*

As he skipped along the path filled with a new sense of anticipation fed by fantasy, Heath entertained what he considered his most fabulous ever idea. Why not kill the brat in front of the bitch mother? He ejaculated spontaneously, without the need to touch himself, and then punched the air. *Yes, yes, yes! Make the bitch watch!* It was genius, inspired. It would be the worst moment of her life, as she watched, helpless, begging for mercy that didn't come. And then he'd kill her too, when he was ready, when he'd had his fun. Maybe record it all on film for the father to see. And the pigs, they could see the results of their failure and witness his greatness.

As Heath entered his Victorian house, he was on

a high, more significant than that engendered by any drug. His mother appeared on the landing as he climbed the stairs, and for the first time in memory, she smiled at him, uttering warm words of reassurance and congratulation, as opposed to the usual morale-sapping criticism with which he'd become so familiar. Heath had never felt more validated or more powerful. He was exalted, a prince amongst men, special in every way.

As he entered the attic, focused on the cage, he believed Lottie knew it too, whatever her unconscious state. She was in the presence of a living god.

It was the greatest moment of his life.

39

'It's too expensive, you said. He won't go back to the house for the third time, you said. Well, he did, he was there last night. The madman actually shat on Lottie's pyjama top and hung it on her mother's frigging clothes line.'

Halliday took a deep breath, in through his nose and out through his mouth. 'I'm in the middle of a call, Laura. Take a seat, and I'll be with you as quickly as I can.'

Kesey sat herself down, still bristling, not quite able to believe he was continuing his very ordinary telephone conversation as if she'd said nothing at all.

When he finally put the phone down about five minutes later, she spoke up insistently, before he had the opportunity to comment. 'I told you Megan Weller needed protection. I sat in this very seat and said it more than once. It was our best chance of catching the bastard. And our best chance of rescuing Lottie too. But would you listen? You were wrong. I want to hear you admit it. You always seem to think you know best.'

For the first time in Kesey's experience, Halliday appeared lost for words.

'What, nothing to say for yourself?'

He averted his eyes to the wall, sitting in continued silence for a few seconds more, before composing himself. 'Do try to calm yourself down, Laura. I'd appreciate you conducting yourself in a professional manner commensurate with your rank.'

'What?'

'I think I made myself perfectly clear.'

'We'd have the abductor in a cell now if you'd listened to me.'

Halliday appeared to be gaining confidence now, as if the early impact of her statement was wearing thin. 'You're the senior investigating officer, Laura. I can only say that you didn't make your case strongly enough. If you had, well, I'd almost certainly have agreed to the necessary funding. If there is a failure, it's yours and not mine. I'm sure the chief constable would agree, should he become involved.'

'You have got to be frigging kidding me.'

'You mentioned cameras. What about the cameras? I thought it was a rather desperate tactic. Weren't they as effective as you'd hoped?'

Kesey sighed. 'Oh, the bastard's on camera all right. He's in clear view despite the darkness. But he's heavily disguised. He's unrecognisable. The one thing we can say is that it's definitely a man.'

'And we know that how exactly?'

'Oh, we know it because he pulled his skirt up and his pants down. He got his dick out and squatted facing the camera. We can see his prick clearly enough, just not his face.'

Halliday picked up a gold fountain pen, turning it in his hand. 'Are you finished?'

Kesey was panting slightly when she looked back at him. 'I've said what I came to say.'

'Well, in that case, perhaps you could move on to

recommend where we go from here. I've had more than enough of your dramatics for one morning.'

She rose from her seat, glaring down at him, oozing disdain. 'Right, you've asked, so I'm going to tell you. I want an officer at the Wellers' house seven days a week, twenty-four hours a day for however long it takes. That's three officers in any twenty-four hour period, and I don't care what it costs. I don't want you whinging about budgets. I just want you to agree so that I can get on and arrange it as I should have in the first place.'

He removed the pen's top for no apparent reason. 'I'll need the full costings.'

'Oh, come on, man, for fuck's sake, grow a pair. I want an officer at that house within twenty minutes. It's time for action not more written reports. Either that or let's knock on the chief constable's door right now. Let's see what he thinks. I'm ready if you are.'

Halliday's face took on a purple hue. 'Very well, Laura, have it your way. But if you ever speak to me like that again, you'll be on a disciplinary charge. I'm the head of this department and don't you ever forget it. Have I made myself clear?'

Kesey looked back on approaching his office

door. 'Duly noted, sir, and thank you for your support. Perhaps now we'll get somewhere. Better late
than never.'

40

Fleeing persecution and terror wasn't an easy option for Jamal.

The journey across the Mediterranean from Syria to Greece in a dangerously small, inflatable boat packed with almost fifty, desperate and bedraggled men, women and children, had been long and arduous. As had his trek across Europe to the French port of Calais, where he camped under thin plastic sheeting for several weeks, before crossing the English Channel, hidden in the back of a delivery lorry bound for Dover. It had taken him another three days and nights to reach Caerystwyth, his destination of choice, where he met up with a family friend who owned a barbershop.

Jamal had been in the pleasant west Wales market town for a little over two weeks when he first saw Martin Heath.

Jamal sat in the large picture window of a corner café popular with locals and stared out incredulously as a man he recognised only too well-strolled past in the summer sunshine as if he didn't have a care in the world. Jamal looked, looked away, and then looked again, a flashback taking him back in time, forcing him to relive events he'd much prefer to forget.

Jamal saw in his mind's eye Heath kneeling down and strangling a young, black-haired boy of six or seven years, and felt his muscles and veins straining against his skin, as blood rushed to his trembling extremities.

For a moment Jamal thought it probably best to forget who he'd seen, to avoid the unwelcome attention contact with the legal authorities would inevitably bring. But as he lost sight of Heath, he had a sudden change of heart, conceding that the killer should pay for his crime in one way or another. Maybe seeing him was an opportunity of sorts, as well as a burden. If not the police, then he himself could inflict some form of retributive justice. A child murderer deserved nothing less.

Jamal drained his cup of strong, sweet, black coffee, before jumping quickly to his feet. He hurried out into the busy street, turning to his right. He spotted his target crossing the road about thirty or forty meters away, up a gradually sloping hill. Jamal picked up his pace, dodging past shoppers, striding out with a newfound determination until he reached Heath's side.

'Do you remember me, killer?'

Heath focused forwards, avoiding the man's accusing gaze. 'Fuck off! I've got no idea what you're talking about. You're mixing me up with somebody else.'

Jamal grabbed Heath's arm as he picked up his pace, attempting to get away. 'I want money.'

'I told you to fuck off. I'm not who you think I am.' Heath looked up into the sky. 'I've told him, Mother, I've told him. What more can I do?'

'You give me money or I go to the police.'

Heath suddenly stopped, and then shoved Jamal into a quieter side street, away from the crowds. He knew precisely who the Syrian was, his face all too familiar. 'You talked to the police in Syria, what good did it do you?'

'I could talk to the British police too, and tell them what I saw. Do you want to take that risk?'

What to do? What the hell to do? Here was a witness he'd never expected to encounter again. He couldn't kill him, not here in the street. 'I can get you one hundred pounds, maybe two hundred at most.'

The Syrian craned his neck, their noses almost touching. 'I want ten thousand pounds cash, and I want it quickly, and not a penny less.'

Heath flinched, as a police community support officer walked past on the other side of the street, more interested in the parked cars than anything else. 'I'm going to need time to get that sort of cash together. I'm not a wealthy man.'

'How long?'

Heath looked Jamal in the eye and had never hated anyone more. He gave him his home address and then said, 'Be at my house at midnight tonight. Knock on the door and wait until I answer. I'll give you money the once but never again. You'll leave this place and never come back. If I ever see you after tonight, I'll kill you.'

41

Kesey heard an urgency in Janet's voice when she picked up the phone.

'You need to come home right now, Laura.'

The detective glanced at the clock. She'd only been in work for a little under half an hour. 'What is it? Is Ed ill again?'

'We've had a letter.'

Kesey scratched her temple with her free hand. 'What, is it something to do with the holiday?'

There was the sound of crying at the other end of the line. 'It's a large brown envelope with what looks like a bloody fingerprint on the back.'

'Oh, shit, have you opened it?'

'No, I've left it on the dining room table. I don't want to touch the damned thing.'

'That's good, Jan, you've done the right thing. Now, I want you to tell me what the writing is like? I'm talking about our address, how's it written? And the postmark, see if you can see where it was posted.'

'Give me a second.'

There was a silence before Jan spoke again. 'It's addressed to you in black ink.'

'What's the writing like?'

'Large block capitals. What's this about? Do I need to be concerned?'

'Could you see where it was posted?'

'It's a bit smudged, but I think it says Swansea, it's definitely Swan, and then the rest's hard to make out.'

Kesey's hair lifted on her nape. 'Right, I want you to lock both the doors and make sure all the windows are closed. Don't leave Ed on his own, even for a single second. I'm on my way.'

Janet was looking out through the lounge window when Kesey pulled up on the driveway about twenty minutes later. She was standing in the open doorway with Edward's hand in hers when the detective exited her car. Kesey did her best to hide her growing anxiety as she greeted her loved ones, leading them back into the house and locking the door behind them.

'What's going on, Laura?'

Kesey sucked air through her teeth. 'Let's put something on the telly for Ed, and we'll go from there.'

Janet fought the impulse to bombard her partner with questions. Kesey was scared. That much was obvious. But why? That was the biggest question, why? 'Scooby Doo's his favourite.'

Kesey smiled at her son. 'Okay, then Scooby it is.'

Edward settled on the sofa to watch his cartoon while munching a packet of white chocolate buttons, an unusual treat at that time of the morning.

Kesey was wearing identical skin tight, thin blue nitrile gloves to those used by Lewis when she opened the letter seconds later. She swallowed, gagged and swallowed again as she began to read:

Dear Miss Piggy,
*   You'll know by now that I know where you*
live. I know where you live, I know where your

flabby pink partner lives, and best of all, I know where your oh so vulnerable little boy lives. Edward, isn't it? One of my most favourite names. I killed a young lad who looked very much like him some years back when my taste for death and destruction first matured.

I want you to know that I've still got Lottie, bound and caged as in my photographs. I'm sure you found them fascinating. I'll tire of her soon, and then she'll die. Does that make you feel guilty, detective? It's your job to find her. Your responsibility to keep her alive. But you're failing dismally. You're a fuck-up, an imposter. Maybe you should leave the job to someone who actually knows what they're doing. I'll need another victim soon enough. A boy, I think, it will make a nice change. A boy with brown hair and green eyes. Does that remind you of anyone? I feel sure it does. I've been watching, and I've been listening. I'm coming after you and yours, detective, and you can't hope to stop me. I'm going to tear your life to pieces. A raging tempest is coming your way.

Love and kisses,
Your worst nightmare X

'What is it, Laura? What does it say?'

Kesey's expression darkened. 'It's... it's from the man who took Lottie Weller. The sick bastard is threatening us; he's even threatening Edward.'

'Oh, for God's sake, how many times do we have to go through this kind of shit. Is any job worth all this danger?'

Kesey fought to retain her composure. 'We've got to take this seriously. Am I right in thinking your brother's still away on that computer course.'

'Yeah, he is, for another two weeks.'

Kesey touched Janet's arm. 'Then I want you to take Ed to stay with your sister in Edinburgh. I want you to go today, and I want you both to stay there until the bastard's safely in custody.'

Janet appeared close to panic. 'Do you really think that's necessary?'

Kesey glanced at the letter and then looked back into her partner's troubled eyes. 'Yes, absolutely, there's no doubt in my mind. Book the tickets, either a plane or the train, whichever suits you best. Use my credit card and do it online. The quicker it's sorted out, the better. And I'll run you both to wherever you need to go to get the transport. You need to be out of here today.'

'I can't believe all this is happening again. How long are we going to need to be away this time? I don't get on that well with Kim's husband, you know that. I feel uncomfortable in his company.'

'Do you want to read the letter?'

Janet turned her head away. 'No, I don't want to touch the damned thing.'

'Then trust me when I tell you we need to do this.'

'I'll phone Kim and then go up and pack. Will you arrange the tickets for us? I can't do everything myself.'

Kesey nodded once. 'Plane or train?'

'Train, I think, and from Cardiff, I don't want to go anywhere near Swansea, even with you with us.'

'Okay, that's the least I can do. We'll get going as soon as we can.'

42

Jamal arrived at Martin Heath's impressive Picton Street home ten minutes early. He considered waiting, but the lure of easy money and the freedom it offered was far too great a temptation to ignore. Jamal knocked and only had to stand on the doorstep for a matter of seconds before Heath checked the street for potential witnesses and ushered him in. The house was in darkness, with only a single candle lighting a sitting room to the right of the hallway. All other internal doors were tightly shut.

'Where's my money?'

Heath could see that Jamal was shaking slightly

as he stood facing him. He pointed at the open door, encouraging the Syrian into the room.

'Why is it so dark?'

'My lights have tripped. It's a common problem. If you want the money, you'll sit yourself down, shut up, and wait.'

'You've got it?'

'Yes, I've got it. But remember what I said to you. This is a one-off payment. I'll never give you another penny. Have we got a deal?'

'You have my word.'

Jamal sat and waited in the darkness, fidgeting with his clothes until Heath returned a few minutes later. Heath was carrying a black leather briefcase with a gold metal coloured combination lock to either side of the handle. He handed Jamal the case, looming above him as he rested it on his lap. Jamal went to open it but found it locked.

'The money's in here?'

Heath nodded in the light of the flickering flame. 'The combination is four-five-seven-one. Open it, and the cash is yours.'

As Jamal focused, squinting, eyes narrowed, concentrating all his attention on turning the tiny dials,

Heath took a recently sharpened carving knife from the rear waistband of his tight linen trousers. He plunged the steel blade deep into his victim's neck, slicing through flesh and sinew until the point made contact with the bone. Heath struck again as Jamal slumped forward, blood flowing from his fatal wounds. Heath repeated the process, raising the weapon high above his head and bringing it crashing down time and again, until Jamal fell from the seat, collapsing to the floor with a mix of blood and saliva bubbling from his open mouth.

Heath was panting hard as he dragged Jamal's blood-soaked corpse across the hall tiles and into a prepared room, the entire floor of which was covered in plastic sheeting. He positioned the body at the approximate centre point of the room, the various items of furniture already pushed aside. He'd switched on the light to illuminate the process but dismembering Jamal's now naked corpse was significantly more demanding than he'd expected.

The hacksaw blade was more than a match for the flesh, but cutting through bone was another matter entirely. It took a great deal of effort, and by the time Heath pushed the final limb aside about forty minutes later, he was utterly exhausted, covered in slowly congealing blood and other body fluids from head to foot. Heath flopped to the filthy plastic, lying prone only inches from the decapitated head, and slept for an hour or so to regain his strength.

Heath rose from his butcher's floor at a little after 1.45 a.m., wrapping each body part in a black plastic bin bag, and secured with lengths of green parcel tape. Heath then placed the gory packages in two family-sized suitcases, ready for later disposal. He stripped off his soiled clothing, showered, and then dressed in fresh attire.

He carried each burdensome case into the street and placed them in the boot of his car, taking every caution to avoid noise that could bring any attention to his activities.

It took him about twenty minutes to reach the river, in a quiet area of the countryside about seven miles from the centre of town.

He had a cautionary conversation with his long-gone mother as he lifted each case from the car in turn, and then dropped them, one at a time, into the fast-flowing mix of salt and freshwater.

'Were you watching, Mother? Did you see what I've done?'

'Do you think they're going to sink, Henry? Did you weigh them down with stones?'

Heath stood on the riverbank, shivering from growing angst as opposed to cold, as he watched the cases slowly sink, but then float just an inch or two below the surface as the tide swept them away. He considered launching himself into the swirling water to retrieve them, but he knew he wasn't up to it. Swimming wasn't a strength he possessed. If he entered the river, he'd drown.

He had a grinding feeling deep in the pit of his gut as he returned to his car, parked a five-minute rapid walk away in the light of a half-moon partly shrouded in cloud.

He didn't know if he'd blown it, but he knew he'd made an error. Maybe it was time to kill the brat, and her bitch mother too. The endgame was fast approaching. Why wait?

43

Kesey handed Lewis his second pint of best bitter as she joined him at the table, keen to talk. 'So, what do you make of the suitcase killer? I don't envy those coracle men fishing that lot out of the river. The body parts were stinking, apparently.'

'The suitcase killer? Is that what they're calling him?'

Kesey nodded. 'Yeah, I guess it's the obvious name. It's all over the news.'

'I'm just glad we're not dealing with it. One major investigation is more than enough to be getting on with.'

'It's fortunate they found the head. Without the

likeness in the local paper, the barber would never have come forward. The victim had only been in the UK for a short time, poor sod. He leaves a war zone for a better life and ends up murdered in Wales. Talk about bad luck.'

Lewis shrugged. 'You've got to admit it's a coincidence.'

'What are you talking about?'

Lewis slurped his beer, savouring the yeasty froth at the top. 'The victim's from Syria, Heath worked in Syria, maybe two and two make four.'

'Oh, here you go again.'

'Sometimes the most obvious links are the right ones, that's all I'm saying.'

Kesey sipped her lager shandy and laughed. 'A lot of people work in Syria, Ray. It's hardly evidence. It's not a criminal offence to be based in the Middle East.'

'I've said it before, and I'll say it again. It's too much of a coincidence for me.'

'You're obsessed with the man. I don't know what the hell's wrong with you sometimes. There's no evidence to suggest Heath's committed any crime, let alone murder.'

'Yeah, yeah, so you keep saying.'

'I keep saying it, because I'm right.'

'How's Janet doing? Is she still in Scotland?'

'Yeah, she's there for the foreseeable future.'

He took another mouthful of beer. 'That must be tough on you both.'

'It's Ed I'm missing more than anything.'

'Trouble in paradise?'

'No, I'm missing Jan too. She's the love of my life.'

Lewis tilted back his head, emptying his glass before standing. 'Right, I'd better make a move. Are you around in the morning?'

'I'm planning to call on Megan first thing. It's about time we had a heart-to-heart. I can't keep avoiding the woman when I'm heading up the investigation searching for her child. It's neither professional nor helpful.'

He pulled his head back. 'Are you sure you want to do that?

She still thinks you're a twat. I can do it for you if you want?'

Kesey frowned. 'No, you're all right, thanks. This is something I'm going to have to do myself. To be honest, I think I should have done it long before now.'

'You know best, boss, although I'm happy to come with you if you want me to? I could meet you there. You know, smooth the conversational wheels a bit.'

Kesey laughed again. 'No, I'm a big girl now. I don't need anyone holding my hand.'

'Okay, if you're sure.'

'I've got a dentist appointment at half eleven. I'll see you later in the day if you're still about.'

'Night, boss, have a good one.'

Kesey waved as he went to walk away. Home was calling. She'd finish her drink, order a takeaway, and then head home herself. Maybe an early night was in order. Tomorrow was going to be a demanding day.

44

Megan's home phone rang at just after eight that morning, waking her from a fitful sleep, interrupted by frightening dreams and dark thoughts that dragged her close to despair. She jumped from the bed, throwing back the quilt and rushing downstairs, just as PC Bethan Rees picked up the phone and said, 'Hello.' The officer listened, and then covered the mouthpiece and said, 'Morning, Meg. It's for you.'

Megan held the phone to her face, surprised to hear Heath's chirpy voice at the other end of the line. 'Oh, hello, Martin, it's early, what can I do for you?'

'Aren't you pleased to hear my voice?'

'Yes, of course I am. I'm just surprised by the time, that's all.'

'Is the piggy police officer listening? It's in their nature. They like to snoop.'

Megan's voice hardened. 'She's in the kitchen getting breakfast, why do you ask?'

'I've got something very important to tell you. Something you'll definitely want to hear. I want you to slip out unannounced and come straight to my house at exactly nine o'clock this morning. I'll be waiting for you. But this has to be between the two of us. Talk to anyone else, the piggy constable, your mother, your ex, anyone, and that's a deal-breaker. I won't be able to share what I know. Are we in agreement?'

Megan inhaled a long breath. 'Oh, come on, Martin, this is all getting a bit weird. I thought we were friends. You're starting to freak me out. If you know something, if it's important, I want you to tell me now.'

'That's not the way this works. Be here at nine and be alone. I've got such exciting news. But there's only one way you're going to hear it. Do what I say and tell no-one.'

Megan sighed, making zero effort to hide her frustration. 'Okay, have it your way. But this had better be good. You'd better not be messing me about. Getting my hopes up and then letting me down would be so cruel. You've always made a big deal about your faith. I hope you're better than that.'

'Just come as I've asked of you. You won't be disappointed. I may even introduce you to Mother. I'm sure she'd be delighted to meet you.'

Megan banged on Heath's front door at precisely the right time, not a second late and not a second early. He answered almost immediately, on her second knock. He was dressed in his father's old clothes, but still had the hint of cherry-red lipstick on his lips. 'Come in, come in, it's lovely to see you. I'm so excited. This is going to be an extraordinary day.'

Megan felt increasingly agitated as she entered the hallway. Why the evasion? There was something about Heath's demeanour that concerned her. He seemed different. So unlike the man she'd got to know. 'What's this about, Martin? I hope you're not playing some kind of ridiculous game.'

Oh, it's a game all right, bitch, but not one you'll want

to play. He led her into the old-fashioned lounge, where a white porcelain cup containing a thick green liquid was sitting on the veneered coffee table. 'Game? No, not at all, you've been praying to find out where Lottie is, and now you're about to get an answer. How good is that? It's a matter for celebration. All your dreams are about to come true because of me.'

Megan's eyes lit up. 'You know something? Where is she? What have you found out?'

Heath looked her in the eye. 'Right, I need you to listen to me very carefully. I want you to sit yourself down, and then pick up that cup. If I'm going to tell you where Lottie is, you'll have to follow my instructions to the letter and without question. Even the slightest deviation from my plan and my mouth will be sealed forever. Tell me you understand.'

Megan's entire body began to shake as she pressed her back against her chair, retreating, making herself smaller. 'Oh my God, it's you. You took her. You had her all along!'

'Ah, so you've finally worked it out. Ten out of ten, what a clever girl you are.'

She snarled at him. 'You heinous bastard! You'll be locked up for the rest of your miserable life.'

'Oh, I don't think so, Megan.'

She reached out, grabbing his wrist, digging in her nails. 'Where is she? Tell me now. Where's my little girl?'

Heath began to laugh as he pulled away, crazed, and then suddenly stopped, the expression on his face becoming thoughtful. 'You can report me to the piggy police if you want to. Feel free, because I won't stand in your way. But I can guarantee you that I'll say nothing if you do, not a single word. The right to silence. Isn't that what you legal types call it? Talk to the pigs if you want to, do it right now, by all means use my house phone. But if you do, you'll never see your helpless little brat again. I'll sit there in what-ever interview room they drag me to and say "no comment" time and again as Lottie slowly dies from starvation and thirst.'

'They'll search your house!'

He laughed again. 'What makes you think she's here? There's plenty of alternative hiding places. Is that really the best you can do?'

'You're a monster!'

'Quite so, you're very probably right. You're not the first person to say it. But it changes nothing. If you want to see young baldy alive, there's only one way to do it. Pick up the cup and drink the contents.'

'Would it make any difference if I beg?'

Heath smiled sardonically. 'Well, it would be amusing. I'll give you that much. But, no, at the end of the day, it wouldn't make a difference at all. Drink or she dies. Make your choice. It really is as simple as that.'

Megan hesitated at first, but then she picked up the cup with a hand that wouldn't stop quivering. 'What is it?'

'Oh, there's such concern on your pretty face, such worry lines. It will help you relax, nothing more. You're going to have to trust me, Megan. Drink it, and when you wake up, you'll be with your daughter. That's the deal, and there's no other way.'

'You'll take me to her?'

'Yes, precisely, I'll take you to her, as you put it so clearly. I've told her to expect you. Now, drink it up. You don't want to keep her waiting for any longer than you have to. This is your one and only chance ever to see your daughter again. Fail to follow my instructions even slightly, and she dies at my hand. And it won't be pleasant. She'll suffer, I can guarantee that much. Inflicting pain is something I'm good at – a skill I've honed with practised glee. I have a remarkable capacity for cruelty when the mood takes me. My mother would tell you the same thing. Now, drink!'

Megan raised the cup to her lips and drank, forcing the sickly sweet liquid down her throat.

'That's it, all of it, down the hatch, every drop, you know it makes sense.'

Heath looked across at his mother's image, seeking her praise as Megan ingested the sedative syrup. When the cup was empty, Megan handed it to Heath, who inspected it and smiled. 'Well, what a co-operative young woman you've become. Give the mixture a minute or two take effect and then we'll be on our merry way. You'll be more compliant that way, weaker, unable to fight back.'

Megan responded in a quiet voice that was barely audible. 'Is it far?'

'No, not far, it's not far at all. Now your phone, give me your phone. Do you know, I almost forgot that for a moment, silly me. We don't want you calling for help.'

Megan yawned as she handed it over.

'That's very good, Megan, today is the greatest of days, and you'll play your part. Everything was leading to this. It's exactly as it should be. Mother is so very proud of me. Can you see her? She's clapping like a performing seal.'

Megan couldn't see very much at all as her eyesight began to blur. She was becoming increasingly drowsy, as she fought to stay awake. Heath watched her closely, studying her expressions and the rhythmic movements of her chest, as her breathing became more laboured. He watched and counted the seconds pass until he decided the time was precisely right.

'Right, up you get. It's time for us to visit my latest plaything. Time for me to have some fun.'

Megan tried to stand, shaking herself awake, but the effects of the drug were already dulling her senses. She fell back into her seat, groaning slightly as she sunk into the soft cushion. Heath took her arm and then leaned backwards, dragging her to her feet in one co-ordinated movement. 'Okay, come on, bitch, up you get, come on, I've been waiting for this! It's playtime.'

'What... what are you saying?'

Heath shoved Megan towards the hall, yelling when she stumbled, struggling to regain her footing. He slapped her face hard with an open hand on reaching the base of the stairs and then pointed to the top. 'If you want to see the little mare, you'll get up there now, one step at a time, that's it, climb, right to the very top.'

'She... she was here all along?'

He pushed her hard. 'Shut your stupid mouth. Get up there, and you may find out.'

Megan climbed the stairs one slow step at a time, focusing on her need to see Lottie, clinging on to hope. Her partially anaesthetised legs felt as if they were weighed down by lead boots, which seemed to get more substantial and more obstructive with every step.

When Megan reached the landing, Heath slapped her again, and then shook her, fearing he may have administered an excessive dose of the medication. He manoeuvred her towards the six-step ladder leading to the open hatch, and then ordered her to climb, jabbing her in the back when she stalled.

Megan's head was swimming now, the entire area an impressionist blur, as she scrambled up the ladder, semi-conscious, with Heath pushing her from behind. She fell onto her knees as she entered the attic room, and began slowly crawling towards the cage on all fours, focused on Lottie's sleeping form. Megan started weeping when she first touched the steel bars. She was desperately struggling to find the strength to free her captive daughter when Heath hit her from behind. He rained down blow after powerful blow until Megan lay unconscious, bruised and bleeding.

'Can you see, Mother? Can you see what I've done?'

She clapped her hands together, shrieking with girlish glee. 'You've done well, Henry. But don't take too long. Kill them quickly and dump the bodies. There's no time for delay. It's time to bring this to an end.'

45

Kesey nodded in greeting as Police Constable Rees answered the front door to the Wellers' spacious house.

'Hello, Bethan, how's it going? I'd like a quick word with Megan.'

The constable's face was ashen. 'I contacted the station. I spoke to DS Lewis. He said he'd give you a ring. Hasn't he told you?'

Kesey checked her phone, which needed charging. 'Told me what, exactly?'

'Megan's not here. She's not in the house.'

'Then, where the hell is she? You're supposed to be keeping a close eye on the woman. That's the whole point of you being here. Didn't Ray make that clear?'

Rees shifted her weight from one foot to the other. 'I'm sorry, ma'am. She slipped out when I was in the bathroom. I was only in there for five minutes at most. What was I supposed to do? I can't watch her every second of the day. And I tried to let you know as soon as I realised she'd gone. What more could I do?'

Kesey linked her hands behind her back. 'Has she done anything like this before?'

'No, we've been getting on great, everything considered. She seemed a little on edge after the phone call. But I didn't think anything of it. She's got a lot to worry about. The last thing I thought she'd do is leave the house without me.'

There was a hard edge to Kesey's voice when she responded. 'What phone call?'

'Martin Heath rang at about eight o'clock this morning. I answered, and he asked to speak to Megan.'

Kesey frowned hard. 'Any idea what about?'

'No, I did ask, just making conversation, really. But Megan wasn't in the mood to talk. She's like that sometimes. They seem to have become close friends. I didn't read anything into it.'

'How long's she been out?'

Rees checked her watch. 'I'd say about half an hour, no longer than that.'

'Have you tried her mobile?'

'Yeah, a few times, but it's off.'

'What's the hell's she playing at?'

Rees looked away. 'I can't claim to know the answer to that one, ma'am. But she's not a prisoner. I can't force her to stay here. If she wants to walk out of the house, she can.'

'Yes, I'm well aware of that, thank you, Bethan.'

The constable's face flushed. 'Do you want me to call at Heath's place? They've been spending a fair amount of time in each other's company. It would only take me a couple of minutes. She could be there. It's only down the road.'

'Just to confirm, you're saying she hasn't sneaked out before?'

'No, never, she's usually stuck to me like glue.'

For the first time, Kesey asked herself if Lewis could have been right all along. Was Heath a suspect? Maybe, but probably not, it still seemed unlikely at best. 'No, you're all right, thanks, Bethan. I'll call on Heath myself. There are a few things I want to ask him. You stay here in case Megan comes back. We're probably jumping to conclusions. There's any number of places she could have gone. Maybe she didn't go to Heath's place at all.'

46

Megan was naked, spluttering, bound, but not gagged, when she woke to see Heath standing next to the cage wearing old ladies' clothes. He was looking down at Lottie with a carving knife in his hand, having just thrown a jug of cold water in Megan's face.

Heath had intended to leave Megan unconscious for hours, planning, maximising his anticipation, but his longing to inflict terrible suffering ultimately proved too strong a trigger. He'd left her mouth unfettered to allow her to scream. The sound was music to his ears.

'Ah, welcome back to the land of the living. I was beginning to wonder if you'd ever wake up at all.'

Megan looked up at her tormentor with bleary eyes, then at the cage, and then at Heath again, as grim reality came into sharp and unrelenting focus.

'Is Lottie all right?'

'The brat? Well, she's still breathing, if that's what you mean. Although she won't be for very much longer. I've waited for long enough, and today's a time for killing.'

'Why, Martin? I thought we were friends. I thought we'd become close. Why would you do such a terrible thing?'

Heath slowly approached Megan, stroking her wet hair as she tried to pull away. 'Can you imagine not being limited by a restrictive conscience? Can you picture the total freedom it would give you to indulge your wildest fantasies without limit? If you can, you'll understand me a little better. I kill because I want to, because I can. Nothing excites me more. I learned that at a surprisingly young age. I murdered and got away with it. I knew then that I had to do it again. And I did, I did. Not soon enough, but it happened in the end. Nursing gave me a ready access to victims. Needy victims who were all too willing to enter my web. And then you came along, you and that little brat of yours – two victims for the price of one. I couldn't believe my luck.'

Megan struggled to free herself, her head pounding, but it was hopeless, absolutely hopeless. The bindings were too strong, the knots too tight, she could hardly move at all. 'If you're going to kill somebody, then kill me. Let Lottie go. She's only a little girl with her future ahead of her. I'll do anything you want me to, anything. Please, I'm pleading with you. I'm not an unattractive woman. Do with me what you will.'

Heath knelt to lick Megan's face, focusing on her eyes, tasting her tears on his tongue. 'That's a very kind offer, so thoughtful, so selfless. Sentiments I fail to understand myself, but ones which you clearly value. It makes no sense to me. Why would I kill only one of you when I can kill you both? But not to worry. You'll live for a few hours yet. I don't want to rush things. You can watch while I strangle the brat. And then it will be your turn to die. You can look forward to that. I'm sure it will come as a relief in the end. Some of my previous victims begged to die.'

He laughed as Megan tried to bite him, her dashing teeth falling fractionally short as she craned her neck towards his nose. 'I wouldn't go giving me any ideas, bitch. Biting, now there's an option I hadn't considered. Why didn't I think of it before? I may even eat you both, cooked or raw, maybe with a light salad. I'm always open to new experiences. Why place limits on depravity?'

Megan shouted. 'You'll burn in hell.'

He grinned on standing. 'Oh, you are full of good ideas. Burning! I love it. I'll go and get my matches. I'm going to be the very best sadist I can be. Mother will approve.'

Megan attempted to tear her hands free as she yelled for help, shouting louder and louder until her words become screams. She screamed and screamed some more, unable to stop as her entire body trembled and her bowel threatened to evacuate its contents.

Heath hit Megan once, bang, hard on the point of the chin, silencing her with one mighty punch, before approaching the hatch. 'I'll see you both in a minute or two. I'll fetch my camera while I'm down there. It seems like a good idea to record events for posterity. I won't bother closing the hatch this time. You're not going anywhere, not all tied up like that with your hands behind your back. But call for help one more time before I return, and I'll cut your tongue out with a blade. You won't say anything else at all after that. You'll just splutter and choke on your blood.'

As Megan looked up, close to unconsciousness, Heath picked up the wig from the floor, beginning his transformation.

47

Heath stopped mid-step as Kesey knocked on the front door of his Picton Street home. He could clearly see her silhouette, but he had no intention of answering. He took a backward step as the piggy detective pressed her face against the glass, willing her to walk away, so he could get on with his day of days. But the officer stayed put, and Heath feared that she'd seen him, dressed in his mother's clothing, dark wig, cherry-red lipstick, black mascara and all.

Heath wanted to cry out a stream of heartfelt abuse when the detective knocked again, a series of short raps of her knuckles this time. But she didn't stop. Bang! There it was again.

Heath searched his troubled mind for an answer to his latest predicament at the hands of the interfering law. He wanted to tear her apart, to inflict terrible suffering for daring to stick her snout in where it didn't belong. But was that wise? Could he get away with it? He knew he had to do something, but what?

'*She's still there, Henry, oink, oink. Your plan is crumbling around your ears – first, the cock-up in Syria and now this abomination. You're losing your touch, my boy. I can't imagine your dear father being nearly as careless.*'

Heath's eyes flashed as he looked up at his mother as she hovered close to the high ceiling. 'Shut the fuck up, Mother, let me concentrate, I need to focus.'

He heard the sound of laughter, a high-pitched female cackle. '*She's still knocking, Henry. There it is again. And I can see her piggy face, look, she's peeping through the glass. Do something, Henry. She's not going anywhere. She's here to stay.*'

Heath was weeping as he peered around a door at the end of the hallway, his camera hanging around his neck on a brown leather strap, a box of safety matches in one hand, and a razor-sharp modelling knife in the other. He willed the interfering pig to go, to walk away, to leave him alone to indulge his desires as he'd planned for so very long. But the pig was still there. She was sticking her snout in. Just as Mother had said. He could see the interfering bitch as clear as day.

Heath glanced behind him as his mother's high-pitched voice rang out once more, filling the house with non-existent sound, so loud that he feared the pig detective would hear.

'The police are out to get you, Henry. I told you they'd come back. They always come back. You've got a knife in your hand. So, why not use it? Cut her piggy throat. Send her to oblivion.'

He blew his nose one nostril at a time, sending snot to the tiled floor. 'Shut up, Mother! She's listening. Please shut up. She'll hear you.'

Heath glared at the front door as the detective knocked again, and then she bent down to look through the letterbox, as her hog sergeant had before her.

'Could you open the door, please, Mr Heath. It's DI Kesey, Laura Kesey, West Wales Police. I'm looking for Megan Weller.'

Heath so wanted to pound her into the ground, to plunge the knife into her body time and again for daring to invade his personal territory when he was so very close to making his ultimate fantasy reality. But he still had his doubts. The threat of prison loomed large in his increasingly conflicted mind. Killing the Syrian was one thing, a pleasant enough distraction, but a pig detective was another thing entirely. 'What shall I do, Mother? Tell me what to do.'

'You'll have to kill her, Henry. Open the door and kill her. That's what you want to do, so why not do it? Less thought more action. That's what's needed. Come on, there's a good boy.'

'Really? Are you sure, Mother? Three in a day? That seems a little excessive, even for me.'

His mother's face swept down, coming within inches of his. *'Aren't you man enough, Henry? Your father wouldn't have hesitated like this. He had the balls for the job when it mattered most. Perhaps you're too much of a worm.'*

Heath screamed as Kesey knocked again, bang, bang, bang. 'Don't mention that man!'

'Open the door, Mr Heath. Open it now, or I'll call for backup to break it down.'

'Did you hear that, Henry? What are you waiting for? You'll have to kill her. Act now, or you'll miss your opportunity.'

Heath felt his core temperature rise as he approached the front door, ever so slowly, ever so cautiously. He stopped, counting to five inside his head before opening it, the knife still gripped behind his back. He squeezed the shaft ever tighter for fear of dropping it.

'I was beginning to think you weren't going to answer,' said the detective. 'Should I call you Mr Heath? Or is there another name you'd prefer me to use?'

Heath took a sudden backward step as the pig detective continued to stare at him, holding his gaze. He knew in that instant that she was suspicious. She looked scared. But there was a determination too. Some victims folded, and others fought. Piggy was a fighter. It was written all over her piggy face.

'Mr Heath is just fine, thank you. I'm a busy man. There are things I need to get on with. Now, how can I help you?'

'I'm investigating Lottie Weller's disappearance.

There are some questions I need to ask you. I'd be glad of your co-operation.'

Heath considered plunging the blade deep into her gut and twisting right there and then. But a small part of him still hoped she'd leave. Killing a pig was never part of the plan, however potentially satisfying. 'What the hell do you want? Say whatever you've come to say and go. You've called at a most inconvenient time.'

But she didn't leave. She stood there staring into his face with accusing eyes which seemed to see everything. Heath threw the matches aside and then removed the wig, flinging it to the floor to the side of the door.

'Can I come in, please, Mr Heath? I'm looking for Megan Weller. I understand she's a friend of yours. You spoke to her by phone earlier this morning. I believe she may be here.'

He tightened his grip on the knife, itching to use it, but still cautious. His loathing for the pig officer was increasing. He imagined her head on a spike and smiled. 'Have you got a warrant?'

'No, no, I haven't, but I could get one quickly enough. Best get this done, don't you think?'

Heath looked back at the detective with a new-found confidence. He snorted, laughing as he prepared to close the door. 'Stop wasting my time. Go away while you still can.'

The detective took a backward step, her body rigid. 'Is that a threat, Mr Heath?'

'You haven't got a warrant. I want you to go. What part of that don't you understand?'

There was a sudden shout from upstairs as Kesey was about to walk away. A cry fraught with fear. 'Help! We're up here, help! We're in the attic!'

Heath attempted to slam the door shut, his sense of panic evident. But Kesey was quick to react. She rushed towards him, shrieking loudly when the door's hard wooden edge collided violently with her knee. She kicked out, hitting the door open and Heath backwards, and then loomed over him as he fell to the tiled floor. Heath scuttled back on his backside and then jumped to his feet as his adversary came after him.

He waited until Kesey was only inches away, before drawing his arm back and striking with the knife, slashing a deep three-inch gash in her right arm just above the elbow. Heath turned and ran for the staircase as Kesey kicked out again, knocking the weapon in his bloody hand with a well-aimed and forceful strike of her foot. He winced, screwing up his face as he continued fleeing, but he somehow held onto the weapon, one finger broken.

'What are you running for, Henry? Stand and fight like a man. That's what your father would have done. She's just a girl, a silly girl. Grow a pair of balls and fight.'

Heath shouted out as he ascended the stairs towards the attic, fully intending to kill his captives as the detective watched, fatally wounded and helpless, worshipping at his feet. Why carry the piggy bitch up the stairs when she could climb them herself? 'Shut your mouth, Mother. I know exactly what I'm doing. Shut your stupid mouth before I shut it for you.'

Kesey was losing a lot of blood as she climbed the stairs after him. He could see she was losing strength now. She was moving more slowly. And her eyes were dimming. They were definitely dimming. The light of life was gradually fading. What a wonderful sight to behold. Heath was boosted by his success. He was excited by the detective's apparent vulnerability. His animalistic senses stimulated by the scent and sight of her blood. He wanted to taste the sweet liquid with its metallic tang, to feed on her life-force, but first, he had to overpower her. She looked close to collapse. How hard could it be?

Heath turned towards Kesey as she reached the landing, stumbling slightly on negotiating the final step. He noted that she still looked scared, but that determination was there too. Despite her wound. Despite her hopeless plight. He watched her as she leant against the wall, panting slightly, regaining whatever strength she could find, dredging it up from her boots. He studied Kesey's pallid face and thought her ridiculous to risk her life for others. She was selfless. So unlike himself. And that made the idea of killing her even more attractive. He planned to do it slowly. To make her suffer. To drive home her failure before she breathed her last breath. He was feeling more powerful now, telling himself that sweet victory would soon be his. He smiled on seeing the warm red blood running down Kesey's arm, dripping and staining the carpet at her feet in a steady stream that wouldn't let up.

'Are you ready to die, piggy? It won't be long now.

You're in my slaughterhouse. A most appropriate place to die.'

Kesey adopted a defensive position, both legs and her one good arm ready to strike. 'Bring it on, you sad excuse for a man. You don't frighten me.'

Heath tried to strike again as Kesey suddenly leapt forward in one adrenaline-fuelled bound, but the knife fell short. He stumbled backwards, hitting the wall hard as the detective threw two quick punches with her one good arm, the first breaking his nose and the second cutting his right eyelid down to the bone.

'Can't you even beat a silly girl, Henry? What kind of a man are you? Or are you still a boy? Fight, boy, fight, kill the piggy bitch.'

Heath attempted to scramble up the ladder as Kesey regained her balance, holding her sore knuckles to her mouth.

He shouted out on reaching the second step, 'Shut the fuck up, Mother!' and then continued climbing, but the detective reached up and attempted to drag him back. He kicked out, landing a glancing blow to the top of her head with the sole of his shoe, but she didn't let go.

As Heath teetered on the very edge of the step, Kesey punched upwards, aiming instinctively, hitting out with all the force she could muster. He doubled over, dropping the knife, as the sickening blow struck his testicles with a force that caused him to gasp and gag. And then as Kesey's sight began to blur, Heath fell heavily to the wooden floor, thumping his head against the carpeted boards, biting his tongue half through.

Heath screeched as she struck him between his legs again, this time with a well-aimed snap-kick which made him puke. Kesey hit him one last time, raising her knee up and stamping down on his abdomen before rolling him over, forcing an arm up his back, ordering him to lie still and securing his wrist in tight metal handcuffs. She forced his other arm wide, attaching the cuff to one of the staircase's wooden balusters, ensuring he was secure.

She looked down at her prisoner and had never loathed anyone more. Every instinct told her to allow him to die as he began gagging on blood from his broken nose. But it wasn't in Kesey's nature. She was better than that. And so she turned him on his side in the recovery position to prevent him from choking. 'You're under arrest, Mr Heath. You're not obliged to say anything, but anything you do say could be used in evidence. It's over, and you lost, you're going to prison for a very long time. It's just a matter of how long for and what happens when you get there.'

48

Kesey stepped over Heath's prone body, avoiding his feet, and began climbing the ladder towards the attic room one slow step at a time. Heath moaned incoherently, more sounds than words, as he engaged in an animated conversation with his dead mother that made no sense at all.

Kesey called out loud enough to be heard above Heath's senseless protestations. 'I'm coming up, Megan, it's Laura, Laura Kesey. Heath's incapacitated. You're safe, and he can't hurt you any more.'

Megan didn't utter another word until Kesey's head suddenly appeared through the open hatch. When she saw Kesey for the first time, Megan's relief was obvious, the tension melting away as tears of happiness freely flowed.

'Oh, thank God. I really thought we were going to die in this hellhole.'

Kesey smiled despite, or perhaps because of the tension. She felt close to collapse. Close to emotional meltdown. And so she chose humour to raise her spirits. 'You should have seen what went on down there. We very nearly did.'

'Is Heath... is he... is he...'

'He's in handcuffs. He can't move. You don't need to worry.'

'I need you to call an ambulance for Lottie, please. She's the one who needs help. I can wait.'

Kesey looked around the attic prison, the cage, the little girl curled up inside, Megan naked and bound. She hid her shock as best she could, sucking in the fetid air. 'My phone needs charging, it's going to take me a bit of time to find another. I'm sure I saw one downstairs. It may take me a few minutes. Does that make sense?'

'Yes, I understand.'

'Right, I'm going to untie you now, and then you

can look after Lottie while I call for the help we
need. Okay?'

Megan nodded, raising her knees to her chest to
hide her nakedness. 'You need to tie something
around your arm, a tourniquet, you're losing a lot of
blood.'

'I'll get around to it.'

'There's only the three of us. If you pass out before I'm free, there's nothing I can do. We'll all die
unless someone finds us.'

Kesey was feeling increasingly faint as she picked
up one of Heath's discarded black stockings. She tied
it tightly above her wound, using both her free hand
and her teeth, and then moved on to untie Megan's
ropes. Kesey struggled: her wounded arm was next to
useless. But she persevered and finally succeeded,
close to exhaustion.

'There you go, that's the last one.'

Megan rushed forwards, opening the cage door
and lifting Lottie out, the tube still taped in her
mouth, a gag of sorts. Megan unwrapped the tape
from her daughter's head and then removed the
tube, taking care not to hurt her in any way. As Kesey
approached the open hatch with a rope in hand,

Lottie opened her eyes, looking up at her mother's familiar face and smiling. Megan lifted her daughter and hugged her to her bare chest, kissing her cheek gently.

'She's going to be okay, Laura. Thank you for everything. You've saved my little girl's life.'

Kesey looked back and beamed. 'You stay where you are. I'll phone for an ambulance and be back with some clothes. Heath will be taken to the police station before you both come down. You won't have to see him. He's going to be locked up for a very long time.'

'I hope you don't mind me asking. What's the rope for?'

'The bastard's hands are secure. This is for his feet.'

49

Both Megan and Dale were sitting at Lottie's bedside in the children's ward at West Wales General Hospital when Kesey entered the room, a box of jelly babies in one hand and a CBeebies comic in the other. She nodded in greeting to both parents and stood at the end of the bed. 'How's my favourite little girl?'

Lottie sat up, resting on her pillows, looking first at the sweets, then the comic, and then at Megan. 'Can I have them, Mummy?'

'Of course you can. Aunty Laura bought them for you.'

Kesey unwrapped the sweets before handing the box to Lottie with the lid open.

'You look ever so pretty, Lottie. Like a princess.'

The little girl popped a sweet into her mouth and chewed as a passing nurse waved to her with a smile.

'Can I have a quick word with you privately, Meg? You can bring Dale up to date when you both get a bit of time to yourselves. Is that okay with you, Dale?'

Dale nodded as the two women went towards the dayroom at the end of the corridor.

'What's this about, Laura?'

'I wanted to let you know that Heath's been charged. Kidnapping, false imprisonment and attempted murder.'

'That's good news, isn't it?'

'He's pleading not guilty despite the weight of evidence. It's going to trial.'

'That means I'm going to have to give evidence.'

Kesey nodded. 'Yeah, I'm sorry, it does. Mad not bad. That'll be the defence's focus. Only a jury can decide.'

'Court holds no fears. It's not something I'm worried about. Actually, I'm rather looking forward to it. I'm going to tell that jury exactly what he did.'

'You and me both.'

Megan hugged Kesey, pulling her close. 'I'll always be grateful to you. You saved us. You gave us our lives back.'

'Oh, you're welcome. Don't even mention it. I'm just glad to be of service. It's all part of the job.'

50

Kesey sipped her hot coffee as Lewis slurped his beer, swirling it around his mouth before swallowing. Lewis wiped his lips with the back of one hand before speaking, 'It's good to see you again, boss. How's the arm, is it any better?'

'It's still not great. He severed the nerves. But I'll be back in work as soon as I get the all-clear. Convalescing isn't for me. I'm bored silly.'

'You should have listened to me. I was right all along.'

'Oh, here we go. I was wondering how long it was going to take.'

Lewis grinned. 'I'm just saying, that's all.'

'You are winding me right up. We can't make arrests based on gut feelings. That's not the way things work. You know that as well as I do.'

Lewis hesitated, his expression becoming more serious. 'I still can't believe the bastard pleaded not guilty, not with all the evidence you found. Heath really thought he was going to get away with it.'

Kesey added single cream to her coffee before stirring. 'A big part of me still thinks he is insane. A secure mental hospital may have been a better option than prison. You should have heard him at the house. He could well be schizophrenic like that one psychiatrist said, that would make sense of it all. I don't think anything else does.'

Lewis shook his head. 'Nah, the cunt knew exactly what he was a doing. He planned everything in intricate detail. All that talking to his dead mother stuff was a load of shit. Prison's exactly the right place for him. He deserves nothing less.'

'I can't say I agree, to be honest, but the jury did, that's what matters. What do I know? Even the expert witnesses were split, one, one way, one the other. Mad or bad, that stuff's not an exact science.'

'What did you make of the sentence?'

Kesey tilted her head at a slight angle. 'It was always going to be life once we nailed him for the Syrian's killing. Twenty-five years is a long time whichever way you look at it.'

'Yeah, but he'll still only be in his fifties when he comes out unless someone does for him inside. It doesn't seem long enough to me.'

'Sentences very rarely do if you know the victims.'

Lewis poured half his pint down his throat. 'How are the Wellers doing, any news?'

'Um, yeah, pretty well, all considered. I visited Megan a couple of days back. She's talking about getting back together with Dale, as much for Lottie's sake as her own. Although, she says she still loves him. I think she always did.'

'Do you think it'll work out?'

Kesey shrugged. 'Who knows? Maybe, or maybe not, we'll have to wait and see.'

Lewis drained his glass, burping on putting it down. 'Is Lottie still oblivious to everything that happened?'

Kesey nodded enthusiastically. 'Yeah, she doesn't remember a thing. She went to bed at home with her father banging on the door and then woke up in the hospital. The time in between hasn't registered. It's as if it didn't happen at all.'

'Well, thank fuck for that. Let's hope it stays that way.'

'You won't hear me arguing.'

'How's Jan? Is she looking forward to the holiday?'

Kesey smiled. 'We all are. I had to change it for somewhere warmer. We're off to Florida in three weeks. I'd never come back to work at all if it were up to her. She'd love me to be doing something different. Anything but police work.'

'That sounds familiar.'

'Yeah, she's been saying the same thing for years.'

He picked up his empty glass. 'Any chance of it happening?'

'None at all. You're stuck with me whether you like it or not.'

Lewis stood with glass in hand. 'Are you going to have a proper drink? We haven't celebrated winning the case yet. Or your pending return to the fold. It's about time, don't you think?'

'They're giving me a commendation. There's even

talk of a medal. Halliday rang and told me. That must have stuck in his throat.'

'That's great, Laura, and very well deserved too. Although you're a fucking crazy woman. You should have waited for backup. How about a glass of bubbly?'

Kesey laughed, amused as intended. 'I'll have half a lager shandy.'

Lewis nodded and smiled. 'Don't ever go risking your life like that again. You're nothing if not predictable. Half a shandy it is.'

MORE FROM JOHN NICHOLL

We hope you enjoyed reading *Mr Nice*. If you did, please leave a review.

If you'd like to gift a copy, this book is also available as a paperback, digital audio download and audiobook CD.

The Sisters, another gripping psychological thriller by John Nicholl, is available to order now.

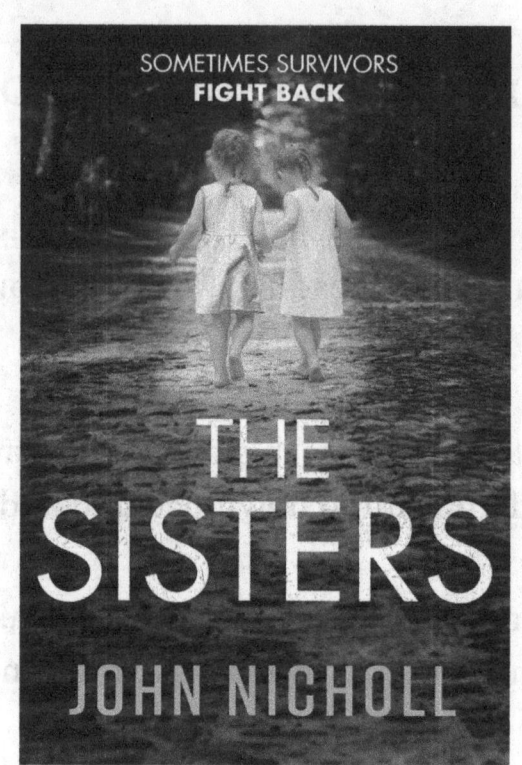

ABOUT THE AUTHOR

John Nicholl is an award-winning, bestselling author of numerous darkly psychological suspense thrillers, previously published by Bloodhound. These books have a gritty realism born of his real-life experience as an ex-police officer and child protection social worker.

Visit John's website: https://www.johnnicholl.com

Follow John on social media:

twitter.com/nicholl06

facebook.com/JohnNichollAuthor

instagram.com/johnnichollauthor

Boldwood

Boldwood Books is an award-winning fiction publishing company seeking out the best stories from around the world.

Find out more at www.boldwoodbooks.com

Join our reader community for brilliant books, competitions and offers!

Follow us

@BoldwoodBooks

@BookandTonic

Sign up to our weekly
deals newsletter

https://bit.ly/BoldwoodBNewsletter

www.ingramcontent.com/pod-product-compliance
Lightning Source LLC
Chambersburg PA
CBHW010700100726
47900CB00010B/2738